Gravedigger's Moon

a novel by

John Robert Schmierer

Copyright 2011, 2013 by John Robert Schmierer

ISBN 978-0-9888981-1-0

Gravedigger's Moon

ONE

ALAN KANE stood naked at the master bedroom's floor-to-ceiling window, close enough to an AC vent to feel the draft, waiting for the chilled air to help clear his head. He stared through the solar-tinted glass out toward Phoenix and watched the glimmer from the city lights fade in the distance. A soft glow backlit the mountains nearby, but there was still a while to go before sunrise. Maybe enough time to gather himself for his first scheduled lesson.

He threw on a robe and headed for the kitchen, the aroma of brewed coffee leading the way. He poured a cup from the automatic maker and picked up the remote control for the downsized flat panel TV mounted beneath a cupboard facing the breakfast nook. A cable business channel flickered to life. Two reporters sat behind a glass anchor desk, the usual morning banter noticeably absent as one of them spoke in somber tones directed at the camera. A ticker-style banner rolled along the bottom of the screen in a repetitive loop that spelled out the headline and a brief summary for those just tuning in. When the studio coverage switched to a live, outdoor feed, Kane turned up the volume to better hear the voiceover while he settled in behind the kitchen table. He caught up with the dialogue and recognized the name.

The reporters were talking about Logan Bigelow, an occasional guest on their show, well known for his successful bootstrap approach to business and his generous contributions to charity. Last night he had crashed his private jet while attempting an instrument approach into O'Hare International. Everyone aboard had died instantly. The weather conditions awaiting the jet in Chicago had been deteriorating, the wind shear, driving rain, and near zero visibility delaying commercial departures and sending their arriving counterparts to alternate destinations. After the storm moved on and visibility improved, the air traffic controllers in the tower were left with a sobering view of the wreckage: a surprisingly compressed heap of smoldering bits and pieces resting not more than five hundred yards short of the runway. Bigelow had been an experienced pilot, as had the copilot sitting alongside of him when the plane went down; nevertheless, pilot error was tossed around as the cause of the crash by most of the aviation experts solicited for their on-air opinions.

The anchors resumed their studio coverage, and Kane lost interest—until they began talking about Logan Bigelow's legacy. Kane was aware that Bigelow's wife of nearly forty years had met her own tragic death in a car accident six months ago, but now he learned there were no surviving children or known business associates queued up for a slice of the empire. After the lead reporter dispensed with the family history, speculation took over and bore down on the estate's current status, its net worth only guessed at but rumored to be closing in on a billion dollars.

More commentators joined the discussion, financial experts this time chiming in on which charitable trusts were likely to cash in and for how much. To the right of the anchor desk the TV screen had divided into three individual frames, each one containing a talking head that competed for attention despite the reporters' attempts to control the proceedings. Words were clashing and running over each other and rising in volume, and Kane felt the first clamp-like squeeze of one of his headaches. He tried to ignore it, but he knew what was coming. His half-hearted denial lasted less than a minute before he slammed his elbows onto the table and covered his head with his hands and gave in to the mounting pain. It offered a strange sort of comfort compared to the violent urge welling up inside him.

The voices from the broadcast were taunting him now, and Kane wondered how they had found out about him and why they were taking such pleasure in humiliating him with their thinly disguised references to the injustices and frustrations he had suffered these last few months. He looked up at the TV and recognized the mirth beneath the words and the smirks on the faces, as if the anchors and the guest speakers could all barely hold back their laughter. He swept the remote and the coffee cup off the table in an uncontrollable outburst. It took every last remnant of his will power to storm past the TV without ripping it off its mountings and hurling it through the closed French doors leading out to the courtyard.

TWO

ARE YOU talking about a mastectomy?"

Benjamin Holt looked over at his wife, Susan, who had a habit of fast-forwarding a discussion when she wanted to get to the point. She seemed to be holding up pretty well, showing no obvious signs of stress while interrupting the doctor sitting across from them behind a polished, clutter-free desk.

But Holt knew better.

Dr. Elaine McCreary's rather stern remoteness lost some of its starch. Her face softened into what Holt perceived as a well-practiced expression that revealed not exactly a smile but more of a knowing kindness. She leaned forward to address Susan directly.

"I'm not necessarily talking about a mastectomy, but I'm most definitely talking about surgery."

Dr. McCreary eased back in her ergonomic chair, as if to allow Holt enough room to resume his place in the conversation. If nothing else, he appreciated the way the doctor was handling the situation. Her white lab coat hanging on a hook near the closed door was the only reminder of the clinical nature of the meeting. She wore her graying hair short, in a no-bother but stylish cut that framed a delicately structured face. The rest of her looked trim and fit, draped in a loose, off-white cardigan over a pale blue blouse. Her desk matched the walnut credenza behind it and somehow managed to be unintimidating. Other than the obligatory diplomas and a few reference volumes, the walls and bookcases displayed less professional paraphernalia and more personal items than Holt would have expected in a doctor's office. Diffused sunlight brightened the room through a translucent shade drawn across the window above the credenza, and it dawned on him that, unlike the waiting area and exam rooms, there wasn't a fluorescent light fixture to be found. He tried to relax into his chair's firm leather upholstery as Dr. McCreary continued.

"Early detection is key, as always, along with a little luck—like having your scheduled mammogram come due just as the mass is beginning to form. You'd never notice it during a routine physical exam." McCreary picked up a thin stack of paperwork and absently shuffled through the pages as she talked. "All indications so far point to *ductal carcinoma in situ*, a noninvasive type of breast cancer."

Holt sensed Susan's inner tension spool down a notch. She said, "I assume that's a *good* thing."

McCreary restacked the papers on her desktop. "If you're going to have cancer, yes, that's a good thing. But while it's not yet an emergency medical situation, DCIS is a serious condition that requires careful attention, especially in your case."

"You mean, because of my family history. My mother . . ."

"There's that. And there's also the type of carcinoma itself. Your biopsy indicates *comedocarcinoma*, which tends to be an aggressive form of the disease. It may not be invasive now, but that can change. We can't allow it to metastasize."

"So can you just cut it out without removing my breast?"

"It's a little more complicated. But we have time to further assess the situation and plan the best way to handle it. There's a good chance we can save your breast, but you need to remember, it's your *life* that's important. We also want to decrease the odds of a recurrence. I'm going to send you home with some literature. The information is pretty generic, but it will give you a good idea about the treatment options available and will help prepare you for our next discussion. As I said, there's time for you to study this and weigh your options as long as you stay focused and make it a priority. In the meantime, I'd like to schedule an appointment for you to see Dr. Troman. He's an oncology surgeon who specializes in breast surgery and is a strong advocate of breast conserving therapy. He has an excellent success ratio. If I were to need treatment myself, he's the surgeon I'd insist on. If it's all right with you, I'll send him your file. I'd like him to go over the pathology report on your biopsy and help us decide the best approach for your particular situation."

Dr. McCreary stood up, indicating the consultation was over. Susan gripped Holt's hand as they rose to follow her to the door. McCreary opened it for them and paused before ushering them through.

"Be sure to stop at the front desk for the reading material we talked about. Karen will have it ready for you, along with Dr Troman's office number. I'm going to call him right now."

* * *

Holt stared at the steering wheel. The key was in the ignition, unturned, as he contemplated whether or not to start the car. Susan hadn't said a word since walking out the doctor's office. He didn't know what to say, how to soften the blow. He figured it best to wait, and after a long silence, Susan finally spoke.

"I guess it could have been worse. Dr. McCreary could have picked up the phone right there and scheduled me for surgery. That's how they did it with my mom. They had her on the table the day after the pathologist saw the biopsy."

"Do you think we should get a second opinion?"

"You mean go through this again, with another doctor? . . . I don't think so. We're already getting another opinion from the surgeon. He'll see the same pathology report that McCreary read, but I'm sure he'll go over the mammogram and biopsy and come to his own conclusions. Besides, I trust Dr. McCreary. She comes highly recommended, and she's just the right age. Not too old, not too young."

"Just right, huh, Goldilocks?"

Susan smiled for the first time all morning. Not a happy smile, but a smile. "You know what I mean. I figure she's what, forty, maybe forty-five? Not much older than I am. She's been around long enough to have gained experience but still young enough to further her education and stay in touch with the latest advances."

"I agree. And she seems to have her heart in the right place for this kind of work. If you're comfortable staying the course with her, so am I"

"Then you'd better take me home—I've got some reading to do. And don't worry about me, at least not this morning. McCreary said we have time to figure this out, and you have your own problems to deal with."

Susan turned away to look out her window while Holt started the car. "I still can't believe what's happening," she said, as if to herself. "And that it's all happening today."

Holt couldn't believe it, either. He hadn't recovered from last night's phone call or the morning news reports, and that was *before* the consultation with Dr McCreary. He started the car. His partners were waiting for him, but he'd worry about them after he dropped Susan at home. For now, he'd busy himself with his driving, concentrate on the traffic and make sure he didn't space-out and cause an accident.

When they pulled into their driveway, Susan gathered her purse and paperwork before Holt could help her.

"I've got this," she said. "You need to get going. Call me when you can." She leaned in to kiss Holt, then pulled away and opened the passenger door with her free hand. There were tears on her face when she looked back at him. "On top of all this, I'm really sorry about Logan."

"So am I," Holt said, "but that's not important now."

He held her gaze as long as he could, then forced himself to put the car into gear and drive away while his eyes were still dry. He made it half a block before the tears came and blurred his wife's reflection in the rearview mirror.

THREE

IT TOOK just over ten minutes to arrive at the glass-walled midrise on Newport Center Drive, where the law firm of Vanderlip, Stratton, and Holt commanded an unobstructed view of the Orange County coastline from the penthouse suites. Holt checked his appearance in the elevator's mirrored interior. He was dry-eyed and composed.

The receptionist barely looked up when he entered the foyer.

"They're waiting," she said, performing a poor charade of appearing busy.

"Don't tell me. Stratton and Vanderlip?"

She nodded. "In Mr. Stratton's office."

"Thanks, Lisa. I guess I don't need to ask what kind of mood they're in."

Holt's response seemed to break the ice. Lisa really looked at him this time and said, "I've never seen them like this. It has everyone on edge."

"Don't worry. It's me they're after. You guys will be fine."

Holt navigated his way past a few awkward encounters with staff members offering condolences on his way to the executive suite. He ignored Stratton's administrative assistant sitting at her desk and opened the closed door behind her without knocking. An abrupt silence greeted him when he entered the room. Chester Stratton was half-sitting, half-leaning on the front edge of his desk. He appeared somewhat stooped. He normally carried his frame, which was well over six feet in height, with a seemingly unstressed ease that belied a chronic back ailment. The lines etching his face now looked furrowed, accentuating the deep crease running down his left cheek. He slid off the desk but maintained his distance as he shoved his hands into the front pockets of his chinos.

"How did it go with Susan?" he said, his voice sounding strained and out of character.

"She has breast cancer. They caught it early, and she has a good doctor. The prognosis is as good as we can hope for."

"If there's anything we can do . . ."

Holt acknowledged Stratton's perfunctory concern with a nod meant to close the subject, then another nod toward Leon Vanderlip holding down the sofa across the room, walking stick in hand and planted on the floor in front of him to help support his considerable bulk should he lean forward or rise. Unlike Holt and Stratton's business-casual attire, Vanderlip wore a conservative three-piece suit. He brushed at something bothering him on his lapel and said nothing. Holt returned his attention to Stratton and caught a glimpse of a manila folder lying by itself on the desktop behind him.

"I see you've been going over Logan's trust."

"That's right, Ben. In fact, this is the first we've seen of your new handiwork."

"It's just an add-on to the trust's portfolio, not an important change."

"Not an important change?" Stratton said, pulling his hands out of his pockets and crossing his arms. "What would *you* call an irrevocable life insurance trust that pays an unknown beneficiary the sum of ten million dollars?"

"I'd call it an addition, a legal contract that stands on its own. It doesn't affect the structure or conditions of Logan's other trusts, or the foundation."

"But it *involves* the foundation. We couldn't help but notice that it's listed as a contingent beneficiary. Do you mind telling us what the hell is going on?"

"Can we sit down first?"

Stratton stood his ground for an extra beat, then acquiesced with a curt gesture toward one of the two armchairs facing his desk. He retreated to his own seat on the other side and leaned back from his desktop, his position centrally framed by the glass wall behind him and the blue-water view beyond.

"So let's hear it."

Holt refused to squirm. He'd done nothing wrong and wasn't in the mood for Stratton's theatrics.

"I'm sorry you weren't brought up to speed on this sooner, Chet, but these last couple of weeks have been very distracting. I'd just finished with the insurance trust when Susan's medical problems surfaced. Nothing has been intentionally kept from you. In fact, I was planning to fill you in last week, then spend a few days out of town to complete my research."

"What research?"

"I'm looking for Logan Bigelow's daughter."

It took a moment for Stratton to respond. "I presume she's illegitimate."

"Yeah, and that's the problem. She was born around thirty years ago and there's not much of a trail. I've come up with a birth certificate, but that's about it."

"Why now?" Stratton said, "after all this time . . ."

"It started a few months ago, after Vanessa died. I think it must have been eating at Logan for years, that he'd fathered a child but couldn't do anything about it. Vanessa wasn't physically capable of childbirth, and as long as she was alive Logan wasn't about to risk breaking her heart. Finding out about an affair would have been bad enough, but if she ever learned that he'd had a child with someone else it would have ruined their marriage. Affair or not, Logan loved his wife. He regretted what had happened and never cheated on her again. I really believe that."

"So Bigelow felt guilty and wanted you to go out and find this long-lost heir to his fortune." Stratton sat up straighter, closer to his desk. "How could he be so naive? I mean, this daughter could be anywhere—a homeless drug addict or in prison or some mental institution. What was he thinking, giving away millions to someone he doesn't even know?"

"He knew he had a daughter and he wanted to believe in the best, not the worst, that maybe she'd inherited some of his better qualities and was living a good life. Logan was only sixty years old. He wasn't planning on dying before he found her. He wanted to meet her."

"Then why the life insurance policy?"

"It was just that—insurance, in case something happened to him first. We talked about the negatives and the what-ifs you just mentioned. If Logan were to change his mind for any reason, all he had to do was cancel the policy or stop paying the monthly premiums and let it lapse. It would have been like it never existed."

"At least that would have kept the foundation's board of trustees out of it," Stratton said. "But as it stands, this exposure could turn into a nightmare, for the foundation, and for our firm. We're continuing on as compensated advisors to the trustees taking control of the foundation, and now *you're* the managing trustee for this goddamned insurance trust. We need nothing less than solid proof of a living heir or an irrefutable death certificate, and we need it now. Anything less has the potential to look bad for us. If we're *conveniently* unable to find the daughter, conflict of interest or some kind of conspiracy theory could be inferred when the foundation is awarded the ten million. And can you imagine the false claims and ensuing media circus we'll have to endure if the news leaks prematurely? Like I said, a nightmare."

"That's not going to happen," Holt said. He hoped he sounded convincing.

"You're damn right it's not going to happen. You're going to see to this personally, whatever it takes short of using an outside agency—we have to keep this in-house. Just find the daughter or find out what happened to her while I try to buffer the situation from our end." Stratton paused, let out a long breath, as if releasing a distasteful but necessary show of authority, and continued on with a more conversational tone. "Now, what do you need to 'complete your research?'"

* * *

Maxine Brennan, the firm's brightest paralegal, was in the loop, waiting for Holt at the conference table when he entered his office.

"Did you get me a flight?"

"You're all set," she said.

"What about the other stuff?"

"Yes, and no. Everything I've found so far is on your desk."

"Any luck with the Social Security number?"

"Only for the mother, *not* the daughter."

"It's more than we had yesterday. Do you have a current address for her?"

"Sorry. I haven't been able to track her down. All the information is so dated as to be nonexistent. What I have is a photocopied address out of the Scottsdale City Directory from 1980 and the name of her last known employers, all from the same era."

Holt scooped up the file from his desk as he passed by to a waiting chair at the table. He sat across from Maxine and sorted through the contents. "Was the card issued in Arizona?"

"Yes, as indicated by the number itself. I cross referenced it with the Social Security Death Index and didn't get a hit. Now

I'm working on marriage license databases to see if I can luck out there."

Holt nodded along, relatively happy with the progress, as he picked up the copy of the birth certificate. "What happened to the certified copy?"

"I filed it here, for safekeeping. I made that copy for you to have handy."

The certificate named Logan Bigelow and Pearl Norwood as the parents of an unnamed child, referred to on the certificate as *Baby Girl Norwood*. According to Bigelow, Pearl had not planned on keeping the baby. What puzzled Holt was that the birth certificate had not been sealed, the usual practice when birth parents immediately gave up their child for adoption. Pearl had not named the girl, which supported the belief that an adoption took place, but there was no paperwork available. Maxine had not been able to find a secondary birth certificate naming the new parents.

"Hand me that memo pad, will you, Max?"

She slid it over, but slowly, and asked, "How are *you* doing, Mr. Holt? Is your wife going to be okay?"

As a rule, Holt didn't confide in work associates. Stratton and Vanderlip were obvious exceptions; they needed to know what was going on and he would keep them informed of Susan's condition and progress. But over the years Maxine had earned her place as his confidant. She had willingly taken on the duties of an administrative assistant, his chief researcher, and friend. Talking to her was easy, no matter the subject.

"It's official," Holt said. "Susan's been diagnosed with breast cancer. When they tell you to come in to the office for the biopsy results, you know it's going to be bad news. But they caught it early and her doctor doesn't seem too worried. I just hope there're no surprises."

"Can't you stay here with her? I could take care of this for you."

"I appreciate the offer, but this is my mess. Stratton will be holding my feet to the fire until I fix it. And he's right. The stakes are high, not only for the firm, but for my future here. Now's not the time to be looking for a new job. The best thing I can do for Susan right now is hold on to my salary and health insurance."

The rest of it Holt kept to himself—he *owed* Logan Bigelow, the one man responsible for Holt's rise to full partner a dozen years ago, despite a lack of seniority and experience. Once they got to know each other, Bigelow had refused to work with anyone else in the firm and made it clear to Stratton and Vanderlip that he'd take his business elsewhere unless he could retain Holt's services exclusively. Holt was now going to make sure his client's last wishes were honored.

He started a list on the memo pad. It would be short one, beginning with Pearl Norwood's last known workplaces and ending with the name of the doctor who had signed the birth certificate. Finding the doctor was a long shot after all these years, and even if he turned up it was unlikely he'd remember anything useful. The only real lead was Pearl's last and longest place of employment on record—Kane Trucking, still in business in Phoenix, Arizona.

FOUR

HOLT SAT close to Susan, facing her from across the corner of the dining room table, both of them ignoring the lunch she'd set out. There were discarded medical pamphlets scattered about, along with a green highlighter and a pen and a few partially-used sheets of notebook paper most likely robbed from their son's school supplies.

"Are you sure you're okay with this?" Holt said.

"I'm good. It helps that you'll only be an hour's flight away."

"Did they call about your appointment yet, with Dr. Troman?"

"I'm still waiting."

"I'll try to be back before you see him. Is there anything I can do before I leave?"

Susan came over and sat on Holt's lap, wrapping her arms around him and burying her face in the crook of his neck, which muffled her voice when she spoke.

"Just get this over with and come home soon."

* * *

Later that afternoon, Holt was looking down at the coastline as the plane banked into a turn and set a course for Phoenix. It had been years since he'd flown on a commercial airline, which brought to mind an overlooked detail about last night: if not for the appointment with Susan's doctor this morning, he would have most likely been on Bigelow's Gulfstream when it crashed.

He sat there awhile wondering why he didn't break into a cold sweat, but his pulse remained steady and a calm assurance washed over him, as if a perfectly good reason why he was still alive lurked somewhere beyond his comprehension. But the more he thought about it, the more he realized that *good intentions* had nothing to do with anything. He was just another cog in the machine, reacting to seemingly random situations, his actions as predictable as the next sunset. Apparently, when it came down to what really mattered, free will was just an illusion, conjured by fate.

He pushed back his seat as far as it would go, not quite so calm, and tried to find a comfortable position to rest his head. A mental image of the live video broadcast he'd seen earlier this morning greeted him the moment he closed his eyes. He felt as if he were hovering over the Gulfstream's wreckage, watching the ghosts of those who had died rise out of the ashes as he recalled their names.

Holt had been part of that group, a member of Bigelow's *Flying Circus*, ready with an excuse to tag along if a flight had anything to do with business. The nickname began as anything but an endearment. It had first been heard several years ago when Bigelow and his team swooped in from out of town and took over a failing avionics manufacturer in Dallas. Not all of Bigelow's acquisitions resulted in open hostilities; in fact, the majority of businesses and corporations that were gathered into the fold found new prosperity. But the name stuck, its connotation suitably wry or serious, depending on the situation.

Regulations governing the Gulfstream had required a copilot onboard during flight operations, and the second-in-command would often relinquish his seat to Holt after they had settled in at cruising altitude. Once Holt found his equilibrium among the dizzy array of dials and gauges and navigation equipment cluttering the cockpit, he got comfortable and began to connect with the *real* Logan Bigelow. The man's boyish enthusiasm was infectious. Holt would never forget the time Bigelow turned to him and said, "You know what? I still get a kick out of jamming the thrust levers to the wall and roaring down the runway in a jet at full throttle—it never gets old."

After Logan's wife died, the conversations turned more personal. Holt learned of Bigelow's past, starting out as a virtual orphan after his father was killed in action over North Korea. Logan never knew his mother. She ran off with a civilian contractor before Logan reached his first birthday. But Logan had fond memories of his dad's best friend, Carl Bigelow, who took Logan in and raised him like his own son.

Carl taught Logan how to fly before he was old enough for a driver's license. Their favorite cross-country destination was Scottsdale Airport, formerly known as Thunderbird Field II, the Air Force base where Carl had trained with Logan's father during World War Two. The old airbase was a two-and-a-half-hour flight in Carl's Cessna from Orange County Airport.

Holt also learned about Carl's foresight to acquire real estate in North Scottsdale before the city bought the airport. The surrounding lots were selling at bargain prices, and by the late sixties he had amassed thousands of acres. After Carl Bigelow died in 1978, Logan began developing the land. It was during a routine layover when his relationship with Pearl Norwood, a waitress at the airport coffee shop, became more than a casual friendship.

* * *

A chime sounded and the FASTEN SEAT BELT sign lit up, accompanied by jolts and sways as the aircraft descended into the warm convection currents over the desert. When he looked out the window, Holt's thoughts dissolved into a cloudless sky that was as vast and empty as the landscape beneath it.

He spent half an hour inside the terminal. A blast of hot jet exhaust hit him as soon as he walked outside. Only there were no jets around, just a line of taxis basking in the heat along the center divider halfway across the Sky Harbor thoroughfare.

Welcome to Phoenix.

The clerk at the car rental counter had mentioned something about the heat, about how unusual it was for this time of year, but Holt didn't get the message. He just nodded along with the clerk, engaged in a little polite conversation, and left it at that. Now he rethought his plan to walk to the rental lot and waited for a shuttle. He found his car without too much difficulty and was relieved he didn't have to sit in the heat while he figured out the air conditioner controls—it came on strong as soon as he fired the ignition.

Curious about the latest hybrids, he'd rented a new Toyota Prius and made sure it had a full map satellite navigation system. He punched in the address to the Phoenician and followed directions to its location on the Phoenix-Scottsdale border.

It was getting dark, the moon rising above the local mountains off to the east, when Holt arrived at the resort. He wound his way past dusky expanses of golf course fairways and greens, glimpsing an occasional water hazard reflecting moonlight. The narrow roadway he was traveling eventually emptied into a large circular courtyard surrounded by the lavish architecture of the hotel itself, which was nestled on the shoulder of Camelback Mountain. Casitas—the Phoenician's high-end suites—took up the higher ground to the north. The entrance to the main lobby opened up at the southern curve of the courtyard. Adjoining corridors led off to rows of rooms that spread out east and west and spilled down the gentle slope.

After settling into his room, Holt scanned a brochure listing the Phoenician's restaurants, grills, and bars; thought better of it, and ordered room service. The room had a private deck that looked out toward the Phoenix skyline. He opened the glass slider and walked outside to wait for his meal. The night air didn't feel quite so hot now. A soft, bone-dry breeze drifted up the slope beneath him and found its way past the railing he was leaning against and through the open door behind him, its last gasps stirring the sheer curtains hanging inside.

While standing there, he pulled out his cell phone, then sat back in one of the deck chairs and called Susan.

* * *

It would have been difficult not to wake up at first light—it was streaming in at full wattage through the open curtains across from the bed. He'd been sleeping in his boxers and figured they covered him well enough for a quick peek at his surroundings from the deck. As his eyes adjusted to the glare, he looked down the slope, past the acres of pools and terraces and fairways, to Camelback Road, and farther on to the flat valley stretched out beyond. Downtown Phoenix looked like a fifteen minute drive away. It didn't appear as inviting as it had last night, with all her lights sparkling in the clear desert air. Looking away from the city, there were only low rooftops taking up the rest of the valley. They were organized into neat rows, the streets seeming to run in perfect north-south, east-west directions and forming an efficient grid. Holt went back into the room to retrieve the street map from his briefcase and returned to the deckchair to familiarize himself.

Maxine had paper clipped a memo-sized sheet to the folded edge. Holt removed it for now and spread out the map itself. The streets were indeed well organized. They all branched out from Central Avenue, exactly sixty-four blocks west of the Phoenician. The roads west of Central and running parallel were labeled Avenues, those to the east were Streets. They were all numbered, starting with 1st. Avenue and 1st. Street, one block west and one block east of Central, respectively. The avenues and streets stretched out diametrically for miles, the avenues numbering into the hundreds. Looking closer, he noticed the numbered blocks were actually spaced a quarter- to a half-mile apart, leaving room for several minor streets in between.

Holt picked up the sheet of memo paper. Maxine had listed the phone numbers and addresses Holt had requested. She had also highlighted their locations on the street map. Kane Trucking was on McDowell, a few blocks south of Camelback.

* * *

The loading docks must have taken up a square city block. Big rigs wheeled around him, barreling along confidently, knowing where they were going, while Holt craned his neck this way and that, trying to see around all that moving bulk and get a fix on his surroundings. He saw a low wooden structure off to his right. Half of the parking stalls surrounding it were full, accommodating normal sized civilian cars. He assumed it was the office and pulled into an open space near the cement walkway leading up to the door. Once inside, he stepped up to a chest-high counter and asked the first woman who looked his way if he could talk to the person in charge. Rather than acknowledge the request, the woman turned to get the attention of a co-worker. Before anything else happened, a door to a rear office opened and a tall man in Levis and a golf shirt stepped into the maze of desks behind the counter. He was studying the top page of a stack of paperwork in his hand as he made his way to the front entrance.

The woman said, "Mr. Kane? Someone to see you," and nodded toward Holt.

Kane glanced up from his papers, appearing distracted as he regarded Holt. He offered a generic smile as he walked over.

"How can I help you?" he said, setting his papers on the counter between them.

Holt was disappointed; he hoped he'd caught himself before it showed on his face. The man in front of him was too young to be of much help, and as Holt looked around the office, he didn't see anyone who looked old enough to have been around when Pearl Norwood worked there. He returned Kane's smile and said, "I apologize for barging in on you unannounced, but I'm looking for a woman who once worked here." Holt handed Kane one of his cards. "It's been years since anyone has seen her, but now my client is in a big hurry to find her."

"Who is she?"

"Sorry, I guess I skipped that part, didn't I? Her name's Pearl Norwood. She's the only lead I have in finding her daughter. It's a family matter, and no one's in any trouble."

"Is that right?" Kane only glanced at the card. "And who's your client?"

"I'm afraid that's a long and somewhat sensitive story. Is there a quieter place we could talk?"

Kane looked back at the card, either studying it closer or trying to decide what to do. He finally looked up and said. "All right, Mr. Holt, come on back to my office."

A counter-height door buzzed next to him and Holt followed Kane as he retraced the path back to his office. The interior was utilitarian and showed years of constant use. An old AC unit rattled in a window behind Kane's desk, stirring a weak current of stale, refrigerated air. Kane stayed at the door to shut it behind Holt and directed him to one of the wooden chairs along the far wall under a wall-sized roadmap of the US.

They sat. Kane said, "Okay, you've got me curious. What the hell's going on?"

"For now, my client would like to keep his name out of this. At least until we find his daughter. He wasn't married to her mother, but now he'd like to find her, and more importantly, his daughter. A lot of time has passed, and he wants to see that she's all right."

"How long ago are we talking about?

"Thirty years."

"Since he'd seen Pearl Norwood?"

"Yes, and from what I understand, she worked here in this office."

"That was a long time ago," Kane said. He remained silent for a long moment, as if thinking it over. Then he smiled, a real one this time. "You know what? I remember the name. Not Pearl herself, just the name. I was pretty young back then—four or five. If you'd like, I could have someone dig through our old files and see what we can come up with."

"You have files that go back that far?"

"My old man was a stickler for that sort of thing. At the close of every year he'd gather up all the paperwork and documents he wanted to save and pack 'em up. We've got the better part of a warehouse filled with cardboard boxes full of the stuff. Each box has a date stamped on it, stacked in chronological order. There must be records back there forty, fifty years old."

Holt's initial disappointment began to fade. Kane walked over to his desk and got on the phone to an office staff member and sent her on a mission to the aforementioned warehouse. He stayed at the desk when Holt asked, "Is your father still involved in the business?"

"He was up until last year. Until the lung cancer. He didn't last long after the initial diagnosis. Just a few months."

More cancer. Holt's train of thought was derailed by the mere mention of the word. Kane seemed to sense his unease while continuing to speak.

"The old man was quite a guy. Turned this into one of the biggest independent trucking companies in the country. It wasn't easy taking on the Teamsters. The unions were big in the fifties and played rough. He was lucky to live through it all and last as long as he did."

"So it's just you now . . . running the company, I mean."

"Yeah, just me," Kane said, heading for the chair behind his desk. After sitting down, he brought a hand up to his chin, absentmindedly let his fingers move back and forth along his jawbone. "I've got a brother, though. We don't see much of each other. But I was just thinking; he's older than I am, and the woman you're looking for—"

Kane's telephone rang. He excused himself and picked it up, spent the next ten minutes listening, issuing orders, and fielding more incoming calls as they stacked up on hold. When he finally got a breather, the door to his office opened and the clerk he'd sent to the warehouse came in and handed him a faded, dog-eared file.

"Sorry about all that," Kane said. He dismissed the clerk, then went through the pages she'd delivered. He found what he was looking for and said, "I've got Pearl's application and W-2 form here, but that's about it." He handed the paperwork to Holt. "Not much there—home address and phone—I doubt if it can help you now."

"You never know," Holt said. "Maybe I'll get lucky." He looked at the address on the W-2 and saw it was the same 71st Street apartment complex listed on the photocopied page from the old city directory. He paused for a moment, then looked up at Kane. "You were saying something about your brother."

"Oh yeah, my brother. Like I said, he's a few years older. He might have a better recollection of Pearl than I do, if he hasn't fried all his brain cells by now."

Holt filed away that last inference before asking, "How much older is he?"

"Close to five years. He had the run of the place until I entered the picture. Being the baby of the family, I probably stole a lot of the attention he was used to getting from our parents. We never did get along."

"Does he still live around here?"

Kane shot Holt an affirmative nod. "Last I heard, he was taking care of a place somewhere off Dynamite Boulevard, in North Scottsdale."

"You have an address?"

"Afraid not. But I understand it's a big house, off by itself. Shouldn't be too hard to find if you ask around."

"I wouldn't know where to start. I'm not even sure where North Scottsdale is."

Kane grabbed a business card out of a desktop holder and began writing on the back. "Maybe this will help. His name's Alan. We share the same last name, but that's about it. As far as I know, he's still a golf pro out at Blackhawk. If nothing else, the folks out there should be able to point you in the right direction."

FIVE

THE COFFEE shop looked inviting. It reminded Holt why his stomach was growling. He parked in the lot and pulled a local newspaper out of a machine on his way to the front door. The early morning rush was over, the available seats as numerous as the parking spaces outside. He picked a booth by the window and ordered coffee while he glanced at the menu. When the waitress went away, he gave the newspaper a try. He didn't find anything that held his attention and tossed it aside. Through the window he could make out the signpost for Scottsdale Road on the corner half a block away. He had to be close to Scottsdale General, now called Valley Community Hospital, the next stop on his list.

The bacon and eggs were a good choice. He was always pleasantly surprised when a cook managed to baste the eggs without scorching them. He took his time over a final cup of coffee after the check was delivered. By the time he was back in the car, he was relaxed and alert, wishing the meeting with Kane had produced better results. He didn't expect much from Kane's brother, but following up the lead would give him something productive to do after he visited the hospital. He was there in less than five minutes.

Once inside the hospital, Holt followed directions from the well-meaning staff and navigated what seemed like blocks of corridors before he finally found the administration office tucked away in an obscure corner on the third floor. The office manager was an older woman with a genuine smile and bright blue-gray eyes that shined with a defiant light from under her weathered brow. Holt hoped she'd had a long career here at the hospital and would remember Dr. Jones, Pearl Norwood's doctor.

"Dr. Jones . . ." the woman said. "I don't know . . . obstetrics, huh? Have you got a first name?"

Holt dug into his briefcase and pulled out the birth certificate. "This goes back a lot of years, and all I have is a first initial." He folded the certificate at the attendant physician's signature line so only the bottom half of the document was visible to the woman. "It looks like an L, or maybe a T—"

"L. Janus," the woman said. No hesitation. "His first name's Leon. I can see how you mistook the last name for Jones." She took the folded certificate from Holt for a closer look. "Yep, that's Dr. Janus, all right. Funny how his scrawl jogged my memory, even if it is a little sloppier than I remember. He was a great obstetrician—busy all the time."

She handed back the certificate. Holt asked, "Is he still around? Do you know where I can find him?"

"You're lucky you ran into me," the woman said. "It's been quite a while—I know he hasn't been here since the changeover and most likely won't be anywhere on the current administration's database. But I've saved a few old lists. Let me see what I can scare up."

Holt scanned the notices thumb-tacked to a nearby bulletin board while he waited for the office manager to go off and search for the information. Ten or fifteen minutes later she returned with a slip of paper.

"This is all I can find; it's his place in Tonto Verde."

"I have no idea where that is," Holt said.

"It must be about twenty miles or so north of here, maybe a little farther, past Fountain Hills."

"Sorry, I don't know where Fountain Hills is, either."

The woman regarded Holt patiently, smile still in place, eyes still shining. "Oh, Fountain Hills is easy to find. Just take Scottsdale Road to Shea Boulevard and turn right. You can't miss it. Shea's the only road going through that part of the desert and will take you right to town. To get to Tonto Verde from there, you might want to stop and ask directions or check a roadmap. It's been quite a while since I've been out that way and I wouldn't want to steer you wrong."

Holt thanked the woman and marched back down the long corridors leading out of the hospital, a bounce in his step. He was suddenly feeling lucky. The temperature outside had risen, reminding him he was in the middle of the desert the instant he stepped out onto the asphalt. He tried to ignore the heat and focused on finding Kane's brother, wanting to exhaust all the leads from Kane Trucking before he concentrated on the doctor.

The golf course where Alan Kane worked was in North Scottsdale, about fifteen miles away, just off Scottsdale Road. Holt went through the now-familiar routine of cranking up the Toyota's air conditioner and punching an address into the nav system before he got underway. Half an hour later he was walking up to Blackhawk Golf Club's impressive clubhouse.

A regulation basketball court could have fit under the massive archway covering the paved entrance leading up to the double front doors. Holt took in all the wood and stonework and felt as if he were entering an upscale hunting lodge. A nouveau Southwestern flavor took over as he walked inside. Plenty of room for more basketball. The ceiling was high, held up by round, knotted pine beams; rough-hewn and lacquered, as straight and as long as telephone poles but with three times the girth. The ends of the four primary beams were joined together under a recessed skylight at the center of the ceiling, forming a cross over the hardwood floor. Across from the main entrance, an open passageway interrupted the curve of the pale stucco wall surrounding the lobby, through which Holt could see a portion of the bar and restaurant. Off to his left was a similar entrance to the pro shop. He walked in past displays of golf paraphernalia and summoned an idle staff member leaning behind a counter at the far wall.

"I'm looking for Alan Kane."

The pro shop attendant behind the counter turned Holt's way. "Do you have a lesson? The school's next door." He caught the attention of a cohort down the counter studying a computer monitor. "Hey Dave, could you show this gentleman to the school?"

Dave stepped out from behind his end of the counter and ushered Holt through a side door and across an outdoor courtyard. They came to a closed door with a placard posted at eye level. The block letters simply read, GOLF SCHOOL. Dave held the door open and introduced Holt to a woman sitting at a desk in the middle of the small office.

"This is Margo. She'll be able to set you up."

Margo looked up from her paperwork, offering Holt an expectant smile. Dave took off. Holt watched him leave, then came up to the desk and inquired about Alan Kane.

"I think Alan is with a student right now," Margo said. "Did you want to set up a lesson?" I could look over his schedule and—"

"I'm not here about a lesson." Holt was about to pass the woman a business card, but thought better of it. He made a show of glancing at his watch. "I'm from out of town. I don't have much time, but if Alan won't be too long . . ."

"Let's see," Margo said, a distracted frown gathering between her eyebrows. She squared away the computer keyboard amidst the clutter piled on her desktop and brought up the current day's schedule. "Yeah, Alan's out on the course. It's a playing lesson—nine holes after a tune-up on the range. He should be through within the hour."

"Does he have another lesson right away? This shouldn't take long, but I don't want to disrupt his schedule."

Margo glanced back at the schedule. "That won't be a problem. His next lesson isn't until one o'clock. You can wait in the restaurant, if you like. I'll tell him you're here, Mr. . . . ."

"My name's Benjamin Holt. And thank you. The restaurant will work out fine."

* * *

Blackhawk's bar and restaurant maintained the same wood and stucco theme of the lobby, but understated, scaled down so as not to distract from a magnificent view of the golf course through a bank of rollaway, floor-to-ceiling windows. No customers in sight, just a couple of waiters wearing bored expressions while they set tables and topped off condiment dispensers. Holt walked by an empty hostess station on his way to the small end of an L-shaped bar.

"Too early to get a drink?"

The bartender polishing glasses behind the bar said, "Not at all," and quickly finished what she was doing, then dried her hands with a fresh bar towel as she walked toward Holt.

"Actually, I'd just like a glass of ice water," Holt said. "Better make it a pitcher—my mouth is really dry."

The bartender filled a tall glass with ice while giving Holt a knowing look. "Where are you from, hon?"

"Is it that obvious?"

"Most people around here know to stay hydrated. Your face looks flushed and dry, and I can tell it's not sunburned. You better take this and sit down." She served him the glass of ice water and backed it up with a full carafe. "Don't let it get *too* cold before you start drinking."

Holt emptied the glass with long, greedy gulps, set it back on the bar for a refill, and chose to remain standing among the available barstools.

"I never knew water could taste so good."

"See there? You let yourself go too long without fluids. That's why they invented those small bottles of water to carry around."

"I better put that on my shopping list."

"Yeah, water and sunscreen, don't leave home without 'em."

"So when does it cool down around here, anyway?"

"It won't be long. It's not unusual for the temperature to spike like this in early October. Sort of like summer's encore." She paused just long enough to hold his attention. A smile began to form. "It's getting pretty nice at night, though."

They continued to chit chat, and an uneasy revelation crept over Holt. *Is she flirting with me?* The bartender didn't look any older than his eighteen year old daughter, Abbey. He knew the girl behind the bar would have to be at least twenty-one to serve alcohol, but nevertheless . . .

As if to erase any doubts, the bartender made one of those not-so-subtle-moves right in front of Holt, combing back her auburn, shoulder-length hair with spread fingers, giving him a perfect view of a body caught in the full bloom of youth. He might have been flattered if he could look at her without imagining Abbey in her place. He knew he was staring, and he had to wonder what the bartender was thinking when she upped the wattage on her smile, turned to fetch a menu, and came back with the menu and a place setting, ready to lean in and arrange them in front of him.

"Staying for lunch?"

"As much as I'd like to, I'll have to pass. I'm here to meet someone, and it's not for lunch."

Now the bartender's smile turned wry, as if to say, *Your loss.* He took advantage of the moment to gather up his water and the half-full carafe and to find a table facing the archway into the lobby. He returned to the bar to retrieve his briefcase from one of the stools. The bartender was back where he'd found her when he first came in. The waiters had gone away.

I'm probably imagining things, Holt thought. The girl was bored and was only being nice, passing the time. He settled in at the table. He pulled out a few sheets of paperwork from his briefcase to distract himself. He shuffled through the papers and tried to concentrate on the task at hand. Kane's business card slipped out of the loose stack. Holt reread the note, set the card on the table, and waited for Alan Kane to show up.

Holt was checking his watch, beginning to wonder, when a man in tan slacks and a white golf shirt with a Blackhawk logo over the left breast approached his table.

"Are you Benjamin Holt?"

Holt rose to shake the man's hand. He could see the bartender out of the corner of his eye, her expression saying, "You're here to see *him?*" He turned his full attention to the man and said, "Mr. Kane? Thanks for seeing me."

Holt returned to his seat and offered Kane a chair. Kane remained standing. He didn't look much like his brother, although the two men shared close to the same height and build. It must be Alan's darker tan and sandier, sun-streaked hair, Holt thought, still not able to pinpoint what was so different—until he took a good look at Kane's eyes. He certainly didn't have his brother's engaging, straightforward bearing.

"What's this about?" Kane said, showing enough agitation to make Holt uncomfortable.

"I'm looking for a woman who used to live around here, a long time ago."

"What makes you think *I* can help you?"

"The woman's name is Pearl Norwood. Her last known whereabouts was her job at Kane Trucking. I talked to your brother, and he sent me here."

"Jeffrey sent you?" Kane relaxed a notch. His initial agitation seemed to simmer down to mere skepticism. "Why are you looking for Pearl?"

"To tell you the truth," Holt said, "I really want to find her daughter. We don't have a clue where she is. We don't even know her name. All we know is that her mother is Pearl Norwood and that she was put up for adoption at birth."

"Okay, so why are you looking for her daughter?"

"She stands to inherit some money," Holt said, immediately regretting his response, realizing he was not in control of the conversation. Kane was asking all the questions, and Holt was obligingly telling him things he didn't need to know.

Right on cue, Kane asked, "How much?"

"That's not important," Holt said, angry with himself for being sloppy. He needed to forget the things weighing on his mind for at least the next five minutes and concentrate on his job. He took a moment to compose his thoughts, to get on track. When he looked at the man across from him, he wondered if his imagination was flaring up again, noticing something invading Kane's vacant stare, something more disturbing than the previous emptiness.

Before giving Kane a chance to ask more questions about the inheritance, Holt changed the subject. "Your brother mentioned that Pearl took care of you guys when you were kids. Was she working for your father back then, or do you remember her working someplace else, especially later on?" Holt was pulling up his briefcase while he talked. He found the copy of Pearl's employment records that Jeffrey Kane had provided. "Your brother didn't have much on her. I can see from her old W-2 form she was hired in 1968, but there's no record of when she quit."

"That was a long time ago," Kane said, "and I wouldn't have been paying much attention to stuff like that."

Holt gestured toward Kane with his best help-me-out-here look. "Do you know where she was living? Did your parents ever drop you at her house? Did she ever take you there?"

Kane shook his head. "Not that I can remember."

Holt slumped back in his chair. "Is there anything *at all* you can tell me about her?"

"Well, that kind of depends," Kane said.

"Depends? . . ." Holt asked.

"Yeah, it depends." Kane stared at Holt, that strange intensity building in his otherwise empty eyes. "It depends on how much you're willing to cut me in on your finder's fee."

Why did I have to mention the goddamned inheritance? Before Holt could further curse his own stupidity, his cell phone rang. It was Susan's ringtone. He stood up to distance himself from the table before answering.

SIX

FOR THE first few minutes, Kane just sat there. The phone call must have been important. Holt had walked out to the lobby almost as soon as he'd answered it. Now Kane had his chair angled for a better view through the wide entrance, and he watched the back of Holt's head over the backrest of one of the lobby's leather chairs. He was too far away to hear even a murmur of conversation. The bartender was gone. Kane figured she was either out back having a smoke or in a storage room gathering beer bottles for the cooler. He was alone in the restaurant. Just himself, and Holt's briefcase sitting on the table, no more that a foot from his folded hands.

The flap closure was folded back, the briefcase itself tipped toward him, the contents visible. Kane couldn't resist a peek. He took enough time to be thorough and had just replaced most of the contents when Holt stood from his chair and shoved the phone into a front pocket. He hurried back to the table.

"Sorry to cut this short," Holt said. "Something's come up and I have to get going."

"Did you get a line on your quarry?" Kane remained seated, watching Holt gather his things.

"How can I get in touch with you?" Holt said, ignoring the question. "If you prove to be helpful, I think we can arrange some kind of financial compensation."

Kane made a show of looking for something to write with. Holt reopened his briefcase and tore out a blank sheet from a notebook. He produced a pen and handed the items to Kane.

"I'll give you my cell number and the home phone where I'm staying." Kane handed back the paper and pen. "I also put down a phone extension here at the club."

"Here's my card," Holt said. "Let's stay in touch."

Holt closed the flap on his briefcase for the second time and slung the shoulder strap messenger-style across his body. Kane hung back and watched him leave. As soon as Holt was out of sight, Kane unfolded the sheet of paper from the briefcase that he'd stuffed into his pocket. It was a printout of a birth certificate. He studied it for a long time after first making sure he'd read the names correctly, then went straight to the golf school and had Margo cancel his one o'clock lesson. Five minutes later he was behind the wheel of his Grand Cherokee, driving north on Scottsdale Road. He figured it would take him just under two hours to make it to Sedona.

* * *

Once he had turned off Scottsdale Road to head west on the less-traveled Carefree Highway, Kane rolled a joint, keeping the steering wheel steady with his left knee. He was disappointed when he reached the interstate—he thought he should have a better buzz going by now. The surge of excitement from finding the birth certificate had passed, and he sat there behind the wheel and wondered why he wasn't feeling much of anything, no different than before he'd lit up. Maybe the pot was getting stale or too dry and losing its potency. What made more sense was that he was developing a resistance and needed increasingly higher doses. Or maybe he'd still been a little high when he lit the joint; it wasn't his first of the day. Then he caught himself wondering whether or not he was even stoned, unnerved by the prospect that he couldn't tell the difference. He needed a distraction and took to ransacking the glove box for a CD, rejecting his current selections as soon as he came across them, finally settling for that old Santana he liked, anxious for the music to do its magic.

He couldn't remember his last visit, and the outskirts of Sedona seemed unfamiliar, especially the new developments south of town. When he arrived at the old downtown section, he turned onto 89A and headed for Oak Creek Canyon.

Here, things hadn't changed at all. 89A was a shaded two lane road running alongside a narrow creek that wound its way down from the Mogollon Rim. Every so often a glimpse of towering sandstone rock formations broke into view through random openings in the canopy of trees shrouding the road. About ten miles out of town, a couple of more miles past Slide Rock, Kane pulled off the road and turned onto a familiar gravel driveway. The weathered sign was easy to miss, posted out by the road amid a small stand of overgrown juniper trees. What was left of the faded, chipped paint covering the raised lettering might have been a dark red, once upon a time. The letters spelled out, RED ROCK LODGE. Kane parked in front of a row of cabins and walked up to the one with the office shingle hanging next to the door.

A spindly old woman looked up and greeted Kane with a *How are you doin'?* as she rose out of a rocking chair facing a portable TV at least thirty years old. It was sitting on a metal desk behind the front counter. The volume was way up, tuned to a soap opera. The cast sounded like they were shouting.

Kane approached her from the customer side of the counter. "I'm doing fine, thanks." He made a show of looking around, as if he were outside. "Nice and cool up here."

"What's that?" The woman craned her neck over the counter to better hear.

Kane gestured toward the TV, raising his voice. "Do you mind turning it down?"

"Oh, is it too loud?"

Without waiting for an answer, the woman shuffled over to the TV and brought down the volume. The picture remained playing. She came back to the counter, made a slight adjustment to the half-frame reading glasses perched near the end of her nose, and glanced down at the registration book on the countertop between them.

"Do you have a reservation?"

Kane shook his head, more out of aggravation than to respond to the question.

"You're lucky it's not the weekend," the woman said. "We're still pretty busy because of all the heat down valley. But I think I can find a room—"

Kane signaled her to stop with a casual wave. "Hold on a second. Before you go to the trouble, do you mind if I ask you a few questions?"

The woman looked up from the registration book and put her hands out on either side of it and leaned on the counter. She peered at Kane from over the top of her half-frames.

"Sure, hon. What's on you mind?"

"I'm looking for someone. Her name's Pearl Norwood. She must be in her sixties by now. You don't happen to know her, do you?"

The woman regarded Kane for a moment, shaking her head slightly before she spoke. "I'm not familiar with the name. Who is she?"

"Would you believe she's my old baby-sitter? She used to take care of me and my brother. Sometimes Dad would bring the family to Sedona, and we'd stay here at the lodge. I remember one time Pearl came along when mom wasn't feeling well enough to handle us kids. That was the last time Pearl took care of us. After that trip, she moved up here permanently. We'd run into her now and again, when we were on vacation, but as time passed our trips to Sedona petered out and we lost track of her." Kane placed his hands on his side of the counter, across from the woman's, and leaned in closer, assuming a staged, conspiratorial tone. "But I learned later on that she had something going on with the guy who owned the place."

The woman's face revealed a faint smile. "Now why on earth would you want to look up an old baby-sitter?"

"I guess I'm just a sentimental guy. I haven't been here for years, and I got to thinking I might drive up to get away from the heat. When I drove past your old signpost, I couldn't resist stopping in."

The old woman's smile became less obvious as she pushed back from the desk and said, "Well, like I told you, I don't know anyone by the name of Pearl Norwood." She waited a beat to time her poker-faced delivery for a full, deadpan effect. "I do know a Pearl Diamond, though."

"Pearl *Diamond?* . . .

"That's right. You could say *she* owns the place now—she's married to Cornel Diamond. His father built the lodge back in the thirties. I'd say she's in her sixties, and it'd be the biggest coincidence I ever heard of if she's not the woman you're looking for."

Kane couldn't believe his good luck. He felt his heart start to pound against his ribcage as he dared to ask, "Do you know where I can find her? Is she here now?"

"Follow me," the woman said, coming around the counter to step outside the office. Kane followed her out the door. She pointed toward one of the footpaths meandering through the complex of guest cabins. "That path will take you to a bridge crossing the creek. When you get to the other side, keep to the path on the left and follow it to the end. you can't miss her cabin; it's bigger than the rest of 'em, more like a regular house."

Kane set out on the path. After crossing the creek he noticed the cabins were more spread out. The surroundings took on a more residential feeling. Not so touristy. He climbed the steps leading up to the porch of the last cabin and rapped on the door.

A loud voice erupted from a back corner of the cabin, calling out, "Hey Pearl, there's someone at the door."

Kane waited awhile. He was anxious to get on with it but saw no reason to knock again. Whoever had called out was still making plenty of noise. It was just too muffled for Kane to make out individual words. Presently, a petite, graying woman of indeterminable years opened the front door. She eyed Kane up and down and waited to hear what he had to say.

"Pearl . . . is that you?" Kane wanted her to be Pearl, trying to remember how she looked and if the woman before him filled the bill. "I'm Alan Kane. Do you remember me?"

Subtle, tell-tale signs of recognition spread across the woman's face. She broke into a lopsided grin and said, "Alan? My God, what brings you up here?"

They both just stood there and stared at each other for an awkward moment, then Pearl snapped out of it and stepped back from the door.

"Come in," she said, taking a quick glance over Kane's shoulder as he entered.

"Who's there?" a voice boomed out. The same voice Kane had heard after he'd knocked on the door, only louder now that he was inside.

"Excuse me a minute," Pearl said. She disappeared through a doorway. Kane waited in the well-tended front room, glancing over the comfortable-looking furniture and the rustic decoration. A further exchange of muffled words sifted out from behind the interior walls. A short while later Pearl reappeared and motioned toward Kane with a follow-me gesture. "Come on out back. We can talk while I finish up."

Kane followed Pearl to the side entrance of a detached two-car garage behind the cabin. Upon entering he could see that it had been converted into a working studio of some kind, complete with skylight. A wall containing two large windows stood where the roll-up door had been, the telltale brackets that had once supported its running tracks still visible. A couple of tall, sturdy tables occupied the center of the room, about three feet apart, taking up the space originally intended for two vehicles. The table closest to Kane was buried under haphazard stacks of paper, drawing instruments, pieces of broken glass, and an assortment of small hand tools. Before Kane could check out the second table he was distracted by the countertops, shelves, and cabinets lining the other three walls and overflowing with more sheets of yellowing paper, reference books and catalogs, and panes of glass of every color imaginable.

Pearl made her way to the second table. There was less clutter here than anywhere else in the room, although a number of projects in various stages of completion took up a fair amount of space on the tabletop. In front of her was a mosaic pattern of colored glass pieces within a rectangle measuring about five by eight inches. The individual pieces were not physically attached; they were grouped close together, sitting on a paper template. Some of the glass pieces were smaller than others, and each one had a metallic border lining its edges, as did the outlining rectangle itself. Next to this arrangement was another rectangle, similar in size, but made up of a dull, gray material. This was the piece Pearl turned her attention to as she picked up a soldering iron out of its tin cradle and went to work.

"I've got to finish soldering this up before the flux damages the copper tape," Pearl said. "It shouldn't take too long."

Kane walked up beside her to get a better view of what she was doing. In a relaxed and friendly voice, the kind of voice he might use to ask for a glass of water, he said, "Do you mind if I ask you a few questions about your daughter?"

At first Kane didn't think Pearl had heard him. She seemed too preoccupied, bending over her work, squinting through tendrils of smoke rising from the thin stream of molten solder flowing off the tip of her soldering iron. Then, in the silence, he heard a faint snap.

"Shit," Pearl said, tossing the iron back in its cradle. "I cracked the glass." She carried the rectangular piece to the other side of the table and doused it with a blue liquid cleaner and scoured it with wadded up newspaper. Colored light began to shine where moments before there was nothing but a formless gray mass. "I let the glass get too hot, dammit."

Pearl left everything on the table and took a seat on a stool next to one of the counters that ran along the wall. She didn't appear very happy. Kane wasn't sure if she was upset with him for his abrupt question about her daughter, or if she was mad about breaking the glass. Of course, she probably wouldn't have messed up her piece had he not asked the question.

He looked closer at the discarded rectangle. It looked like a miniature stained glass window. The patterns of colored glass took on the abstract rendering of a flower arrangement. It was beautiful, even Kane could recognize that. He could also see that the individual pieces of glass were interconnected, and he realized Pearl had been in the process of soldering them together and that each piece relied on the other for support. Replacing the small sliver of cracked glass without inflicting too much collateral damage wouldn't be easy.

He looked over at Pearl and said, "Sorry about that."

Pearl remained silent. Kane shifted around, feeling uneasy, about to speak, when she finally looked at him.

"Is that why you're here? This is about my *daughter*?"

Kane didn't answer. They both let her question hang in the silence.

Pearl finally spoke. "I don't *have* a daughter."

"I know about you and Bigelow," Kane said. He pulled up another stool and sat across from her, leaning his back against the table she'd been working on. "A lawyer talked to me today. He's looking for you."

It seemed Pearl tried not to react. Then her mouth started to open, as if she were about to say something but couldn't find the words.

"I don't know why he's having such a hard time finding you," Kane said. "It's like you've dropped off the face of the earth. I don't think he knows where you've been since your job at Dad's place. That's where he talked to Jeffrey, who sent him to me."

Pearl finally found her voice. "What did you tell him?"

"What *could* I tell him? I didn't know anything. All I had was a hunch. Thought I'd check it out for myself."

"Good God," Pearl said, staring past Kane as if she hadn't heard him. "Why would Logan be looking for me after all these years?"

"You mean, you don't know?"

Pearl's blank stare remained intact.

"Logan Bigelow was killed in a plane crash," Kane said. "It's been all over the news. I don't know how you could have missed it."

Pearl got up and walked back to the table and stood near the damaged piece. Kane could see she needed a moment. He watched quietly as she gathered herself. She picked up the piece and ran her fingers lightly over its surface.

"I don't pay much attention to the news, even though Cornel's always watching cable TV in his room."

"Is he your husband? The guy in the other room?"

Pearl nodded. "He had a stroke a while back. I think he's recovered more than he lets on—he can sure shout loud enough, despite the emphysema. Anyway, he spends a lot of time in the bedroom. I try to encourage him to get out more. It's not that hard getting him into the wheelchair, not with all the weight he's lost, but he's just not up for it. I know it's a hassle to drag along his portable oxygen bottles and mess with the hoses and all, but I think it's depression more than anything else." Pearl turned to look through the open door of the studio, toward the main cabin.

"He doesn't know anything about Logan and me. He'd have no reason to tell me if he saw something about him on the news."

"He doesn't know *anything* about your past?"

"What past?" Pearl said. She put down the piece and returned to her stool. "The time I spent with Logan didn't last much longer than the blink of an eye. Wait till you get a little older, you'll see. A few months here or there can get lost very easily in the course of a lifetime."

"What about the baby?"

"What *about* the baby?" Pearl said. "Why do *you* care?"

Kane wasn't sure what to say, but he knew enough to be careful. Finding Pearl had been such a long shot that he hadn't considered what to do if he actually found her. Yet here she was, right in front of him. There was also a big payoff right in front of him; he could feel it. He just needed to figure out how to proceed. Maybe telling Pearl the truth would be a good start.

"If they can find her, your daughter could inherit some money. I thought there might be something I could do to help out."

"*Some money?*" Pearl said. She stared past Kane for a moment, as if thinking it over. "I'll bet there is. Probably a lot of it, seeing that, according to you, Logan's death was such big news, not to mention all this fuss about a lawyer looking for me. Logan was no slouch back when I knew him; over the years I imagine he did pretty well for himself."

Kane nodded. "I think that's safe to say."

Pearl's faraway stare found something to focus on. She looked directly at Kane and said, "And this help you're offering . . . what, exactly, do you expect in return?"

"I haven't had time to think that far ahead. Like I said, I was just following up on a hunch. I didn't really expect to find you so easily. But now that I have . . ." Kane shrugged his shoulders, his words trailing off into silence.

Pearl continued to stare at Kane, until the flicker of a smile brushed her lips. "If I know *you*, Alan, you've already worked out something with the lawyer. What's your percentage? Is that going to be enough, or will you want something from my daughter's end as well?"

Kane shook his head slowly. He tried to play it straight, casting his eyes down at the floor, losing the battle to suppress a smile of his own.

"Little boys don't really grow up, do they?" Pearl said. "You haven't changed a bit."

SEVEN

KANE ACCEPTED Pearl's invitation for a late lunch. On the way back to the cabin, he asked her what she was working on in the studio.

"I call them my candle lamps," Pearl said. "Sort of a take-off from the original Tiffany lamp. I buy the glass, modify some of the pieces to suit my needs, then cut and fit them together with the same sort of technique Tiffany used. That lantern I was working on is my standard four-sided candle holder. I make a variety of shapes and sizes, including rounded styles. The round ones require working with wood molds, and the technique is a little more difficult to master. I also get more money for them."

Kane pulled open the back door and held it for her. "So you sell them, huh?"

Pearl walked by and shrugged. "It's no big deal. Not like a business, or anything. I have a friend in Jerome who owns a small gallery. She'll keep a piece or two on display for me, on consignment."

Kane nodded and followed her into the kitchen. She showed him a seat at the table and washed her hands at the sink before opening the refrigerator. He watched her pull out a Tupperware container as he spoke.

"I'm beginning to see why you're so hard to find—tucked away in Oak Creek Canyon, selling consignment goods under the table. When's the last time you filed with the IRS, anyway? And what about your income from the lodge? Does your husband file separately?"

Pearl placed the Tupperware container on a countertop by the sink and went back to the refrigerator for a pitcher of iced tea. She brought a couple of glasses to the table, poured the tea, then sighed heavily and sat across from Kane. She lowered her voice when she spoke, and Kane remembered her husband, Cornel, lying in the bedroom.

"I guess this is all going to come out, eventually," Pearl said. "so I might as well tell you now. Cornel and I aren't really married, not legally. At least I don't think so. I'm not sure how common law marriages work anymore."

"How many years have you been together?"

"Who's counting? It seems like forever. We just never felt the need to make it official. Our friends and the people we do business with have assumed we've been married for years. We never told them otherwise. And after I began signing my lamps *Pearl Diamond* . . . well, what else could they think?"

"Catchy name," Kane said. "I can see how that would go over big with the crystal gazers around here. Whose idea was it, anyway?"

"The name? I think Cornel appreciated the commercial potential. I thought it was kind of a kick. After a while, I started signing everything that way. It could only happen in a place like this, under just the right circumstances. It reached a point where Cornel and I thought it would be, oh, I don't know, sort of deceitful to have a ceremony after everyone assumed we were already married. After all, we did go along with it. So we just let things stay the way they were."

Pearl got up, returned the pitcher to the refrigerator, then poured the contents out of the Tupperware container into a large saucepan and set it on the stove. She looked at Kane after firing the burner.

"I was thinking—I can't remember the last time I renewed my driver's license. I'm not even sure where it is. Cornel owns the one car we have between us, and up until recently, when he had his stroke, I didn't do much driving. I had sort of forgotten about my license until I had to start taking Cornel to the doctor and run the routine errands he used to take care of. I figured it didn't really matter if I found my old license or not; it must have expired years ago. If I thought about it at all, I told myself I'd go down to Prescott for a new one after Cornel was in better shape."

"That doesn't leave you with much of a paper trail," Kane said. "I'll bet you don't have any credit cards in your name, either."

"Nope. I just use Cornel's. We never saw the need for me to apply for one. Never had much use for them, anyway. Nowadays we use his debit card for picking up cash and paying for groceries—and the groceries don't amount to much seeing as how we pad the lodge restaurant's supply orders for most of our necessities."

"You are truly invisible, Pearl. Sorry I had to come up here and disrupt your life."

Pearl stirred the stew reheating on the stove. "No big deal; it's not like I'm on the run or hiding out. We just live a simple life. I'd appreciate it, though, if nothing comes out about my consignment deals in Jerome. It's been going on for years, and I wouldn't want anyone getting into trouble."

"Your secret's safe with me," Kane said. He watched her fuss with the meal and eventually she set down a bowl in front of him.

A comfortable silence invaded the kitchen as the two of them ate. After she finished her meal, Pearl retrieved the pitcher of iced tea to refill their glasses. Kane leaned back from the table, thanked Pearl for lunch, then brought his voice down to the level she had used earlier, respectful of the fact that Cornel Diamond was within ear-shot and didn't know about Pearl's daughter.

"What can you tell me about her, Pearl? Do you know who adopted her or where she is now?

Pearl returned to her seat and talked in low tones. "I don't know where she is. During my pregnancy I didn't want to know any of the details about the adoption or anything else. I know that sounds foolish, but I thought it would be easier that way. The only good thing that came out of that time of my life was meeting your parents."

"How did that happen?" Kane said, mildly curious and wanting her to keep talking.

"When I was admitted to the hospital, they put me in a room with your mother on the maternity ward. She was there to have you, with the same doctor taking care of both of us. I'll say one thing about Logan; he made sure I got a good doctor and would have insisted on a private room if there had been one available. Anyway, your mother had a rough time of it. She had to stay a couple of extra days, and it overlapped with my time there. It gave us a chance to get to know each other. It was thanks to her I got the job working for your father."

"I didn't know that," Kane said. "I though you were just one of the office girls Dad recruited for baby sitting."

"No, it was my idea to take care of you when I could. Your mother was apprehensive at first, not sure how I'd handle it. After all, I should have been taking care of my own child. I guess that I wanted a taste of what I'd given up. To find out what it would be like as a real mother. Right away I felt close to you, like part of the family. It was the whole experience—your mom and me having our babies together, sharing some of our feelings on those quiet nights in the room. She was a real friend to me." Pearl paused to look deep into her glass of iced tea. "I don't know why, but I was never able to warm up to your dad. I don't think he liked me. We seemed to get along best if I kept my distance."

"I hear *that*," Kane said, nodding along in agreement. "It must have been tough sometimes at the office."

"Like I said, it was your mother who got me the job. I'm sure your dad went along with it to appease her. It turned out he did me a favor. I didn't want to go back to waiting tables. No matter what, I'm thankful to him for getting me out of that."

"Have you ever wanted to find out what happened to your daughter?"

"You're not going to let it go, are you Alan? What do I have to say to convince you that I have no idea what happened to her and no way of finding out now?"

"Well, who made the arrangements for the adoption? And what about the doctor? Somebody has to know what happened."

"Maybe somebody does," Pearl said, "but I don't know who it would be other than Logan or the doctor. There were some complications before delivery, and all I can remember is the doctor telling me everything had been arranged and to just focus on myself and getting through it. When he said I needed a c-section, I told him to knock me out for the procedure. At that point I wanted it over, and I didn't want to know or remember *anything*. Afterwards, in recovery, he told me I gave birth to a healthy baby girl, that she would have a good home. I didn't ask any questions. I just wanted to believe everything happened for the best and get on with my life. If I've had any regrets, or if I ever wanted to know what happened to her, it doesn't matter. The fact is I gave her up. I never held her. I never looked at her. What could I possibly say to her if we were to meet?" Pearl shook her head, tears welling in her eyes. "No. That day can never come."

"Okay, that would be tough," Kane admitted, thinking Pearl's guilt might be the real cause of her memory lapse regarding the adoption. "But what if you could tell her how rich she's going to be? What if *you're* the reason she receives her rightful inheritance?"

Pearl looked across the table at Kane. They held each other's stare until she finally said, "You're right; it would be tough, even if I were giving her good news." More silence while she thought it through, her face hardening with what Kane hoped was newfound resolve. "But I'd do it. I'd do the right thing. And I'd be happy for her if it turned out that way. But I don't see that happening. I really don't know anything that can help."

"What, exactly, do you remember about your doctor?"

"I can't even tell you his name—just that he was already an old man those thirty-some years ago. If he's still alive, he's certainly not practicing medicine anywhere."

Kane could think of nothing else to say.

Pearl cleared the table and went to work at the kitchen sink. "Don't look so glum, Alan. I'm sorry I wasn't much help, but I'm sure things will work out the way they're supposed to. The important thing is to have your heart in the right place."

"Meaning my motives shouldn't be so self serving," Kane said.

"Something like that. It might sound corny to you, but doing a nice thing for someone can be rewarding in and of itself. If you make a habit of it, your perspective will follow. You'll automatically begin to focus on the positive. How can anything but good be born of good deeds?"

"You've been hanging out with the crystal gazers too long, Pearl. Offer a helping hand in the real world and you'll pull back a stump. Times have changed, and not for the better."

Pearl dried her hands and walked back to the table. "People can change too, for better or worse." She reached behind her neck and unhooked a thin gold chain and said, "I want you to have this," while handing Kane the chain and the attached stained glass object. "It's a moth, sort of my trademark since Tiffany already has a lock on the butterfly. I set them in some of my candle lamps. You know, like a moth attracted to the flame."

Kane held the stylized little moth to the light, turning it back and forth to catch the subtle glints of amber and gold shinning through its delicately veined wings, spread out in perpetual flight.

"I don't know what to say. It's very nice, but I'm not quite sure what I'd wear it with."

"It's not to wear—its a little feminine for you. Just put it where you might come across it once in a while and think of me. You were too young to remember much of anything when I was around, but I have fond memories of those days. I'll feel good knowing you have this little reminder."

Kane thanked her, appreciating Pearl's gesture, an example of the positive energy she'd been talking about. He admitted to himself that he felt better than he had a while ago, pissed about the slim prospects of finding her daughter. He thought now's the time to leave, on a note of goodwill, before his true feelings resurfaced.

Pearl accompanied Kane as far as the front porch and said her good-byes from the railing as he stepped down to the path leading back the way he'd come. She had neglected to introduce him to Cornel, and Kane was reminded of his presence when he heard the now familiar voice off in the background calling Pearl's name.

The afternoon sun had dropped behind the canyon walls, along with the air temperature. As if relieved from their duty of shading the footpath, the surrounding trees were now free to bend and sway, ushering in the first cool breeze Kane had felt since early last May. He took his time along the path and stopped at the middle of the bridge crossing the creek. He leaned against the railing and stared downstream. He felt helpless. There was no way he was going to find Pearl's daughter. He could call the lawyer and let him know where Pearl was, but for what? To do a good deed? It wouldn't matter anyway; Pearl was a dead end. As he thought it over, Kane realized he hadn't learned anything new from Pearl at all. In fact, he knew more than she did. He had the doctor's name. Everything else they had talked about was merely confirmation of what he'd already read on the birth certificate. The birth date was a surprise—it hadn't registered when he first read it, too distracted by the other information and his mounting excitement. As soon as he saw Bigelow's name, nothing else mattered.

He watched the water flow by awhile longer—water under the bridge—then pushed off from the railing, followed the footpath to the parking lot, and headed back to the Valley of the Sun.

EIGHT

KANE CHANGED his mind about going home. He turned off Dynamite Boulevard at Alma School Road and headed south along the base of the McDowell Mountains. He worked his way toward Reata Pass, originally part of an old stagecoach trail that passed between Pinnacle Peak and Troon Mountain. There was still enough light to make out the granite boulder perched atop the peak. The rock was the size of a midrise office building and cast a long shadow across the entrance to Whiskey Flats. Kane turned in at a dirt road that snaked along for a quarter mile of twists and turns past broken down horse stalls, barbed-wire enclosed barnyards, and a ramshackle trailer before the road widened out into a large parking area. The lot was empty. Kane drove by and pulled into a another wide lane that led up to the Flats. Here he found a dozen or so cars parked near the entrance. He recognized Gunnar Warburton's Harley leaning on its kickstand, next to the front door.

The door was actually a wooden gate hanging on heavy, wrought-iron hinges that opened to what at first glance resembled an outdoor picnic area. Wood tables and bench seating took up most of the hardpan surrounding a low concrete fire ring. There were a few patrons scattered about, eating burgers and drinking beer. Kane glanced their way looking for a familiar face as he walked along the raised, old-west style boardwalk at the front end of an ancient bunkhouse that now served as a cowboy bar. Kane found who he was looking for as soon as he walked inside.

"Hey, Gunnar."

Gunnar Warburton glanced back over his shoulder, keeping his elbows on the bar, not bothering to straighten up. "Hey, man; how you been?" He freed an arm to pick up his bottle of Pacifico and drained it before hoisting it toward the bartender in the universal salute requesting another round. "Better make it two," he called out. "Looks like my friend could use one himself."

He slammed the bottle on the bar and wheeled around and clasped Kane's hand in a brother handshake that quickly turned into a mock Indian-wrestling bout. They both knew who could kick whose ass, but that's not what the ritual, macho bullshit was about; it was just Gunnar's way of showing affection. After they'd settled down and picked up their beers, Kane held Gunnar's stare for an extra second and nodded toward the door. Gunnar glanced at the pile of bills he'd left on the bar, then followed Kane out to the picnic tables. They picked a lonely spot on the far side of the fire ring. Both of them sat on the same side of the table for a good view of the patrons coming and going along the boardwalk. It was getting dark enough for the outdoor lighting to make a difference.

"What's the matter?' Gunnar said. "You outta dope?"

Kane shrugged. "I'm not really out. I'm just not enjoying what I've got. What's the sense of smoking the shit if it doesn't get you high?" He kept his eyes on the boardwalk while he talked, following the progress of a small group of women in western riding gear drumming their boot heels across the wood planks. "I'm hoping you can come up with something decent this time."

Gunnar just shook his head. "Don't try to feed me that happy horseshit. You're just turning into a scratch pothead. Like a *scratch* golfer, get it? I'll bet you're firing a joint before you get up in the morning. If I were you, I'd watch it. The way you've been stumbling around lately and losing track of what you're saying . . . you're smoking it too much, man."

"What do you suggest? A little crank, maybe?"

Gunnar leaned back and opened his arms, palms up. "Works for me."

"Maybe so. But it's not my style. I can't play golf on speed. It'd be even worse coming down. And could you imagine taking a lesson from a tweaker?"

"Yeah," Gunner said, "golf is sort of a laid-back sport, isn't it?"

"It's how I make my living. Not the lessons, so much, but—"

"Yeah, yeah, yeah, I know all about it. The fat cats looking for a little wager."

"Not always so little," Kane said. "And I have to be ready. You never know when the right opportunity might show up."

"And you can pull it off stoned on pot all the time, huh?"

"I'm not stoned all the time," Kane said, feeling like he had earlier, on the way to Sedona. And then he remembered how it was first thing this morning, when he really *was* straight. He hadn't thought about it all day—he couldn't think about it all day—but he'd really lost it. He wondered what Gunnar would have said about his little breakdown in front of the TV. He tried to push it all out of his mind and kept talking. "But even if I've had a few hits, I can still play. Sometimes I think it helps my concentration. Keeps me focused."

Gunnar snorted. "Yeah, sure. Keep telling yourself that."

Kane took a long pull on his beer. The girls in the riding gear were congregating next to one of the tables across the way, deciding who should go inside for the drinks and what they were having. Gunnar pointed his bottle toward one on the blondes.

"Isn't that Ashley Sherbrook?"

Kane looked over, straightened up a little when he saw Ashley. "It sure is. I didn't recognize her in the western get-up. I liked her better in her English riding breeches."

"Oh yeah," Gunnar said. "The English know how to do it, don't they? Those skin-tight pants, knee-high boots, and cute little jackets. I even like the helmets. Ashley looked great in that shit."

Kane couldn't agree more. "I wonder why she's changed camps."

Gunnar appraised the rest of the girls in the group. "It looks like she's taken up with the cutters. It's the cool thing now. A couple of the big ranches around here have jumped on the band wagon—breeding, training, the works. One of them even has a mechanical cow for practice."

"A *mechanical* cow?"

"Yeah, it runs on rails, remote controlled. The horse is supposed to chase after it like it's cutting out a real cow."

Kane set his empty bottle on the table and regarded Gunner with a sideways stare. "How does a guy like you know so much about this stuff?"

"A guy like *me*? What the fuck, Kane. You think I'm some dumb-ass hillbilly who doesn't get around? I know a *lot* of shit."

Yeah, Gunnar knew a lot of shit. Like how to tear down a bike and rebuild it into two-wheeled artwork; how to end a discussion anytime he wanted, with a glance or a fist, whichever was necessary or enjoyable. And he especially knew how to play his customers—yuppies and older executive types, weekend wannabes longing for that slice of authenticity that came with the signature work he'd do on their Harleys. There was more to Gunnar than met the eye, an intelligence Kane respected. Maybe that's why Gunnar liked him.

"What's the matter?" Gunnar said. "You got laryngitis or are you gonna offer me another beer?"

"Sorry," Kane said, "I guess I spaced-out for a second."

"See there? You see what I'm talking about? You better stop smoking that shit, man. You just sit tight—I got this."

Gunnar stood up to go for more beers. Kane said, "I know what you're up to. You only want an excuse to walk by and terrorize those little cowgirls. Don't scare them away."

"I've got something that might scare 'em all right, but don't you worry; some of those horsy types know how to handle a real man."

Gunnar geared into his best swagger as he made his way by the girls' table. He stopped and said a few words to Ashley, like he'd just noticed her sitting there, then looked up and gave Kane a wink before continuing on to the bar. He came back and set two beers in front of Kane, keeping another two for himself as he sat down.

Kane said, "Do they really go for that bare-chested act of yours?"

"What . . . ?" Gunnar leaned back again and struck his open-armed, palms up pose; his unbuttoned Levi vest hanging open, fluffy chest hairs unable to hide the bedrock of solid pecs. "You think this is an act?"

Kane broke into his first real smile of the day. He offered Gunnar an unspoken toast and they clicked bottlenecks. "Now can we get down to business?"

* * *

The crowd had arrived in earnest, taking up most of the outside tables, when Ashley Sherbrook sauntered up to where Kane was sitting, a beer in one hand, cigarette between her lips. She dragged in a lungful, grabbed the cigarette with her free hand and blew out the smoke before she said anything.

"Where's your friend?"

Kane remained seated, impassive. "Gunnar had to step out for a while; he should be back pretty soon."

"You going to offer me a seat?"

"Sure, make yourself comfortable."

Ashley settled in next to Kane on the bench where Gunnar had been sitting. She put out her cigarette in a tin ashtray and scooted it aside, put her beer bottle down in its place. When she finished arranging things, she turned toward Kane with a little head toss to flick a strand of hair out of her eyes.

"It's been a while," she said.

"Yeah, I guess it has."

A short silence. Ashley kept looking at Kane, glanced at her beer, back to Kane. "Maybe I shouldn't have come over."

"No, it's okay. I'm glad you did. I've just had sort of a weird day, and then seeing you here . . . it surprised me, that's all."

Kane paused for a quick swig of beer, looked everywhere but Ashley's direction, then finally rested his bottle and turned toward her. "You're looking even better than I remember, in spite of your new outfit."

"Yeah, how 'bout this?" Ashley leaned back, reminiscent of Gunnar's earlier pose. "From English rich-bitch to Western shit-kicker. Who would've thunk?"

"Why the change?"

"Decided to be a cowgirl. Arizona's not the right place for serious show jumping. It's more of an East Coast thing. Or Europe. And it takes a different kind of horse. Warmbloods rule the roost over there. A quarter horse can't compete with them, not on the higher jumps. On the other hand, quarter horses are perfect for cowboys—good cutters—and there are some great breeders right here in Scottsdale." Ashley took a delicate sip of beer, set the bottle down and stared off in the direction of the boardwalk. "My little English fantasy was fun while it lasted, but that's all it was, a fantasy."

"And now you're in the real world, huh? Hanging out with the shit-kickers and reliving the days of yore."

"It's not like that, Alan. I'm meeting some good people. You'd be surprised who's involved."

"Well, I've had some English fantasies of my own," Kane said. "I guess there's no hope for them coming true now."

Ashley flashed her secret smile, the smile only Kane could see, or so he liked to think. She said, "English fantasies? You?"

"Yeah, you know—riding through the heather on a misty afternoon with a cute English lass; turning out the horses afterwards and lingering on in the stable, watching her braids come undone, hair falling over her shoulders; unbuttoning buttons, taking off those high riding boots—or better yet, tearing at her clothes with no time or thought for taking off her boots while she urges me on, talking dirty to me in a thick British accent."

Ashley's smile widened. "You're dreaming, all right. You won't find any misty moors around here."

"I'll settle for a fake British accent and the riding boots, if you promise to take the spurs off."

"Boy, absence *does* make the heart grow fonder."

"Like you said, it's been a while."

"And now you regret dumping me, huh?"

Kane shook his head. "That's not how I remember it."

Ashley looked away. She fiddled with her beer bottle but didn't take a drink. "Maybe it's best not to remember the details." She seemed to be talking at the beer bottle, as if it were some kind of microphone. "At least not that part."

Kane reached over and gave her forearm a gentle stroke. "You're probably right. But I still like thinking about the good times."

"Me too."

She had been trying to hold her smile, but it was different now, a little forced, very vulnerable, and Kane groaned inside. She's got it going tonight, he thought, that smile. One look and it could break your heart. There weren't words for what she could express with the slightest movement of her mouth. Kane would have said something if his own works weren't caught somewhere between his chest and his throat. He washed them away with a last swallow of beer and set the empty on the table.

"Join me for one more?"

Ashley kept her smile and Kane went for the beers, thankful for the chance to walk away and compose himself. He fell in line behind the customers queued up in front of the bar, vying for the bartender's attention, the intro to an old *Outer Limits* rerun he'd seen on TV just the other night replaying in his head like a song he couldn't shake:

There is nothing wrong with your television. Do not attempt to adjust the picture. We are now controlling the transmission.

Don't fight it, Kane told himself, just flow with the situation. He hadn't seen Ashley in months and wasn't quite sure what she was up to, but he was willing to go along with her program. He tried not to think of the pleasant possibilities, wary of the frustration he was getting so good at creating for himself.

He scored the beers and threaded his way back through the crowd, half expecting Ashley to be gone, relieved when he saw her still sitting at the table, nailing him with a glance that sent something like a warm chill right through him. He sat down next to her and kept an eye out for the smile. It felt good to let go.

. . . we control the horizontal . . . and the vertical . . .

NINE

IT WAS almost eight o'clock when Holt finally touched down at John Wayne Airport. Phoenix Sky Harbor had been a mess. Over-bookings, delays, even a security issue that backed him up an extra hour before he could enter the departure gates. He called Maxine Brennan on her cell as soon as he slid behind the wheel of his car.

"How did it go?' he asked. "Any luck with Dr. Janus?"

"I've got a line on him. That signature fooled all of us—I'm looking at a copy of it here on my desk. Those doctors love to scribble, don't they? Still looks like Jones to me, even after I know better."

"You're still at the office?" Holt wasn't surprised. He knew she'd be working late after he called her on his way to Sky Harbor this afternoon.

Maxine ignored his question. "It's just as well you didn't waste time driving out to Tonto Verde; I don't think he's there. He has another house in San Francisco. Presidio Heights. The trouble is, I can't raise him at either location. I called both places as soon as I found the home phone numbers. The Tonto Verde number just rings, and I'm getting an answering machine in San Francisco. My guess is everything's shut down for now in Arizona."

"I hope he's not on a cruise in the Mediterranean," Holt said. "We need him. I pretty much ran into a dead end regarding Pearl Norwood."

"Nothing more from the golf pro?"

"Just what I'd told you. He remembers Pearl, but I still don't think he's telling me everything. I was about to press him when I got the call from Susan."

"Have you seen her yet?"

"No. I'm on my way home as soon as we finish this call. But I'm going to follow up on Kane. I let it slip about the inheritance, and he wants in for a piece."

"How are you going to play it?"

"Anyway I can. I just wish I'd kept my damn mouth shut."

After he finished the call, Holt eased out of the overnight parking lot. A few minutes later he was driving down MacArthur, the old way home. He usually avoided MacArthur for just that reason. It was the old way, to his old life. Lisa, his ex-wife, and his two daughters, Abbey and Cindy, lived up on top of Spyglass Hill. The house looked down on MacArthur, past Newport Harbor, and on to the coastline beyond. The house was all Lisa's now, and Holt was glad he'd been able to afford the settlement and pay it off for her. It helped with the guilt. It also helped if he caught the toll road and took Newport Coast Drive to his new home on Pelican Hill, avoiding any potential confrontation with his emotions. He wondered why he chose the alternative tonight.

He couldn't actually see the house from MacArthur, it was too far away to make out the details, but he knew just where to look. He stole a few glances as he drove by. He had promised to provide for his daughters' educations. He'd be there for them whenever they married. He mentally added future expenses to the alimony and child support he was already paying—he'd even picked up the property taxes last year, and for the first time in recent memory, he was scared.

Things were going to change at Vanderlip, Stratton, and Holt. He'd be lucky to keep his name on the letterhead. Without Logan Bigelow's account, he had no idea what was going to happen. As long as he was able to resolve the life insurance issue, he should be good for six more months or a year working out transitional details for the foundation's board of directors. After that, he'd have to bring in new business to fill the void. If he failed, he wouldn't last a month, probably less than that, knowing Stratton.

Pacific Coast Highway came up. Holt turned south, resisting the urge to pull over at every bar he passed along the way. When he arrived home, his son, Benny, ran up and hugged him around the thighs before he had time to close the front door.

"Mom's hurt." Benny looked up, a concerned frown creasing his brow. "She's been crying."

Holt patted the boy's head. "Mom's fine, Benny." He squatted down on his haunches to look Benny in the eye. "As I recall, I think I've seen *you* cry once or twice. You were okay afterwards, weren't you?"

"Yeah, but . . ."

Holt saw Susan turn the corner, waiting on the far side of the foyer. Holt held Benny close, a hand on his shoulder, as he walked over to hug his wife.

She held on tight. "Thanks for coming home."

"Sorry it took me so long. It was still only an hour flight. The problem was getting airborne."

Susan squeezed harder. "You're here now. That's all that matters."

Benny stood at their sides, concerned as ever. Susan smiled down at him. She reminded him of their deal: *you can stay up until your dad's home, then off to bed.* Holt picked him up this time and carried him upstairs. When he had Benny tucked in, he found Susan sitting on the sofa in the family room, the TV on for background noise.

He sat next to her. "How did the appointment go?"

"There's more to this than I thought," she said. "I read all the material Dr. McCreary gave me. I knew they might give me radiation. Or Chemo. But when I actually heard it from the surgeon . . ."

"How bad *is* it?"

Susan didn't respond at first, other than to look at Holt with a gesture that said, *Give me a moment*. She put on her game face.

"It's not that bad, not for them. Not for the doctors. They see this all the time, and yes, they caught it early. They're very encouraging. But nothing's for certain and they aren't giving me any guarantees. Not until they operate and see everything first hand and test all the margins. That's the key—making sure they remove not only the tumor, but all the cancer cells in the tissue surrounding the incision. That means radiation."

Holt wished he'd read the breast cancer material himself, thinking, at the time, that he would have a chance when he returned from Phoenix. Now Susan has already had her appointment with Dr. Troman, a signal that this was serious. Holt was well aware of how long it normally took to see a doctor, and he'd been surprised by Susan's call and upset that he wouldn't be able to go with her.

"Have they scheduled the surgery?"

"Friday morning, bright and early."

"What have you told Benny?"

"I'm not sure what to say. I think we should be honest with him. He needs to be prepared, in case something goes wrong."

"He's only six years old. He doesn't need to know worst case. Besides, everything is going to work out fine."

"How can you possibly know that? You weren't there today, hearing what they're going to do to me—and I'm talking *best* case. If everything goes as planned—if they can save my breast—I start on the radiation treatments right away. That's every day for *five weeks*. I'm going to need help, for both me and Benny. I know he's scared. He can tell something's going on. I'm scared too."

Holt pulled Susan close. They sat quietly on the sofa for a long time, then Susan led him upstairs. They undressed like they usually did, on either side of the bed, only more deliberately. They hadn't said anything for quite a while now, as if they both knew that words would kill the moment. When her blouse came off, Holt smiled at her and hoped she could read his mind. *Nothing changes, not between us.*

TEN

ALAN KANE closed his cell phone and returned it to the nightstand. He sank back into the pillows propped against the headboard and looked up as Ashley came into the bedroom with a cup of coffee.

"Who was that?" she asked, handing Kane the coffee.

Kane waved the coffee toward the nightstand. "A lawyer."

"A lawyer? Jesus, Alan, are you still obsessing?"

"It's not what you think."

No, he was beyond that now. At least he thought he was up until yesterday morning. But when people on TV start talking to you, well, you've got a problem. Paranoid schizophrenia. That's what the shrinks would call it. Kane would, too, if he didn't know better. The amounts of alcohol and drugs he'd been consuming would drive anyone batshit, but he'd rather blame it on his old man. It hadn't been that long ago since he'd died, and the obituary read a lot like Logan Bigelow's, one more reminder of all the years Kane had spent in pleasant contemplation, waiting patiently for his just deserts. When his father died, it didn't take long for Kane's soaring expectations to come crashing down in bitter disappointment. Jeffrey got the business and the family house on Central Avenue, the remodel underway before the old man's body was cold. Alan Kane had to find a job. Ashley was around at the time, and she was right about the obsessing. Probably what drove her away.

He realized she was waiting for more of an answer. He said. "It wasn't *my* lawyer on the phone."

"Yeah, sure."

As she shook her head, Kane wondered if she was responding to what he'd said or if she was pissed about the partially smoked joint still smoldering in the ashtray next to the coffee cup. If it was the joint, he expected to hear echoes of Gunnar's lecture from last night.

All she said was, "Getting an early start?"

"Oh, that? Gunnar got me some pot last night. Thought I'd roll one up and see if it's any good."

"Is it?"

It's good, all right. He had taken a few hits just before the phone rang a few minutes ago. He'd had the presence of mind to end the conversation quickly; a serious high was sneaking up on him and he managed to hang up before his impaired ability to respond to the lawyer's questions became obvious. Now he had to put Ashley at ease, but talking was difficult. It was getting so he couldn't put the right words together before they were lost in a swirl of conflicting thoughts and pot-paranoia. He pulled Ashley closer. He kissed her, tentatively at first, until she responded with a hungry enthusiasm that sent Kane into a realm of expression that required no words at all. They now communicated in a more basic language, where a sigh hinted at a wish and a groan signaled approval. Their bodies searched for a compatible rhythm, ultimately finding a steady groove that built to an urgent intensity, fueled by gasping breaths and clutching limbs. Kane savored every moment, losing all train of thought in the sensory overload, reluctant to return to reality when it was over. A few minutes later, Ashley stirred next to him and rolled out of bed.

"Maybe a little sip of the weed *is* a good way to start the day," she said, looking down on Kane. She came down closer and kissed him. "Kind of like old times. Makes me wonder what happened to us."

She turned and headed for the bathroom before Kane could answer. When she returned, Kane had his feet on the floor and the coffee cup in his hand. The coffee had turned cold, but he was after the caffeine and drank it anyway. He was coming down from his high. He felt spent, and not just from the sex. From everything. The high hopes. The quick trip to Sedona and the subsequent let-down. Partying last night, drinking all that beer and staying up with Ashley till dawn. And then getting high this morning. He wasn't sure if Gunnar had done him a favor, or not.

Ashley came back with her hand out. "Let me take that and get you a fresh cup."

"Thanks," Kane said. He handed her the cup. "How 'bout I meet you in the kitchen? I could use some breakfast."

* * *

Kane felt better after cleaning up and having something to eat. He kicked back from the table, working on his third cup of coffee, looking the place over while Ashley was off in the bedroom getting dressed. He saw his Cherokee through the kitchen window, parked next to Ashley's Explorer. Still an SUV world, he thought, despite the gas prices. Beyond the vehicles an open expanse of dirt roads and white-railed fences stretched out as far as he could see. He walked over to the window for a better look.

He wasn't quite sure where he was. His memory of following Ashley from Whiskey Flats was fuzzy, at best. There wasn't a paved road in sight from the window, just a lot of hardpan and more white fences. He couldn't get his bearings until he stepped outside and saw that Ashley's place was connected to a long row of stables, like the living quarters for a ranch hand. That's when he noticed how quiet it was. There was no one around, not even another parked vehicle. Kane saw the main house up on a knoll a few hundred yards past the stables and training rings. It had a winding driveway leading up to a covered front entrance that gave the place a sort of regal bearing, like a castle looking down on its fiefdom. Kane took it all in while he finished his coffee, then turned back to the kitchen door of Ashley's bungalow. She was just coming in from the bedroom as he stepped inside.

"You're coming up in the world, Ashley. What are you doing, working for a living?"

"Not hardly," she said, looking more cowgirl than ever in her tan boots, Levis, and snap-buttoned white shirt. "The owner of the ranch is letting me stay here, as a favor."

"So what happened? The old man finally kick you out?"

"The divorce lawyers are still squabbling over the house, making it too tense to hang around any longer. We'll have to sell it anyway, so why not split now? I was already boarding my horse here when Kyle offered to help me out for a while.

"Kyle"

"Yeah, Kyle Nabarro. He owns the place. Haven't you heard of the K-Bar-N Ranch? They breed and sell some of the finest horses in the Valley."

"I must have missed the sign when we drove in last night."

"It ain't the Ritz, but it'll do."

Kane glanced out the window again. Learning the name of the place didn't stir his recollection of how he got here. He said, "By the way, where the hell *is* everybody? It seems pretty quiet around here for a horse ranch."

"Big horse show in Nevada," Ashley said. "They caravan out there every year in a herd of RVs, SUVs, pick-ups and horse trailers. It lasts about a week. There's still a couple of Mexicans around to take care of the rest of the horses and keep an eye on things." She came up close to Kane and held up the half-smoked joint form the bedroom ashtray. "I think we should burn this evidence. Wouldn't want any illegal substances falling into the wrong hands."

"I though you gave it up."

"I though so, too. Until this morning. Now I'm thinking a little taste would be nice, for old-time's sake."

"It won't take much," Kane said, settling down at the kitchen table.

Ashley sat across from him, the ashtray between them. Kane smiled.

"Gunnar really outdid himself. He must have taken it as a personal challenge when I told him I wasn't getting high from the last stuff he got for me."

He lit the joint for Ashley. She took a long hit, held it, and sat back in her chair. After a slow, drawn-out exhale, she said, "So, what's the story?"

Kane reached over for the joint. "What story?"

"The story about the lawyer."

Kane took a hit. That was going to be it for him. Just a refresher to top off what he'd smoked earlier. His words came out with the exhaled smoke.

"You mean the phone call?'

"Quit stalling. Why the wake-up call?"

Kane passed the joint, signaling Ashley to keep it. He leaned over to pull out his wallet, produced Benjamin Holt's business card, and set it on the table next to the ashtray.

"This guy came by the golf course yesterday looking for me." Kane watched Ashley pick up the card for a close look. "He'd already talked to my brother, and Jeffrey told him where to find me. I think he's one of those heir hunters. You know, someone who tracks down lost heirs to fortunes."

"Who's he looking for?"

Kane changed his mind, taking the joint for another hit. He told Ashley the whole story while they finished it off.

That's when the car drove up. Kane heard the tires crunch across the gravel road that led from the highway. He looked out the window at yet another SUV pulling up next to Ashley's Explorer. A fine cloud of dust from the vehicle's wake drifted past the window as an older-looking guy got out and stepped onto the hardpan.

Kane looked at Ashley. She didn't seem surprised.

"Who the hell's that?" he said.

"Wentworth Tellington. He boards a horse here."

"Oh, really? Here in your bungalow?"

"I've got a key to the tack room. Kyle keeps it locked while everyone's away."

Just then the kitchen door opened after a quick, perfunctory knock. Wentworth Tellington leaned in from the stoop and stuck his head across the threshold and looked in. He was about to say something, then hesitated half a beat when he saw Kane sitting at the table.

Ashley said, "How are you doing, Wentworth?"

Tellington tore his eyes off Kane. "Hey, Ashley. Riding today?"

"Maybe later." Ashley got up from the table. She walked over next to the door to grab a key ring from a row of pegs mounted on the wall. "Would you mind bringing the key back after you unlock the door? Don't worry about locking up later. I'll keep an eye on things."

"Sure thing." Tellington grabbed the keys. His eyes darted back to Kane before he turned away from the doorway and headed out to the tack room.

When he was gone, Kane said, "Intense dude."

Ashley came back to the table and sat down. "Oh, he's harmless."

"You sure about that?"

Ashley stared out the window. Kane looked over in the same direction and watched Tellington opening a door at the far end of the stables across the way. Keeping his eyes out the window, Kane said, "You don't have a problem with him barging in here like that?"

Before Ashley could answer, Kane thought of the obvious and caught her in his gaze. "Hey, you guys don't have something going on, do you?"

"Are you kidding? He's old enough to be my grandfather."

"He didn't look *that* old."

"He's pushing sixty, if he's a day."

"That would only make him old enough to be your father."

"Let's not split hairs. I'm not sleeping with the guy."

"Whatever. But I'm sure ol' Wentworth would like to change that. And he sure didn't look too happy when he saw me sitting here."

Kane was leaning back in the chair, his eyes out the window again. Then he saw the light. "Wait a minute." He straightened up, leaned in next to the table. "He's not the reason you're being so goddamned nice to me, is he?"

"What are you talking about?"

"Come on, Ashley. I'm not *that* stoned. I can see why you might be a little concerned—out here all by your lonesome, your horse buddy sniffing around, looking for the first opportunity to get into your pants. Hell, I can't say as I blame him."

Kane waited. Ashley said nothing.

He was about to break the silence, but stopped short when out the window he saw Tellington approach the kitchen door to return the tack room key.

Ashley saw him as well and this time jumped up to intercept him outside. She came back with the key ring and replaced it on the peg. She stood by the door, keeping her distance.

"I *am* glad you're here, Alan. And I won't deny how glad I am that Wentworth saw you sitting here. You're right about him—he's been getting way too familiar with me."

"So this is what it's all about? Last night, and this morning—just keeping me around to scare off the old man?"

Ashley shook her head. She came closer to Kane, pulling a chair with her so she could sit down and affectionately stroke his arm while saying, "I'm glad you're here, regardless. Last night I was planning on staying with one of the girls you saw me with at Whiskey Flats—"

"Until you spotted me, sitting there with Gunnar."

Ashley locked eyes with Kane, shaking her head slightly. "It doesn't make any difference now, does it? Whatever the reason, we're together again, and it feels pretty good." She looked down and grabbed one of his hands with both of her own. "I should have been upfront about Wentworth. I'm sorry about that. And forget what I said about him being harmless. Don't let his age fool you. There's something about him—I don't know—under the surface. Something you don't want to mess with."

ELEVEN

KANE PLANNED on spending the rest of the day at the K-Bar-N with Ashley. It was slow out at Blackhawk this time of year. Not many snowbirds yet and the overseeded rye grass still needed a couple of weeks to properly take root. Kane had only one other private lesson scheduled with a local. He had the number for the man logged in his cell phone's speed dialer and was able to reset the lesson for another day without going through Margo at the school.

Ashley conducted him on a tour of the ranch, stopping first at the stables to introduce Kane to her new quarter horse, then continuing on to the training facilities. They didn't see a trace of Wentworth Tellington until he reined up next to them on their walk back to Ashley's bungalow. He sat astride a huge Appaloosa.

Kane had to lean back and crane his neck in order to take it all in. "That's quite a horse you've got."

"Over seventeen hands," Tellington said. "A credit to his breed." The horse let out a loud snort and reared his head sharply against the tight rein. He couldn't keep his hooves still. They shuffled and stepped in place and kicked up small swirls of dust off the hardpan. Kane stepped back a full pace to give the horse more room. Tellington smiled down on him. "He's feeling a little frisky today. Do you ride, Mister—?"

"I'm sorry, Wentworth," Ashley interjected. "I guess I should have introduced you." She nodded toward Kane. "This is Alan Kane. Alan, Wentworth Tellington."

Tellington offered his hand, making Kane come back and reach for it. The horse seemed to get even more skittish when the man's vise-like grip clamped down on Kane's outstretched hand, and Kane could have sworn he saw Tellington's spurs jab the animal's flank. The horse was prancing in place now, ready to bolt, while Tellington kept him reined in with his left hand and held on to Kane with his right. Kane felt a stab of panic as he pictured the horse taking off, Tellington continuing to hold on, dragging him alongside those pounding hooves. Kane managed not to rub his hand after Tellington finally let go, at least not until Tellington turned toward Ashley and said, "What are y'all doin' for lunch?"

"Sandwiches and beer, at my place. Why don't you join us?"

Tellington considered the request for a brief moment, then smiled. "Sounds good, but I'll need about twenty minutes or so." He reached down to stroke the horse along the side of his neck and gave Ashley a quick wink. "I gotta let Hannibal cool down before I curry off the sweat. Can't go putting him away wet." He dismounted and led the horse on foot toward the stables.

Kane and Ashley resumed their walk. When Tellington was out of earshot, Kane said, "Why did you have to do that"

"Do what?"

"Invite your *friend* over for lunch."

"Since Wentworth's been hanging out here, I've been nice to him." Ashley paused when she saw Kane's expression. "Not *that* nice, just sociable. But it wouldn't do for me to stop being polite, now, would it?"

Kane shrugged. "How long have you known him?"

"Not that long. I didn't run into Wentworth that much at first—maybe I just didn't notice him. It wasn't until I moved in myself, right across from the tack room, that I realized he was out here almost every day."

"Doesn't he have a job, or something?"

"No, he says he's retired. He lets on that he had some kind of government job, but he makes a point of not being specific."

"Government, huh?"

"Yeah. Like the FBI or CIA or something. Something secret. At least that's what he wants you to believe."

"Do you?"

"I don't know. The guy's definitely been around, but I'm not sure what to think. He sounds like he knows what he's talking about sometimes when he's telling a story and starts getting into details. But then he'll stop himself short, like he just caught himself giving away things he's not supposed to. That's when he'll give you that little wink of his and change the subject. To tell you the truth, I don't know if he's for real or just trying to impress me."

Kane opened the door for Ashley and followed her into the kitchen. The odor of stale marijuana smoke from their earlier session hit them as soon as they walked in out of the fresh air. Ashley opened some windows and Kane said, "Let out the smoke and bring in the horseshit."

"I love the aroma of horseshit in morning," Ashley said, giving Kane a little wink of her own. "But don't worry, the wind usually blows away from the stables and I get a nice, clean breeze through here."

Kane found his chair at the table. Ashley opened the first beers of the day and started making sandwiches. They were both at the table, working on their second beers, when Wentworth Tellington walked in, this time without the knock.

Ashley told him to help himself to a beer from the refrigerator and Kane checked him out as he walked over, thinking his Levi's were too tight and his aftershave was too strong. Kane could smell him from across the room, disliking him more by the second. He didn't like the blow-dried silver hair or the meticulously trimmed silver mustache. He didn't like the way Tellington carried himself with that arrogant, cock-sure manner that suggested just how desirable the man thought he was to women—in his dreams. And he especially didn't like the way Tellington had shaken his hand, looking down from his high horse, graciously offering Kane a small sampling of greatness.

Before he shut the refrigerator door, Tellington turned toward the table. "How's everyone doin' on beer? I'll bet you can use another one, huh Kane?" He grabbed an extra beer without waiting for an answer and came over to the table, sliding a fresh bottle in front of Kane. "Here you go, pardner."

Kane's absolute dislike of the man was now complete. He watched Tellington take a seat across from him. Ashley sat midway between them, on Kane's right. Now that the asshole was down off his horse he didn't look so imposing. He was still a big guy—probably outweighed Kane by thirty or forty pounds—but it was that middle-aged, paunchy kind of weight, although well distributed and looking fairly solid.

"So how 'bout it, Kane?" Tellington said, setting down his beer and wiping traces of foam off his perfect mustache. "What's your interest in horses? Are you a rider, or just an admirer?"

Kane finally noticed the man's eyes. They looked like black steel beads and Kane felt that if he looked at them too long they'd bore a hole right through to the back of his skull. He instinctively averted his gaze, as if he'd been staring a welder's arc. He looked at Ashley, remembering what she'd said: *something you don't want to mess with.* When he answered Tellington's question, his eyes were on Ashley.

"I'm not interested in horses at all. I'm just here to see my girl."

"Okay, I get it. But what *are* you interested in? That is, when you're not busy with your girl?"

"I'm a golf pro. I work out at the Blackhawk Golf Club."

"You're still not answering my question. I don't care about your job. I want to know what gets the fires burning. What is it, for you, that makes life worth living? Surely it's more than chasing after a fucking golf ball."

Kane didn't know what to say. He didn't even know what to think. His mind went blank and he sat there as if he were paralyzed from the neck up, unable to summon forth an answer to Tellington's smug, condescending questions.

Ashley broke the silence by noisily pushing back her chair. She got up for the platter of sandwiches she'd placed on the counter. When she set them on the table, she asked Tellington, "What about *you*, Wentworth? What floats your boat? Surely it's more than riding horses."

"Hey, no fair. You guys are teaming up on me." Tellington reached for a sandwich, smiling good naturedly. "It's not just riding horses. It's the whole nine yards: the breeding and nurturing, watching a young colt or filly grow to maturity . . . it gives me an excuse to be here, out in a natural environment, away from our artificial society."

Ashley dealt plates in front of the two men and rejoined them at the table. "Maybe Alan could say the same thing about golf."

Tellington bit off a mouthful of sandwich. Between chews, he said, "Is that it, Kane? Is golf some kind of Zen thing for you?"

Why, Kane thought, couldn't they just leave it alone? He took a long pull on his beer, set the bottle down, and fidgeted with a sandwich before putting it on his plate without taking a bite. He finally said, "Golf's been good to me. I'm not on the tour, or anything, but I get by. As for the Zen angle, I don't know what you're talking about. Golf's just an enjoyable sport that I happen to get paid for teaching."

"Now if you can teach people to *enjoy* golf, you must be one hell of a special guy. Golf's got to be one of the most frustrating endeavors mankind has ever created. I should know—I've tried it a couple of times myself."

"To be honest with you," Kane said, "it's the betting that's enjoyable."

"So you're a hustler, huh?"

"Let's just say there's people out there who like to play for money. I like to accommodate them."

Tellington looked out the window for a moment, chewing on his sandwich, then regarded Kane. "So how does someone set up a match with you? Is it like that old movie, *The Hustler*? You know, with Paul Newman, where he had the manager—I think it was George C. Scott—who bankrolled him and set up the pool matches. For a big percentage of winnings, of course."

Kane shook his head. "It's nothing like that. I'm talking about friendly matches, one on one. Sometimes the stakes are pretty high. There's a subculture of golfers out there looking to make big bets. They learn who's who at a variety of different courses around the country and for whatever reason think they're good enough to take 'em on. They'll show up with their egos and vanity handicaps and very often wind up being the ones taken—straight to the cleaners."

"And those are the guys you like to play, is that right, Kane? The guys with the egos and the vanity handicaps. Fat cats you know you can beat. You're a hustler, all right."

Tellington picked up his beer to wash down a swallow of sandwich. When he lowered the bottle his unblinking stare bore into Kane with the certainty of a man who knew the answers to his questions before he bothered to ask them.

"When's the last time you made a *real* bet? When you put it all on the line, not knowing for sure how it was going to turn out?" Tellington paused for Kane's response. When none came, he continued. "I heard a story once. I was in a bar, and a golf match was on the TV. It was years ago, and Lee Trevino was lining up a putt that could win the tournament for him. I remember it was Trevino because the guy on the stool next to me told me a story about him while we watched. I had commented to the guy about the unbelievable amount of pressure Trevino must be under, knowing what was at stake. The guy next to me sort of laughed and then told me the story. It was more of quote, really. Supposedly, Trevino had once said, 'Pressure isn't having to sink a putt to win a million dollar tournament—pressure is five dollars on the front nine, five dollars on the back, and five dollars for the eighteen; and all you've got are two dollars in your pocket.'"

Tellington lifted his bottle for the last of the dregs, then slammed it on the table. "Now *that's* what I'm talking about. Laying it on the line. Feeling alive. You ever done that, Kane?"

"Like you do, *Tellington*?" Kane spit out Tellington's name like a piece of rotten meat. "Is that what you're really all about? I don't buy it. Trade that horse of yours for a flashy ride and drive up to Blackhawk's bag drop some weekend and I'll have a hard time separating you from the rest of the bloated bullshiters I deal with everyday."

Tellington calmly finished his sandwich. He picked up a paper napkin off the small stack next to the platter. He concentrated on wiping his mouth and hands, then discarded the napkin and returned his stare directly at Kane. "You keep using that tone with me, son, and I'll come over there and bury my boot so far up your ass you could use my spurs for earrings."

Kane felt the blood rush to his head. He didn't say anything. He didn't do anything. He sat there and let the initial moment pass, that all-important moment when he should have acted, when he should have done something—anything but sit there. But moments are fleeting, and as soon as this one passed it was too late. Tellington owned him.

Another long moment dragged by in silence. Then Tellington said, "Great sandwiches, Ashley. They really hit the spot. You mind if I help myself to another beer?"

"Not at all," Ashley said. "Stay put and I'll get it for you."

Kane started in on his sandwich and kept quiet while Tellington and Ashley bantered back and forth in polite conversation of no importance other than to dissipate the tension in the air. They were so casual about it, Kane wondered if the tension had even been real. Maybe Tellington had been kidding around, had one of those senses of humor that didn't always come across as funny, especially if you were the brunt of it. Kane chewed on his sandwich and sneaked glances at Tellington out of the corner of his eye. The man was completely relaxed, leaning back in his chair, smiling and gesturing as he talked. Then he winked at Kane when he noticed him watching, without so much as missing a beat in the conversation with Ashley. Kane felt his face redden again. He got up, dropped off his empty plate in the sink on his way to the bathroom. When he came back he opened the refrigerator for another beer.

"I have to get going," he said.

Ashley looked at him, a trace of a smile still on her lips from something Tellington must have said while Kane was out of the room. "What for, Alan? Didn't you clear your schedule?"

Kane wanted out of there. If Ashley was going to laugh at Tellington's jokes after what had just happened, she could deal with him on her own. "I've still got that other appointment."

"What are you talking about, your lawyer? I thought you shined him on."

"I told you, he's not my lawyer."

"You also told me you blew him off. What gives?"

Tellington, looking bemused, jumped into the conversation. "What's the matter, Kane? Getting sued? Hit somebody with a golf ball?"

"It's nothing like that," Ashley said. The way she looked at Tellington, Kane could almost see the wheels turning inside her head. But he couldn't believe it when she said, "Alan's stumbled onto quite a *situation*." She looked over at Kane. "Maybe you should tell Wentworth about it—see what he thinks."

"What good would that do, other than maybe start a rumor I'd rather not be responsible for."

"Now I'm intrigued," Tellington said.

"Come on, Alan," Ashley chimed in. "Wentworth might know something, or somebody, that might be able to help you."

Kane came back to the table, bringing his beer with him. He took a pull and considered Ashley's expectant face. He studied Tellington as you would a feral dog in an open field, with nowhere to run. He ignored his better judgment and started talking, all the while silently berating himself for trying to impress the asshole sitting across from him. But he couldn't deny the satisfaction he felt when Tellington responded to Bigelow's name.

"Let me get this straight," Tellington interrupted. "This lawyer, he tells you he's looking for the rightful heir to an estate, and he doesn't know that *you* know it's Bigelow's."

"That's the long and the short of it," Kane said. "He didn't give me any pertinent information on purpose. That phone call came at just the right time. He answered it and left the room. Otherwise, I wouldn't have had a chance to get to the birth certificate."

"And you have it with you?"

Kane said nothing.

"All right, Kane, go ahead and play it like that."

Tellington turned to Ashley and had her fetch something to write with. He asked Kane to go back to the beginning and start over. When Kane got to the part about finding Pearl, how she was off the grid and how lucky he'd been to find her, Tellington began interrupting him with questions. He asked Kane for a full physical description of Pearl—what did she look like, how old, how tall. Tellington wanted to know all about the Red Rock Lodge—exactly where it was located and the best way to get there, how many people were employed, how many guests were registered. When he heard about Pearl's side business, he wanted to know about that. As soon as Cornel Diamond's name came up, Tellington asked about him. Tellington kept writing as he fired off questions, able to do both tasks concurrently and with what appeared to be a practiced ease. Kane gave him everything he knew, caught up in a vague sort of excitement as he watched the man work.

"So," Tellington said, looking up as soon as he had finished with his notes. "This Benjamin Holt—what did he want when he called you this morning?"

"First thing he did was apologize for having to leave so abruptly yesterday, before we finished our meeting. Then he wanted to know if I'd remembered anything else about Pearl."

"And you said . . . ?"

"I said I didn't know anything."

"You didn't tell him you saw Pearl yesterday?"

"Pearl's a dead end. She can't help him. I wanted to get off the phone, so I skipped the details."

"I'll take that as a *no*."

Tellington tossed the pencil he'd been using onto his notes and leaned back in his chair, appearing to think it all over. He sat in stony silence while Ashley busied herself with the dishes and threw out the empty beer bottles that had piled up. Kane went for another fresh beer and paced off nervous energy.

After several minutes, Tellington said, "I want you to listen to me, Kane. Listen good. How'd you like to cash in on this? Bigelow's estate is worth millions. What if—"

"Don't you get it?" Kane blurted out. "There's nothing there. I tried the finder's fee angle and there's nothing to work with."

"Slow down, cowboy. I'm not talking about a finder's fee. That's chump change. I'm talking about collecting the inheritance."

"Are you crazy? There's no way—"

"This is where you've got to listen to me, Kane, and listen good. I'm not crazy. There *is* a way."

Tellington motioned Kane back to his seat at the table. Kane sat down and kept his mouth shut. Tellington leaned forward, letting his forearms slide up on the table, and said, "You need to call back that lawyer. Pester him a little bit about the finder's fee."

"I told you, man, that finder's fee is—"

"Goddamnit, Kane, hold your water, will you? Shut up and listen to me. You need to use Benjamin Holt to make this work. All he knows or has to believe is that you want a piece of the action. Like you said, he doesn't know you're wise about Bigelow, so just act accordingly. After you remind him about the finder's fee, tell him you've found Pearl." Tellington shot a cold stare at Kane, daring him to say something. Satisfied with the silence, he continued. "Try to set up a meeting for tomorrow at her cabin in Sedona. It's got to be past mid-afternoon, at the earliest. Later is okay, but no earlier than say, four or five tomorrow."

"What should I tell Pearl?"

"You won't have to tell Pearl anything. Just go up there with Holt and act like a guy helping him find Pearl's daughter. Whatever happens, and I mean *no matter what*, keep your mouth shut. Don't give it away that you know about Bigelow. Holt will have his guard down if he thinks you're unaware."

"But I've already told Pearl. She knows this is about Bigelow's estate."

"Don't worry about that. We're going to play another angle. I'd tell you more, but first I need to work out some details and see what's possible. I'll try to give you a heads up sometime before you guys meet with Pearl. By then we'll know whether to go ahead or forget about it."

"I still don't get it. What good is it going to do to meet with Pearl?"

"It's our *in*." Tellington said. "Just take this one step at a time and see what happens. I'm not sure of anything yet or if I'll be able to set it up. All I know is we have to act fast. If this opportunity turns out to be real, it won't last long. A few days at the most." Tellington picked up the pencil. "What's the best way to reach you? You got a cell phone?"

They exchanged numbers. Tellington folded the sheet of paper he'd been writing on and stuck it in his shirt pocket. He got up from the table and announced, "All of a sudden I've got a lot to do today. Right now this is only a wet-dream, but you never know."

"You're serious, aren't you?" Kane said.

"Damn straight, Kane. Fuck this up and I'll show you just how serious I can be."

TWELVE

HOLT FOUND Susan at the kitchen sink scraping off the breakfast dishes from earlier and loading them into the dishwasher. He came up from behind her and gathered her in his arms.

"How about we send for your mother?"

Susan stopped what she was doing and twisted inside his embrace to look at him. "What for? We can handle this. The surgery won't be any worse than the biopsy. I'll probably be back home the same day."

Holt stepped back, still holding on to Susan's shoulders as he studied her face. "What's the harm? She could be a big help around the house and taking care of Benny while you're undergoing the radiation treatments."

"Since when have you become buddies with my mom . . . wait a minute, have you already told her?"

"Yes."

Susan spun away and went back to the sink to rinse the coffee cups, glancing through the countertop window. "You know how she gets. I'd rather not worry her. I wish you would have let *me* handle it."

"Look, I'm sure Friday is going to work out fine. It will turn out to be minor surgery with a stellar prognosis. But just the same, I thought it would be better to let her know what's going on now, rather than break it to her all at once after the fact." Holt waited a moment, then told her the rest. "She wants to help, said she could fly out tomorrow morning."

Susan turned toward him. Now she was the one doing the face studying, and Holt was only too aware of how easily she could read him.

"You still have more work to do, don't you? In Phoenix."

"Yeah, but that's not why—"

"You promised that you'd be here for me. That it would be you, not my mother, with me on Friday."

"I'm not breaking any promises, no matter what. I meant what I said and I'll be here. But we still have some time before Friday, and something's come up that needs my attention. I'll have to go back to Phoenix to take care of it."

"How long?"

"A day, at the most. I need to get there by this afternoon."

"All right, Ben. But I'm holding you to your promise. *You'll* be here, not just my mother."

* * *

Kane was parked at the curb near Southwest Air's departure area at Sky Harbor when his cell rang. Caller ID announced Tellington's number.

"Are you alone?"

"Yeah, I'm still waiting for Holt. He's due on the two o'clock arrival."

"Good. Now don't forget to hit him up for some money first— your so-called finder's fee. You need to sell him on why you're doing this. The more you distract him, the better."

"I get that, but I still don't know what good it's going to do."

"I don't have time to fill you in with the how and the why right now, but by the time you're in Sedona there will be a *new* Pearl Norwood in play."

"*A new Pearl?* What do you mean by that?"

"Just what I said, Kane. We're putting in a substitution, a new player who'll lead Holt where we want him to go."

"What about Pearl, the *real* Pearl? Where will she be?"

"Somewhere safe and out of the way. I've got it all worked out. Take Holt out to the lodge in Sedona and follow our girl's lead when you get to the cabin. I've got to go now. Still a lot to do."

Before Kane had time to digest the phone conversation, Benjamin Holt showed up outside the second set of departure doors down the block. Kane shifted the Cherokee into gear and drove over to pick him up.

Holt threw his carry-on in the back and climbed onto the front seat. "I see why you like the departure drop-off. No cars or busses lined up for the arrivals."

"It works pretty good," Kane said. "And if there's no departures at the time, there's not so many cops around to keep the waiting traffic clear of the curbs."

Holt leaned back in his seat and faced Kane. "So why did you hold out on me?"

Kane didn't have an answer.

"I'd like to know why you didn't tell me about this when we first met."

"I didn't think about it until after you'd left," Kane said. "And then, since you were already gone, I decided to check it out myself. To tell you the truth, I didn't think anything would come of it. I hadn't seen Pearl for years and figured it was a long shot she'd still be around."

"So where are we going?"

"Sedona. About a two-hour drive. But before we go, there's the matter of my fee."

"Okay, Mr. Kane . . . can I call you Alan?"

"Sure, why not."

"Okay, Alan, what have you got in mind?'

"You mean, how much?"

"That would be a good place to start."

"I figure ten percent."

"Ten percent of what, exactly?"

"Ten percent of the inheritance. I mean, without me, Pearl's daughter wouldn't be getting anything, right?"

"That's one way of looking at it. The thing is, that inheritance money doesn't belong to me. It belongs to the beneficiary of a trust agreement and I'll never have access to it. Any deal we strike has to be between the two of us."

"So I'll just take a percentage of *your* fee."

"I'm afraid it doesn't work like that, either. I'm on retainer. I'm not collecting any fees. I'm only doing my job. If I think the information you give me is worthwhile, I'll have to pay you myself."

"So I have to take you all the way to Sedona to meet Pearl with no guarantees, nothing in writing? I don't even know how much you're willing to pay."

"How does ten thousand dollars sound?"

Kane took a moment to think about it. Tellington was right, a finder's fee was chump change. Kane remembered the newscast from the other morning, before he lost it, when they were talking about a billion dollars in cash and assets. Whatever this inheritance amounted to, it had to be big for Holt to be flying back to Phoenix on a moment's notice to check out a lead.

Kane had to ask. "How much is the inheritance?"

"I can't tell you that, Alan. What's important, for you, is to understand what I think your information is worth. You're only taking me to meet the mother, not the actual beneficiary I'm looking for. If we were going to meet the daughter, we'd be having another conversation. As it stands, I still have to find her. Pearl may or may not be able to help. I'm operating on blind faith here as much as you are. Under the circumstances the ten thousand is a generous offer."

"Can I at least see the money?"

"Even if I carried that kind of cash around, that's not how I do business."

"Okay," The lawyer was getting testy and Kane figured he'd pushed it far enough. "Can we at least shake on it?"

They shook hands, then Kane pulled the Cherokee away from the curb. Not much was said while Kane navigated the freeway interchanges on the way to I-17. But once they were headed north, Holt said. "So now that we're on the same page, what else can you tell me about Pearl Norwood? What's the *real* story? How did you find her?"

"Like I said, it's been years, and I wasn't very old when I'd last seen her. But some of it came back when I started thinking about it. I remember my mother liked her a lot, but after one of our vacations in Sedona, I never saw her again. Later on, I heard my folks talking about her moving up there, at the lodge we stayed at."

"What did you tell her?"

"What do you mean?"

"When you found Pearl, what did you say. Didn't you tell her why you were looking for her?"

Keep your mouth shut. Tellington's admonition was practically ringing in Kane's ears. *Whatever happens, keep your mouth shut.* Kane realized he was in the middle of an elaborate improvisation, and he was already getting too loose-lipped. He had no idea what the plan was or what was going to happen next.

"What *could* I tell her?" he said. "I was surprised I found her. All I knew is that you were looking for her daughter, and that's all I said."

It fell silent again inside the Cherokee. Despite Tellington's advice, Kane couldn't imagine traveling all the way to Sedona without a little conversation. As a diversion, he told Holt to feel free to check out the CDs in the glove box. Some of them were pretty old, and thinking Holt looked a good ten or fifteen years older himself, he might even find something he liked.

"I haven't heard this in a while," Holt said, holding a copy of *Riding With the King*, an old B. B. King – Eric Clapton double act. He pulled the CD already there out of the player and waved the *Santana* at Kane. "Boy, you're old school. This is even before *my* time."

"I like that stuff," Kane said. "That's Santana's first release, from '69. Doesn't have a title, really. Just *Santana*, the name of the band."

Holt changed his mind about B. B. and Clapton and shoved *Santana* back in the slot. He found the track for *Soul Sacrifice* and turned up the volume. Kane smiled to himself, toying with the idea of offering Holt a joint. When the disk had finished, Holt replaced it with his first pick. It was on the last track when the exit for Sedona came up.

"We've still got a ways to go," Kane said. "Just a local highway now, about ten miles to town, and a few more out through Oak Creek Canyon."

THIRTEEN

O NCE THEY were on 89A, Holt couldn't believe they were still in Arizona. They'd left the desert behind. The trees, the creek, and the imperial red rock that crowned the canyon walls and encroached upon large swaths of impossibly blue sky—it took him by surprise. He felt a slight tug of disappointment when they turned off the road and cut short their journey up the canyon. But when they had parked on the Red Rock Lodge's gravel lot and were out of the Cherokee, and when Holt had paused a moment to stretch out the kinks and take a look around, the pleasant feeling he'd experienced on the road grew stronger, like a physical embrace. It must be the fresh air, he thought, having to catch up with Kane already on his way to the cabins across the creek.

Holt stood off to the side while Kane knocked on the cabin's front door. An older woman welcomed them inside.

"You must be Mr. Holt," the woman said, offering her hand. "Just call me Pearl. I think there's already been enough confusion regarding my last name. I've been using Cornel's for so long, it's second nature."

Holt glanced at Kane before he spoke. "I wasn't aware of that. And who's Cornel?"

"Cornel Diamond, for all intents and purposes, my husband. We've been together over twenty-five years, just haven't gotten around to making it official."

"That might explain why we've had such a hard time finding you."

"Well here I am," Pearl said. "But I hope you won't be too disappointed if I'm not able to help you. From what Alan told me, it's my daughter your after, and I have no idea what happened to her after she was born."

"If you don't mind," Holt said, "I've got a few other questions I'd like to get out of the way before we talk about your daughter."

Pearl had shut the door and they were all standing in the small entryway to the living room. Pearl offered Kane and Holt the sofa while she sat down in a well-used stuffed rocker across from a low coffee table. There was an interplay going on between Kane and Pearl that seemed off, not what Holt had been expecting. He couldn't put his finger on it, but it was noticeable, especially when Kane started sweating. Holt could see the stains spreading under his armpits. Now that they were seated, Holt turned his focus to Pearl.

"The first thing I need to do is confirm your identity."

"Makes sense," Pearl said. "But I'll have to excuse myself and dig around the place and see what I can find. All our business papers and such are in Cornel's name, and I've lost track of my driver's license. It expired years ago, anyway."

"You must have something," Holt said. "A Social Security Card, an insurance policy, old doctor's bills under your former name—"

"I think I've still got my Social Security Card."

Pearl rose from her chair and walked out of the room. Holt had an oblique view of her through the doorway to the kitchen, rummaging through a small, roll-top desk, pulling out and replacing drawers and checking the pigeon holes above the desktop. She found what she was looking for and returned to her chair holding a cigar box. After setting it on her lap, she lifted the cardboard lid and dug into the contents, discovering musty looking envelopes and faded photographs and stacking them on her lap as well, behind the box.

"It's been a long time since I've gone through these things," Pearl said. She held up one of the photographs for a closer look, a wistful expression on her face as she placed it on the growing stack. Then her face brightened when she peered into the next envelope. "Here it is," she said, and handed a small card across the coffee table to Holt.

It was a Social Security Card issued to Pearl Norwood. Holt handled it gingerly, afraid it might crumble to dust. It looked ancient, the printing faded, the edges worn and frayed. But Pearl's name was still legible, and Holt felt a pleasant rush cross his ribcage when he read the same number he'd memorized from Pearl's old W-2 forms. Holt was no expert on forged documents, but the card appeared to be the genuine article to him. He knew there were talented people out there who were capable of creating authentic-looking fakes, but Holt couldn't imagine that an obscure golf pro and a Sedona recluse could produce a flawless and accurate forgery on such short notice. He handed the card back to Pearl.

"Hold on to this for now. Just don't lose it."

Pearl tucked the card into the envelope she'd taken from the box, then replaced the stack she had started, placed the envelope on top, and closed the lid. She stood up, walked into the bedroom for a few minutes, and came back without the box. She shut the door behind her, careful to be quiet, and said, "Why don't you make yourself at home, Alan? I want to show Mr. Holt my studio and talk over a few things. Be careful not to wake up Cornel; he's had a rough night."

"Sure thing," Kane said.

Holt stood up to accompany Pearl to the studio. Once inside, he asked, "I gather Cornel's not well."

"He's had emphysema for years, now the stroke . . ."

Holt looked away, examined the clutter, and to change the subject asked about some of the items strewn around the workbenches. Pearl gave him a brief summary about her candle lamps, holding up one of the partially completed pieces and pointing out items of interest. But she seemed distracted, and soon put down the piece and lowered her voice.

"This is part of the reason I want to speak to you privately. I've been making these lamps for years now. Over time I've done business with some folks around here, friends of mine who sell them for me. It was no big deal at first, but over the years I've sold a fair amount. I've never reported any of it to the IRS. We never paid taxes on the income."

"How do your friends sell them for you?"

"It's all on consignment, little tourist shops here Sedona or over in Jerome. We split the proceeds, off the books. I'd hate to see them get into trouble on my account. I never really thought about it before, until yesterday, when Alan showed. up."

Holt remained quiet, waiting for her to continue.

"When he told me you were looking for my daughter, that there was an inheritance, I thought it best not to say too much until I found out exactly what he knew. He didn't seem to know anything about Logan."

"Logan?"

"Come on Mr. Holt. *Logan Bigelow*. I might live out in the sticks, but I'm not out of touch. I saw the news. The next day Alan shows up wondering where my daughter is. I can still put one and two together and come up with the right number."

"So you didn't tell him?" Holt asked.

"Not a word. At first I thought surely he must know, but when I thought about it, I saw there was no way Alan or anyone else would even suspect that I'd had a relationship with Logan Bigelow. And so far the news hasn't reported anything of the sort. That's the other reason I wanted to talk out here. There's no reason for Cornel to overhear any of this."

"Your secrets are safe," Holt said. "All of them. I don't think Alan knows anything."

Pearl let out a sigh of relief. "I like Alan. He's kind of charming, in his own way. But I was very nervous about him being involved in this. When I first heard Logan had died, I felt bad, but removed. We had never stayed in touch. He was good to me while I was pregnant, then after the baby was born I never saw or heard from him again. It never occurred to me that he'd want to leave something to his child. He was so careful about covering it up, what with his wife and all—"

Holt got the message. "And what you're saying is, you'd like to keep it that way."

"Yes I would," Pearl said. "I don't want to bring any attention to my life here. I may be a little out of touch with the real world, but I know how the media works. If they got hold of this, they'd leave no stone unturned, poking their noses into my business and those I do business with; talking to the neighbors, dragging Cornel into it—the poor man doesn't know anything at all about this, and with his medical condition . . ." Pearl shook her head slowly, a faraway look in her eyes.

"What if I keep you out of it? Holt said. "Will you help us? Believe me, we don't want publicity any more than you do."

"You're not working on your own?"

"No, I'm not. And *everyone* is anxious to get this settled."

"Do they want *me* for anything? Or just my daughter?"

Holt smiled to himself at Pearl's roundabout way of asking if she was included in the inheritance. Who wouldn't be curious? Even a few scraps out of an estate like Bigelow's could amount to serious assets.

"As far as I know," Holt said, it's just your daughter."

Pearl nodded. "Just as well. And I want to do the right thing. If my daughter has something coming it would be wrong of me not to help."

"Do you know where she is?"

"I have no idea. I never saw the baby after it was born. I thought it would be better that way, since I was giving it up. I thought the less I knew about its situation, the better. I overheard a conversation, though, at a lawyer's office in downtown Phoenix. Logan sent me there. He was out of town and called to give me directions to the place. Said I had to sign some papers. I was pretty well along by then, just about due to give birth."

"Do you remember the name of the lawyer?"

Pearl appeared to be thinking about it, then shook her head. "No, it was so long ago . . . I remember his office, though, somewhere on Central. And I also can remember a phone conversation I heard through a closed door while I was waiting in the outer office. I was sitting close enough to the door to make out most of what the lawyer was saying. It was kind of sketchy. You know how it was back then, the way people would talk over the phone when they were looking for pot or something, thinking they were being careful but not fooling anybody who might be listening."

Holt *didn't* know—the sixties were before his time. But he nodded agreeably. "Did you think that was strange, like there was something illegal going on?"

"I didn't know *what* to think. And I couldn't help asking questions after he hung up and came in the room. He reassured me that he had found a good home for the baby, that they'd come out from Los Angles and take it right away with, as he put it, 'No paperwork, no fuss—other than this document I need you to sign.'"

"Did he mention who they were, the new parents?"

"No. But I overheard a name during the first part of the phone conversation, when the lawyer asked for the man he was calling. It was Bryce Saunders. *That* name I've never forgotten."

* * *

It was quiet in Kane's Cherokee. Holt was eager to get back to the airport, where he could call Maxine and begin the search for Bryce Saunders. It had taken a fair amount of will power to leave Pearl's cabin before making the call then and there, but Holt didn't want Kane listening in on the conversation. To take his mind off it, Holt looked over and said, "You did good, Alan, I couldn't have found Pearl without you. If this checks out, you'll be taken care of. I promise."

"You willing to put that in writing?"

"Trust me, will you?"

"*Trust me*? I can't believe what I'm hearing—from a lawyer, no less. First you're talking about good faith, now trust."

"Like I said, it's a two-way street. I have to trust you, as well. Pearl's concerned about her privacy, and I told her I'd respect it. That's why she didn't tell you everything. She wants to stay in the background and keep out of this as much as possible."

"So I'm out of it now," Kane said. "I don't get to know what this is all about?"

"Don't worry, you'll find out soon enough. In the meantime, Pearl asked me to keep this quiet. I hope you'll follow suit and not tell anyone."

"What could I say? I don't know anything."

Holt saw no point in answering a rhetorical question and turned toward his window to watch the view pass by. It was getting dusky in the canyon and would be dark by the time they hit Phoenix. Kane took over the music selection. He put on something more up to date—The Foo Fighters, at an ear-splitting volume. Holt's ears were still ringing after Kane dropped him at the now familiar departure lane at Sky Harbor.

He found a quiet corner in a vacant waiting area and called Maxine.

"You gotta pencil handy? We're looking for Bryce Saunders. Last known address, somewhere in LA."

"Last know when?"

"Over thirty years ago, but who's counting? He'll have to be easier to find than Pearl—I've never encountered anyone *that* far off the grid."

"I wouldn't be so sure about that," Maxine said. "We were lucky. And your friend, Alan Kane? He's just as hinky. All I've been able to pull up on him is a PO box. Employment records and credit checks were sketchy as well. But I did find something interesting—after his father died, he contested the will. The old man owned Kane Trucking and left everything to his other son, Jeffrey. Alan got nothing. In fact, he was stuck with some hefty fees after his litigation failed."

"I guess that would explain their strained relationship," Holt said. "It's kind of disturbing news, though, considering the circumstances."

"I thought so, too. But it's just a weird coincidence, right?"

"About all this sudden interest in an inheritance? It has to be. Kane doesn't really know anything. Besides, we started our search for Pearl Norwood on our own. I'll bet whatever happened to Kane was still on his mind when I approached him. It must have motivated him to try to cash in on this. He was definitely hoping for a bigger payoff."

"Did he go for the ten thousand?"

"Yeah, and it'll be well worth it if Saunders knows where the girl is. But just in case, we need to stay on top of Janus. Have you made contact yet?"

"Not exactly, but I found him at a hospital in San Francisco, about to undergo major surgery. I'd left several messages on his home answering machine and his daughter finally returned my calls—they were probably becoming a nuisance."

"You're kidding me," Holt said. "For every step forward we're taking two back. So what's his prognosis? Will he pull through?"

"It sounds serious. Annie—that's his daughter, Ann Warren—told me he's got an aneurysm in the aortic artery just below his ribcage."

"Annie, huh. You two are already on a first-name basis?"

"She insisted," Maxine said. "If you get the chance to talk to her, you'll see what I mean. She's concerned about her father, of course, but she also comes across as a warm, caring person in her own right. That's why I felt I could take a chance with her."

The line fell silent. Holt finally asked, "What do you mean, exactly, by *taking a chance*?"

More silence. Then Maxine was back on the line, her voice not quite brimming with its usual confidence. "I made a judgment call; I felt I had to. I went ahead and told Annie why we needed to talk to her father."

"You told her everything?"

"I didn't know what else to do. I would have taken the next plane to San Francisco myself if I'd been able to see Janus before he went under the knife, but I couldn't make it in time. He's an old man, in his mid eighties, undergoing a risky procedure for a man his age—for any age."

"So you asked his daughter to find out what he knows, in case he doesn't make it."

"Yes. I didn't put it quite like that, but she agreed to tell him about our inquiry if she gets the chance and if he's lucid enough to understand her. I felt I had to give her all the details, including Bigelow's name, for him to have any chance at all of remembering something that happened so long ago." Another pause. "I hope you're not mad at me."

"I'm not mad, just a little nervous. I probably would have done the same thing myself."

"I told her how important it was to keep all this confidential, but frankly, I don't think our little drama is of much concern to her at the moment. Our last conversation took place a few hours ago, and I suppose the old boy is in the thick of it right now. All we can do is wait it out."

FOURTEEN

KANE WAS surprised to see all the messages on his cell phone. He'd just walked into the bedroom and noticed the phone when he emptied his pockets. The calls were from Tellington, sent while Kane was on the way back from Sedona with the music cranked up way beyond the range of a cell phone chirp. Kane listened to the most recent message. It was short. Tellington's voice sounded tense.

"I'm at Ashley's. Get over here, now."

Kane pocketed the phone and turned for the door. Ten minutes later he was driving up to Ashley's bungalow, his headlights washing over Tellington's SUV parked by the kitchen door, his empty stomach turning queasy from an ominous sense of dread.

Tellington's voice called out, "It's open," before Kane had a chance to grab the doorknob. He walked in and found Tellington sitting at the kitchen table.

"Where's Ashley? I didn't see her Explorer out front."

"Never mind about her," Tellington said. "How'd it go in Sedona?"

"Okay, I guess. It would have helped if I'd known sooner what you were up to. Who *was* that woman, anyway. And where's Pearl?"

"Sorry about taking so long to fill you in, but I had a lot to do and not a lot of time. We barley made it as it was." Tellington's steely eyes bore in on that spot the inside of Kane's skull. "Did Holt buy it?"

Kane grew more uncomfortable standing there, unsteady on his feet. He took the seat across from Tellington and felt like he was climbing into bed with the devil.

"Yeah, he bought it. He thought she was Pearl. Whoever she is, she's good. I almost believed her myself."

Tellington stare softened, his eyes showing a hint of relief. He continued looking at Kane and said, "What's he doing now? He tell you his plans?"

"He didn't tell me anything and I don't know anything. The woman took him out to Pearl's workshop and they talked out there awhile. I don't know what went on."

"Okay," Tellington said, his stare hardening again as he stood up. "Follow me."

He pushed open the kitchen door and stood there and held it. Kane didn't like the idea of brushing by him on the way out, but Tellington wasn't moving. Another one of those moments, Kane thought, feeling it slip away as he acquiesced to the man's will. They walked across to the tack room, its door lit by a bare bulb over the transom. Tellington pulled the key out of his pocket and unlocked the door, holding it open once again for Kane to pass through.

There was no mistaking the tension now, and Kane was suddenly afraid—not like before, but *really afraid*. He could smell his own fear, recognizing it for what is was without ever encountering it before. Sweat flowed from his armpits and ran down his ribcage, its odor drowning out the scent of Tellington's cologne and increasing in potency as he entered the room.

Then he saw Pearl lying on the floor.

The assault on Kane's senses ramped up when Tellington flipped on the interior switch and lit up the room. It was far more than his own fear that Kane was smelling; it was death. The stain of body fluids darkening Pearl's clothing below the waist and the red stain visible through the clear plastic bag covering her head made it obvious at first glance, which was all Kane could handle before sagging against a saddle stand, feeling lightheaded and in danger of passing out. Tellington stood over the body and glared at Kane.

"Take a good look at it, Kane, and get it over with."

The two of them stood silent. When Kane got his breathing under control he tried to say something. The words wouldn't come. Tellington finally broke the silence.

"I didn't want it to happen this way, not like this. There was no reason she had to die." Tellington was staring at the body. After a short pause he looked over at Kane. "But it happened, and now we'll have to deal with it."

For the moment, Kane had a bigger problem to deal with—his own sanity. Sheer panic actually had a desirable allure. He pictured himself letting go, running out the door screaming, allowing nature to take its course. What's the worst that could happen? He'd been afraid for good reason. He must have sensed, on some primal level, the pall of death as soon as he heard Tellington's voice summon him to the ranch. Only it was Pearl, at least for now, who had ended up lying on the tack room floor. He looked at Tellington, still unable to speak. Even if he survived the night, he would still be involved in a murder.

"You don't look so good," Tellington said, "Let's get some fresh air."

He guided Kane out of the tack room. He turned off all the lights, including the bulb over the door, and they sat in the darkness next to each other on the stoop.

"You're still looking kinda pale." Tellington gave him a pat on the shoulder. "Get your head down below your knees for a minute. Get the blood flowing again."

Kane did as he was told. The fresh air was doing him good and the clammy lightheadedness began to go away. He brought his head up and looked across the hardpan at the miles of white fences suddenly aglow with a radiant purity, and he was confused at first about the source of the light. He then noticed how bright everything was around them and how the shadows were cast from the stable roofs and he almost laughed when he realized it was just the moon cresting the ridge behind the ranch and now shining across the valley. It remained relatively dark under the eve where they sat. Kane kept staring at the fences as Tellington spoke.

"We gotta get rid of the body, Kane."

Kane didn't answer.

"Let me rephrase that," Tellington said. "*You* gotta get rid of the body."

Kane turned quickly toward Tellington, but now the man looked away, staring off in the distance as he continued.

"I don't have time to help you, other than to lend a hand loading the body in your Cherokee and tidying up around here after you take off. At least I was able to get her head covered before she bled all over everything." He paused for a moment, like he wanted a response. When none came, he said. "Well, what are you waiting for? Get your vehicle over here so we can get goin'. I've got things to do in LA that can't wait."

Kane finally found his voice. "You mean you're still going through with this?"

"*We* are going through with this, Kane. There's no backing out now; we're committed. And thank your lucky stars I'm not leaving you here holding the bag all by yourself. Do you have any idea how easy it would be for me to walk away? There's nothing to tie me to any of this."

"What about the woman you sent up to Pearl's place?"

"What about her? Do you know who she is or where she's from? Do you know how fast she can disappear if I call her? No, you'd be stuck, Kane, with a lot of explaining to do. Like what happened to Pearl and what were you doing with Holt up at her place. If he finds out you set him up with an imposter, he won't be happy."

Tellington gave Kane a full minute to let it sink in. After the prolonged silence, he said, "But I don't know why we're talking like this. Nothing's changed. Not really."

"How can you say that?"

"Look," Tellington said. "I know this is rough, and it's not the way I planned it, but there's no reason why we can't go on."

With that, he turned to Kane, and although his face remained in the shadows there was enough moonlight reflected off the hardpan for Kane to recognize, or at least *think* he recognized, the first sincere expression he'd seen from the man when he said, "Do you have the slightest idea how much Bigelow was worth?"

"They said a billion dollars on the news."

"The *news* tends to exaggerate, but what you heard wasn't that far off. Bigelow's been on the Forbes 400 list and climbing steady for the last ten or twelve years. Their last listing had him at a net worth of nearly 850 million dollars." Tellington paused for effect. "If he leaves his daughter—his only living heir, by the way—if he leaves her say, ten percent of his fortune, that's 85 million right there. It obviously could be a lot more, but I'm being conservative here, thinking worst-case. And the guy was smart. You gotta figure everything's set up in trusts to beat taxes, so figure the full 85 mil is up for grabs. Who knows how much it *could* be; I'm afraid to even think about it."

The 850 million dollars was a potent reminder of what this was all about. But Kane also knew the dangers of getting your hopes up. He couldn't help but recall that morning in the attorney's office, waiting for his name to be mentioned among the other beneficiaries of his late father's trust, and after that didn't happen, anticipating to at least show up on the supplemental will, which of course also passed him by. He knew there was no such thing as a free lunch, but he was robbed of what was rightfully his. This situation now offered it all back, in spades. Call it *poetic justice.*

He matched Tellington's stare and said, "How are we going to do this?"

"Get rid of the body? Hell, Kane, look around. We're in the middle of the desert."

"Forget the body. How are we going to collect the goddamned inheritance? The stakes have gone up and I need to know how you plan on pulling this off."

"Hey, that's right. This isn't one of your sure things, is it, Kane?"

"Don't fuck with me. We're talking about murder and who knows what else you've gotten me into. I have a right to know what's going on."

Tellington smiled, a big, wide smile that gleamed in the indirect light. "Good for you, Kane. I believe you're growing a backbone. I respect that in a man. And you know what, I'd like to sit here and map the whole thing out for you, but like I said, we don't have a lot of time."

"You better *make* the time, because I've about had it. Otherwise, if you want to end it right here, go ahead."

Kane held his breath. He'd either get an answer, or sudden violence.

"All right, Kane, I'll tell you how we're going to parlay the situation. This is going to work because I've already got a ringer for Bigelow's daughter. I thought about her as soon as you started sharing your little story with us yesterday. She's the daughter of a friend of mine, the woman Holt met up at Pearl's cabin."

"You're shitting me," Kane said. "You just happened to know her?"

"It came to me in a flash, Kane. It was one of those things— right time, right place. This friend of mine? I've known her for years. In fact, we've worked together before. I also knew she had a daughter around thirty years old, but I had to find out exactly how old he she was to see if we had a shot."

"A shot at what?"

"It's complicated, Kane. You see why I don't have time for this? I can't take all night explaining it to you."

"Give me the short version."

"Then pay attention. I've got to be in LA tonight, so I'll only go over this once." Those steely eyes were back, making sure Kane was listening. "Anyway, the girl we're talking about, my friend's daughter? Her name is Mona. The first thing I did yesterday was call my friend and get Mona's birthday, and wouldn't you know it, she was born in 1981. I knew we were in business.

"But Bigelow's daughter was born in 1980."

"That's okay. We can work with this. If Mona were too much older, it wouldn't work. But *this* works because of the next stroke of luck—hell, its more than luck. This is on a much grander scale than mere luck. This is fucking cosmic. You see, Mona didn't have a birth certificate, not until her parents were ready to enroll her in school. When Holt and his buddies research Mona's background, all they'll find is a delayed birth certificate for her. We'll provide the rest, a solid explanation that will satisfy anyone who's interested."

"You lost me at the delayed birth certificate."

"Don't worry about it. *Holt* won't be lost. That's all that matters."

Kane had forgotten for the moment there was a body lying on the other side of door. He was concentrating on what Tellington had said, and even without fully comprehending the plan, he saw a major complication already.

"Let's say this works—the people in control of the estate think they've found Bigelow's daughter. What happens when the *real* daughter finds out?"

"The real daughter probably doesn't know anything about it. A lot of parents don't tell the kids they're adopted, much less tell them who the birth parents are. They usually don't know themselves."

"What if they find out?"

"Nobody's shown up yet, have they? And if they figure it out after it's in the news, it'll be too late. The real daughter will have a harder time proving who she is than my friend's daughter. Don't forget, Mona's DNA matches her mother's—the woman Holt will have already confirmed as Pearl Norwood."

"Won't there be adoption records? Some kind of paper trail?"

"That's the beauty of the plan—it's *simplicity*. We're going to use Mona's own documents. This is classic misdirection. Once Holt believes he's found Pearl, it's all over. We don't have to sell him on Mona. Her records will be in order and where they should be. Like I said, if they want a DNA match for conformation, Mona's and *Pearl's* will match."

"What about Bigelow's DNA? Won't they want to use that?"

"Let's hope they can't. The explosion and the fire after the crash left nothing but crispy body parts. From what I've read in the papers, the fire was so hot that DNA testing might turn up inconclusive for identifying them."

Kane had another question, but Tellington cut him off.

"There's more, Kane, if you want to hear it. I believe the real adoption was illegal. There's a good chance the foster parents don't know who the birth parents were and I doubt there's any conclusive paperwork at all."

"How can you possibly know that?"

"Think it through. You told me Bigelow's name is on the birth certificate. If a legal adoption had taken place right away, that certificate would have been sealed and a new one issued naming the new parents. All the other stuff—attending doctor, dates and places—would remain the same. That's the only certificate Holt would have been able to find, and all he would have needed to track down the daughter. After finding her, he'd want the original certificate for corroboration, but that would take a court order and a little time even if it were rushed through the system—more time than he's had, so far."

Kane sat quietly. He studied the white fences and listened to Tellington's steady breathing beside him. After a while he said, "But there's no way to be sure, is there?"

"No, Kane, there's no way to be sure. And you're right, the stakes have gone up, but I see the rewards far exceeding the risks."

Then Tellington flashed Kane a quick wink; at least Kane thought he did. It was hard to tell in the soft light under the eve. But he had no trouble hearing Tellington say, "Kinda makes you feel alive, don't it?"

FIFTEEN

THERE WASN'T another vehicle in sight along Dynamite Boulevard. Kane kept his eyes on the rearview mirror, waiting for a set of headlights to appear off in the distance and steadily gain on him and then burst into a bright, pulsating array of reds and blues followed quickly by a far brighter wash of white light from the ubiquitous searchlight mounted on the cop's cruiser.

He knew it was only paranoia; after all, how many times had he been pulled over and rousted by the police? He told himself it hadn't happened yet, and there was no reason for it to happen now. Why would they pull him over anyway? He was just driving down the road in a nondescript Cherokee, minding his own business and obeying the traffic laws like he'd done a thousand times before—except for the pot he sometimes kept stashed under the driver's seat and the times he might have had a bit over the legal limit of alcohol running through his veins. No, if something went wrong tonight, he could be sure Tellington was behind it. Whether it was paranoia, or a healthy dose of mistrust, it kept Kane watching the rear view until he turned off Dynamite and onto the long gravel drive that led to his current residence, the only man-made structure on an otherwise pristine desert hillside patchworked with sun-bleached scrub and stunted mesquite. When the two-story house came into view, appearing as quiet and secluded as ever, Kane breathed easier, though he knew it would be a long time—maybe forever—before this night was completely behind him.

He pulled into the garage and got out of the Cherokee, leaving the garage door up, waiting for the automatic timer to turn off the interior light. He walked around to the back of the vehicle and was about to open the tailgate, then hesitated a moment when something occurred to him. He ran into the house, reentering the garage a couple of minutes later wearing an old pair of cowboy boots. He opened the tailgate and rolled back the screen covering the cargo area. He pulled out Pearl's body and slung it over his shoulder and balanced it properly before setting out for the open desert behind the house.

He'd have to hump the body a long way up the slope to make sure of crossing the property line before he started digging. The house stood on a ten-acre lot on the north shoulder of the McDowells, and Kane had a general idea where the perimeter was drawn. His load was light enough starting out, but a weight far surpassing that of Pearl's body soon rode on Kane's shoulders as he pressed on. It felt like the weight of every evil deed that had ever been committed was now bearing down on him. His earlier fear and paranoia began to fade and he no longer thought of just himself but of what he was doing. The moon shone brightly, lighting his way through rocky gullies and past thorny mesquite branches and all the other prickly obstacles threatening his passage. But the light reflected off that spent rock orbiting the earth held no warmth. It was as dead and cold as the body he carried over his shoulder.

Kane made it to a shallow ravine that had to be well past the property line. Breathing hard, he used the last of his energy to climb up the other side and continue on a few paces, where he found a good spot for the grave. He dropped Pearl's body unceremoniously onto the ground. Flesh and bones hit hard with a sickening thud that echoed in the now soulless center of his very being. He sat down an a rock across from the body and looked over at what was left of Pearl Norwood while he tried to catch his breath.

The body was wrapped tight in a shower curtain from Ashley's bungalow. It had been the best he and Tellington could come up with at the time, knowing they had to keep Kane's vehicle free of any forensic evidence. And as Kane now stared at the body, still able to make out the dark outline of Pearl's face through the translucent shower curtain and the drycleaner's plastic bag Tellington had earlier placed over her head, a sense of unreality took hold of him. Everything had happened so fast. Wasn't it just yesterday morning when he was getting high with Ashley, telling her about Pearl and Bigelow? It had started out as nothing more than an interesting story, Kane thought, something to talk about over a joint at the kitchen table. He had admitted as much, hadn't he? Ready to forget the whole thing. Why the fuck had he paid attention to Tellington? A man he'd never met and knew nothing about.

Kane kept staring at the body as if it could answer his questions. When he looked away, he found no comfort in the harsh, moonlit landscape. If anything, it heightened the feel of unreality continuing to close in on him. It was the middle of the night yet light enough to read newsprint, and he suddenly felt exposed and vulnerable. He took a last look at the body, figured it would be safe enough where it lay for the time being, and set off for the house. He soon hurried his pace, nervous about finding his way back to the body as he noticed a bank of gray clouds drifting over from out of the southwest and threatening the moon.

He tried to take the same route he'd just used so as not to spread his tracks all over the place. Thinking about where he could find some tools, the former house-sitter came to mind. He'd been a more active caretaker than Kane, taking on a few substantial projects the year before Kane had replaced him. Most of the labor was dirt-work, like shoring up the railroad ties that formed the low retaining wall behind the house; or collecting the native rocks and running them alongside the gravel driveway and finishing the job with low-voltage lighting. The tools he'd used were still hanging on one of the garage walls. Kane pictured them in his mind and knew where to look. As soon as he entered the garage, he grabbed a digging bar, a pick, and a spade. He hoisted them onto his shoulder and headed back out.

The clouds were reaching for the moon as Kane dumped his load next to Pearl's body. He'd been in too much of a hurry to think about grabbing a flashlight, but when the first stray clouds scudded beneath the moon it didn't seem to matter. He still had plenty of light to dig. He scratched out a likely border between a medium-sized rock and a mesquite tree and went to work. His heart sank when the spade bounced off the hard ground.

Kane took a moment to reevaluate the grave site, but this place looked the same as everywhere else—rocky and hard. He threw down the spade and picked up the digging bar, a seven-foot length of solid iron weighing about thirty-five pounds. One end was wider and heavier than the other, squared-off and fashioned with a crude, blunt tip. Kane held the bar vertically in front of him with both hands, hoisted it as high as he could, and drove the tip into the ground, letting the weight of the bar do most of the work. The tip stabbed through the surface easily enough, and Kane felt the first trace of hope since his ordeal had begun. He started working the bar in a steady, relaxed rhythm, knowing he had a long night ahead of him. He needed a deep hole.

He hadn't told Tellington where he was taking the body, thinking it best to keep that information to himself. Tellington had shown no concern about it. Like he'd said, *We're in the middle of the desert*. Tellington's only expressed worry was of the body being discovered. Kane figured that burying it would be best, weighing his options while he and Tellington had been packaging Pearl for her last ride in the Cherokee. He knew it would be risky driving to his place with a corpse behind the back seat, but he could get there quickly and not have to worry about his activities being discovered once he got there.

The biggest risk was having the body buried close by. If suspicions ever implicated him, the authorities would be all over the place, possibly with cadaver dogs or ground penetrating radar to look for the grave site. But they'd have to cover ten acres of rugged terrain before even thinking of extending the search, where they would have to deal with potential legal hassles concerning warrants and find the manpower to comb the vast and nearly inaccessible surrounding properties. As long as he was careful, Kane felt they wouldn't have much of a chance finding anything.

The body could always be uncovered by erosion or new construction, neither of which Kane believed would be a factor in the foreseeable future. That left the animals to worry about, and visions of a pack of coyotes digging up Pearl's body and strewing her bones all over the landscape kept Kane motivated to dig deep. He had his shirt off now, the sweat flowing freely, dripping off his brow and running down his torso, where the top of his chinos wicked it up and spread a wet stain below his belt.

The digging was easier now that he'd broken the surface. He was just beginning to make some real progress when off to one side he hit the first big rock. The digging bar wasn't able to pulverize this one, and when Kane started digging around it, looking for an edge so he could pry it out, all he uncovered was more of the rock. For all he knew, it could be the rounded dome of a huge boulder—they were everywhere. Some of them looked like they'd rolled down the mountainside, scattered here and there where gravity dictated. Others were half-buried extensions of more substantial formations, one of which, Kane realized, he could be standing on. All he could do was angle away from the rock and hope he didn't encounter any more like it.

He kept digging at a steady pace until some time around midnight and finally had to take a break. He sat on the edge of the hole next to his pile of freshly excavated rocks, his feet dangling freely inside. He had more digging to do and hoped his hands would hold up. They were hardened from years of golf, but the digging bar and the handle on the shovel had eaten up the calluses hours ago. Kane was almost afraid to look at the blisters, amazed, nevertheless, at how well he could see the details on his upturned palms. The moon had climbed high behind the broken gray clouds that now filled most of the sky. But the clouds were only thick enough to diffuse the moonlight rather than block it out. And as Kane turned his gaze into the hole, he saw that the cloud cover also diffused the shadows. He could see clearly every nook and corner down where he had dug, the light eerily filling the empty space, where not even the faintest of shadows were cast from the vertical walls of the grave, nor from his own body as he leaned over the opening. Just enough light to see what I'm doing, Kane thought, thankful for this measure of good luck. He looked around again, reappraising his surroundings, trying to feel confident that under the softened moonlight he looked no more conspicuous than one of the saguaros standing nearby.

* * *

Dawn was still a few hours away when Kane lowered Pearl's body into the grave. He shoveled in loose dirt until he no longer heard it drum against the shower curtain, then tossed back the heaviest of the rocks he'd dug out, hoping to create a barrier between the body and the most determined, hell-bent pack of coyotes he could imagine. After he finished backfilling the grave, Kane scattered the remaining dirt displaced by the body. He broke off a dead mesquite branch and used it as a crude rake to blend the freshly turned soil with the lighter colored surface dirt, knowing that in a day or two the desert elements would complete the process of erasing any signs of his handiwork. He then gathered up his tools, took them back to the garage, and returned to the grave site for a final look around. He picked up the mesquite branch for one more sweep, this time obliterating his footprints the best he could, the smooth-soled cowboy boots not leaving much to begin with. He'd be sure to get rid of them first thing in the morning.

SIXTEEN

HOLT AND Maxine had agreed to meet early on Thursday morning, well before Stratton or Vanderlip normally arrived at the office. Holt wasn't in the mood for seeing either of them. He was waiting at the conference table in his office when Maxine walked in.

"I've got something for you," she said, handing Holt sheet of paper. "A friend at the Registrar's office fast-tracked it for me."

Holt quickly scanned the heading on the copied document. "A delayed registration of birth?"

Maxine took her seat while Holt finished reading.

"Mona Saunders," he said. "What do you make of it?"

"The only thing bothering me is the year of birth—1981."

"Maybe there's a practical explanation. It's only a few months later than the November, '80 date on the original."

"You want this to be it, don't you?"

"It would be nice. But I've been wondering why there's an original certificate in the first place. Since there is, and if this delayed certificate belongs to the right person, why didn't the registrar find the original and reject the application for this one?"

"How could they?" Maxine said. "The original's from Arizona, and there's no federal database for this stuff. Besides, all the names are different and so is the birth date." She reached over and stubbed a line of the copy with her index finger. "And look here, they didn't apply for this until May of 1985."

"But why *is* there an original? It should have been sealed."

"Not if the adoption took place off the books."

"That's about the only thing that make sense," Holt said. "I guess the hospital in Arizona could have already issued the birth certificate before the arrangements were made." He took a moment to think it over, trying to remember exactly what Logan had told him. "It would have been nice if Logan had filled me in, but we never got that far into the details before he died."

"It doesn't matter. All we have to do now is explain the birth date discrepancy. Maybe Bryce Saunders can help us out with that."

"You've found him already?"

"He's in the LA phone book, if it's the right guy. He was so easy to find that I had time to run him through a few search engines. Found his name on a search though the state's union archives. He's a member of the American Federation of Musicians, Los Angles Local 47."

Maxine handed Holt another sheet of paper.

"So he lives in Beverly Hills, huh?" Holt kept talking as he scanned the sheet. "This looks promising."

Maxine said, "I'm working on his birth and marriage certificates and DMV records. I should have photocopies available for you soon."

"We also want a Social Security number issued to Mona Saunders. We need more than just a delayed birth certificate. We need a certified copy of the whole form. By itself, this won't be accepted as evidence in any proceeding involving estates of decedents, or in any proceeding to establish heirship, unless the affidavit of at least one person who knew the facts was filed at the time the delayed certificate was registered. Similar rules govern Social Security numbers. If Mona has a number, it probably means her delayed registration has already passed the test. It would be good to know this as soon as possible, and I'll bet you can find out if she has a number a lot quicker than it will take to receive all the support documents for the certificate."

"Makes sense," Maxine said. "I'll get on it."

* * *

The drive to Beverly Hills was almost therapeutic. The traffic on the 405 was moving at a reasonable pace and the fact that he'd missed running into Stratton had already made Holt's day. He drove by rote, barely aware of checking his mirror or braking and accelerating with the flow of traffic. He pigeonholed all the things on his mind for later access and relaxed into his seat. He had a lot to do and not much time. No matter what, he'd be there for Susan come Friday morning.

His nav system alerted him when the Wilshire Boulevard turn-off came up. He turned off the audio once he was he was on the surface streets. He had a general idea where he was going and preferred to use the system's map as a visual back-up rather than follow spoken directions. He found the residential street near La Cienega Boulevard. He had to smile when he came up to the weed-choked lot. Beverly Hills, huh? he mumbled to himself, shaking his head as he climbed out of his Mercedes.

At the rear of the lot, a good twenty or thirty yards back from the street, stood a graying, wood-framed, two-story duplex. What was left of the paint peeling off the siding was pretty much the same color as the weathered surface beneath. The windows had a lifeless look about them, stained and dusty and unable to shine in the morning sun. Holt walked the narrow sidewalk cutting through the knee-high weeds, straining to check for a number next to either of the doors facing the street. He climbed the stairs to the porch. It was hard to tell if anyone lived inside. If there were curtains on the windows they were drawn back, out of sight, the panes standing too high from the ground and too far away from the porch for Holt to see into them. There was a small window, though, in the upper portion of one of the doors. It was glazed with a crusty film of dirt and neglect. Holt craned his neck and peered inside. It was like looking through old dishwater. All he could see was the bottom of an interior stairway. After stepping back and taking another look around for identifying markers, Holt finally went over and tried the door to the first-floor residence.

He waited half a minute after ringing the bell, then rapped his knuckles against the door a few times before going back to the door with the window. Not able to hear a chime from the other side, not sure if the doorbell was out of order or if the chime was too far away up the stairs to be heard, he pounded loudly against the door. Probably should have called first, he thought, but he still believed the wise thing to do was initiate the first contact with Saunders in person. After standing on the porch for a reasonable amount of time and not getting a response from either of the units, Holt walked back down the sidewalk leading to the street. Halfway to his car, he turned around for a last look and saw a man in threadbare, colorless sweatpants and a faded red tee shirt standing on the porch. The door to the upstairs residence stood open behind him.

"Mr. Saunders?"

The barefoot man stepped down to the sidewalk, an inquisitive expression fixed on his face. "Yeah? What can I do for you?"

Holt walked back toward Saunders. The man was as gray and faded as the old sweatpants he wore, as much in need of an overhaul as his surroundings. Holt wondered what instrument he played and tried to picture him in a musical setting, but his imagination wasn't up for the task. It was more likely Saunders hadn't had a gig since his front lawn disappeared. Holt tried to sound upbeat when he introduced himself.

"A lawyer, huh?" Saunders said, turning the business card over in his hand, like he might find a message written on the back telling him why Holt was there.

"That's right. I'm trying to find your daughter."

Saunders glanced up quickly. "Mona . . .why? What's she done?

"She's not in trouble, Mr. Saunders, at least not that I know of. I work with a law firm trying to locate her—"

"What for?" Saunders said. He looked like someone had just told him his dog had been run over.

Holt regarded the man's pathetic stare for a moment, then smiled calmly. "Look, could we step inside to discuss this? I think we'd both be more comfortable if we sat down and I told you what this was about."

"I don't know . . ." Saunders ran a hand through his unkempt hair, and Holt waited patiently, noticing the sweatpants looked like they'd been slept in—many times. Lint and other nonspecific pieces of fluff clung to what was left of the fabric's fuzzy nap. He must have just rolled off the couch to answer the door, Holt thought, as Saunders finally glanced over to the porch and spoke in that direction.

"I haven't had breakfast yet." He turned to face Holt. "While I clean up, why don't you go over to the restaurant down the street and grab a table. I won't be long."

Holt didn't like it, but what could he do? "Okay," he said. "Where's your restaurant?"

"You know your way around here?"

"Not really."

Saunders pointed up the street, the same direction Holt's Mercedes was facing. "About a block up the street you'll hit San Vicente. It's kind of a tricky intersection because San Vicente runs almost parallel and cuts across at a weird angle. Anyway, once you're on it, head north for about another block and veer to the right where it turns into La Cienega. You'll see the Beverly Center on your left; you can't miss it. Across the street, on your right and as you get close to Beverly Boulevard, there's a place called Tony's. You can usually find a place to park in the drugstore parking lot around the corner."

Holt nodded along. "Sounds easy enough."

"I eat there all the time," Saunders said. "Give it about fifteen minutes and order me a cup of coffee."

They split up; Saunders back upstairs and Holt to his car. Holt had no trouble finding the restaurant, and sure enough, there was an available parking space waiting for him in the drugstore parking lot on Beverly. He idly wondered about Saunders's motives for shooing him off to Tony's. Maybe he was embarrassed about having him in, or perhaps he wanted to call his daughter and see that she was all right. Whatever the reason, Holt decided he really didn't care as he walked into the restaurant. He was just glad he'd found him on the first try.

Saunders proved to be as good as his word, walking up to Holt's table no more than fifteen minutes later. Saunders smiled at the cup of coffee waiting for him. He appeared more alert, his jowls freshly shaved, his hair damp. Holt was encouraged. They both remained silent while Saunders settled in, stirred sugar into his coffee, and took his first sip. Holt busied himself with the menu.

"What's good here?"

Saunders set down his cup. "I like the *big mix-up*. It's scrambled eggs and whatever else they feel like throwing in at the time. If you want something lighter, their croissant breakfasts are pretty good."

They both ordered. When the waitress went away, Saunders sat back in his chair and said, "So what's going on with my daughter?"

"I apologize for this," Holt said, "but first I'm going to have to ask you some rather personal questions." He moved his own coffee cup aside and folded his hand on the table. "I hope you'll bear with me; you'll understand why in a moment."

Saunders shrugged. "What do you need to know?"

"Is Mona your adopted daughter?"

Saunders was about to pick up his cup. He looked sharply at Holt instead. "How'd you find out about that? We never told anyone, not even Mona."

"Before I answer you, can you tell me about the adoption? Who your contacts were, that sort thing?"

"What's this all about?" Saunders forgot about his coffee, leaning forward now, locking eyes with Holt. "I don't know who you are or who you work for or why I should tell you *anything*. What business is it of yours, anyway?"

Holt sat back in his chair and drew in a deep breath and took his time exhaling before he shook his head apologetically, "Sorry about that. I guess I'm coming on a little strong, aren't I? It's just that it's been very difficult getting a line on your daughter, and I haven't been given much time to find her. Now that I'm getting close . . . well, I hope you can excuse my lack of tact. The thing is, I need to be reasonably sure I've found the right person before I can clue you in."

"What do you mean, *right person*?" Saunders waited half a beat for an answer, then thought of something before Holt could respond. "Does this have something to do with Mona's birth parents?"

"Not really. It's all about Mona. That's why I'm talking to you. If you can tell me where she is, that would be great. It would also be a big help to know the details of her adoption. I need all the information I can get to confirm her identification." Holt paused to weigh the last part of his appeal, then said, "I don't want to get too far ahead of ourselves, but let's say this involves an inheritance."

The waitress came by to top off the coffee cups. Saunders leaned back, brought up is right hand and did nervous little things with his fingers on his lips. When the waitress was gone, he said, "I'm not sure the adoption was exactly legal. Is that going to be a problem?"

"It all happened a long time ago, Mr. Saunders. You've got nothing to worry about. And if it turns out Mona's the one we're looking for, the circumstances surrounding her adoption will not affect the outcome one way or the other. Why don't you just tell me how it took place?"

Saunders pressed his lips together and nodded resolutely. "All right, where should I start?"

"Who handled the adoption for you?"

"I can't remember his name. It was one of those friend-of-a-friend things. I think he was some kind of lawyer. You see, my wife and I wanted a baby—okay, my *wife* wanted a baby, and we weren't having any luck. Don't get me wrong, I thought having a kid around might be a good idea. I was on the road a lot, and having my wife busy raising children would keep her occupied while I was gone. You know, keep the home fires burning, and all that. But I didn't want it as badly as she did, and it got to the point where I knew we wouldn't stay together much longer if it didn't happen. Our friends knew about our situation, including a guy I'd run into every now and then during studio sessions. He introduced me to the lawyer."

"Why not use a legitimate agency?" Holt said.

Saunders shrugged. "We'd already tried. A lot of red tape, and a lot of waiting. Not only that, being a sometimes-unemployed musician wasn't the kind of lifestyle that generated good vibes during the interviews. When this other opportunity came up, we decided to go for it. The guy said he could smooth over our qualifications and present us in a more favorable way, if we could overlook a minor detail."

"What was that? The birth certificate?"

"Yeah, he said they were *light on documentation*."

"Did he tell you why?"

"Just something about it being too late to arrange all the paperwork. But he said I could turn it to my advantage and save a lot of money and hassle. He told me the parents just wanted a good home for the kid and to remain anonymous. Then the lawyer told me a few ways I could apply for a birth certificate later on, once we were established and there was no way to connect the real parents."

Holt's briefcase was sitting on the chair next to him. He pulled out the copy of the delayed registration of birth and handed it to Saunders. "Look familiar?"

After cursory glance, Saunders smiled knowingly. "That's it. We applied for it when Mona started kindergarten. It worked out like the guy said it would."

"How were you able to corroborate the birth place and date.?"

"We told them Mona was born at home and that we'd hired a midwife, only to learn she didn't have her citizenship in order yet and wasn't willing to sign off on the birth registration at that time. Later on, when we applied, the midwife had her green card and she cooperated with us."

"So at that time she signed the required documents?"

"Yeah, it was all they needed. Later on we got a certified copy of the delayed certificate in the mail. Never had a problem using it for enrolling Mona in school or getting a driver's license for her when she turned sixteen."

"She has a Social Security number."

"Yep."

"So where can I find her?"

"She lives in Ojai," Saunders said. "Her place is outside of town, kinda hard to find. I don't see her too much, but I know how to get there. I'll have to give you directions. She's married to a guy named Jim McBride. He's a local tree surgeon. I guess they do all right."

"Any kids?"

"Not yet. They're sure not in a big hurry about it."

"How about you, Mr. Saunders? You still married?"

"Not to Mona's mother," Saunders said. "Not to the second or third Mrs. Saunders, either."

The waitress brought their food, asked them if they had everything they needed after setting down the plates, and hurried off to her other tables.

After the interruption, Holt asked, "How long as it been since you saw Mona?"

"It's been a while." Saunders set down his fork, that troubled look creeping back onto his face. "You know, we never told her she was adopted. I'm not sure now how to break it to her. She was so young when we got her; it was like she was really ours from the beginning. We kept putting off telling her the truth, and when Clarissa and I split up neither one of us wanted to confuse her with more bad news. I don't know how she's going to take it after all these years."

Holt's cell phone chirped. He apologized to Saunders and answered the call. It was Maxine.

"Can you talk?" she said.

"Not at the moment."

"Then just listen. If you're not sitting down, grab onto something to steady yourself. I've been talking to Ann Warren and she has a message from her father. He's in intensive care, recovering from the surgery, and he's extremely agitated. Annie's not sure if he's going to make it. The message is, and I quote, 'They're making a terrible mistake. I need to talk to somebody right now and set things straight.'"

* * *

Two hours later Holt was back at his office. He phoned Susan, told her he'd be home soon, and then called for Maxine. She walked in a few minutes later and set a clasped manila envelope on his desk before taking a chair facing his desk.

"Here's everything I've found so far on Bryce Saunders and his wife. Still working on the Social Security number on Mona."

Holt glanced at the envelope. "Any more surprises?"

"Not on Saunders."

"Any further word from Ann Warren?"

"Nope. It's been quiet around here. What about Mona Saunders? Did you get a line on her?"

"Her name is now Mona *McBride*. Her husband, Jim, owns a local tree trimming business. No kids."

Holt produced the contact information Saunders had given him and wrote out copies for Maxine. She waited quietly while he collected his thoughts.

"The thing is," he said, "Mona doesn't *know* she's adopted; at least that's what her father told me. After hearing your message from Janus, I thought it best to regroup and see what develops before seeing her. I don't think she'll be going anywhere."

"Is there anything I can do?"

"I think you should take the first available flight to San Francisco. You've established a rapport with Ann Warren; maybe she can get you into the IC ward to see her father before it's too late. In the meantime, I'll be at home or with Susan. Her surgery is scheduled for tomorrow morning."

SEVENTEEN

ALAN KANE woke up to the smell of cigarette smoke. He was groggy, his head filled with thoughts and images still present from a nightmarish sleep. He got up on an elbow, scanning the room, trying to see in a thick, blue-gray haze that shouldn't have been there. Late afternoon sunlight streamed through the partially opened slats of a shuttered window and cast bright geometric streaks against the smoke, lending a surreal tone to his escalating concern. He breathed a sigh of relief when he recognized Ashley sitting in the wing-backed chair facing him from across the room.

He dropped down on his pillow and said, "What are you trying to do, give me a heart attack?"

When Ashley didn't say anything, he got up on his elbow again, looking closer this time. He couldn't be sure, but she seemed to be shaking. No, more like trembling. His eyes were burning, and he realized she must have been there for quite a while to fill up the room with so much smoke.

"I guess I should tell you that the people who own this place don't appreciate smoking inside the house."

"I already figured that out when I couldn't find an ashtray." Ashley punctuated her remark by stubbing out her butt inside the rim of a metal wastebasket she had set at her feet. She leaned back, picked up the cellophane cigarette pack off her lap, saw that it was empty, and tossed it into the wastebasket as well. She tuned toward Kane, a blank stare on her face, tears beginning to glisten in her eyes. Even her words trembled.

"Alan . . . I'm so scared."

"I can see that."

Kane got up and grabbed his pants. After he pulled them on he turned out a straight-backed chair from in front of an antique desk and pointed it toward Ashley and sat down. He had a nice room—the desk, the reading area where Ashley was sitting, the private bath. He could hole up there quite comfortably on the few occasions both he and the owners were around at the same time. It was set up for a caretaker or in-laws, giving all parties involved a measure if distance from each other. There were two ways into the room: a door off an interior hallway, or another door leading directly to a covered courtyard at the rear of the house. Rarely using it, Kane always kept the exterior door bolted. Before he could ask Ashley how she'd got in, she was out of her seat and down on her knees at Kane's feet, clutching his legs, burying her face in his lap, her words barely audible as they came rushing out in a jumbled torrent.

"God I'm sorry I had no idea he would do something like that so sudden without any warning and that poor woman the way she just dropped like those animals you see on TV when they shoot them and they just fall hard right now down in the dirt their knees buckling and the sound of her head being hit so hard—"

"Whoa, whoa . . . not so fast." Kane took Ashley's face in his hands, turning it up to face him. "Take some deep breaths. Try to calm down. It's okay. No one can hurt you here."

Ashley's face was wet with tears. Words gave way to sobs. Kane let her rebury her face. He stroked the back of her head while she cried.

After she was quiet for a while, Ashley looked up at Kane, her voice a harsh whisper "Who was she? Do you know?" She pushed away to sit on the floor, her back against the wall as she drew in her knees hugged them close to her chest. "He hurt her. He hurt her real bad." Again the tears surfaced, but this time Ashley choked them back. "I'm sure she's dead, and there was nothing I could do. I watched the poor woman die right in front of my kitchen door. There's no way I'm going back, not ever."

Now Kane had his own head in his hands, bent over, elbows on his knees. He looked up and said, "You were there?"

"Goddamnit, Alan. What do you think I've been talking about? Hell yes I was there, watching a fucking maniac beat a woman to death. I don't know how I could make it any clearer."

Ashley's fear was quickly turning to anger. To whom it was directed, Kane couldn't be sure. "Okay," he said. "I got that. But let's start from the beginning. Try to stay calm and tell me what happened."

"All right," Ashley said, finding some resolve, sniffing, wiping the tears from her face, taking in a few deep breaths that seemed to catch in her throat before she could expel them. "It was getting dark. I was at my place, around back of the big barn behind the stables, where we keep the trailers. I had my Explorer back there to hitch one up. I was going to a meet the next day and I wanted to be ready for an early start. I heard a vehicle go by and didn't think much about it. I figured it was probably one of the Mexicans coming in to finish up with his chores. I was surprised to see Wentworth's Escalade in front of the tack room. I was coming back to get a flashlight, walking along in back of the stables. Wentworth was standing by the tailgate, facing away from me, when the woman stepped down from the passenger seat. That's when he dropped her. He came up fast and hit her over the head with a tire iron. She never saw it coming." Ashley had been staring into a void as she talked, but now her eyes found Kane's. "I was close enough to hear the tire iron break through her skull."

It took a long moment for Kane to ask, "Did he see you?"

"He was facing the other direction, but I still don't know how he missed me. I was standing right out in the open, frozen stiff. I couldn't move, except for my hands. I had to get them up to my mouth in a hurry and press hard to hold in the scream. I just stood there while he stepped over the woman and walked up to my kitchen door. He opened it almost as easily as if he had a key. I knew he didn't have one because he had to work at it for a few seconds, but that's all it took, and then he was inside. As soon as he stepped in, I backtracked to my ride and unhitched the trailer as quietly as I could. Then I crept out of there, no lights, real slow. The barn blocked me from view if he looked out a window, and as long as he was inside I didn't think he could hear me. But I have no way of knowing if he did or didn't."

"Did you call the police?"

"I wanted to see you first. I tried calling you but just got your voicemail and didn't leave a message. The I came by, and you weren't here—"

Kane must have been on his way back from Sedona—same problem with the phone that he'd had with Tellington's calls. Not that it mattered. Even if Ashley had warned him in time to avoid Tellington at the ranch, Kane would still be just as involved. If Tellington were caught, he'd drag Kane down with him. The way Kane had played Holt didn't leave any explanation other than that of an accomplice.

"—Are you listening to me?"

Kane had let his head fall back into his hands. He looked up again and said, "I heard you. Where did you go after you came by here?"

"I went into town and found a motel. I didn't know what else to do. I couldn't go back to my husband. And by then I figured I couldn't go to the police—I'd have too much explaining to do." Just as she seemed to be regaining her composure, Ashley turned pale again. "It's better that I kept a low profile and didn't talk to them. If I'd ratted on Wentworth and he found out before they caught him, I'd be in real trouble. He's a lot scarier than the police, believe me. I can't help wondering what he has planned for me as it is."

Kane was thinking the same thing—what *were* Tellington's plans? The reality of the attack on Pearl, the cold, premeditated brutality of it, was beginning to sink in. Tellington had obviously planned it that way all along, and Kane had somehow believed, or at least wanted to believe, that it had been some kind of accident, like maybe Pearl had been struggling with Tellington and fell and hit her head. Hadn't Tellington implied something like that? Hadn't he expressed regret, like it wasn't really his fault? Kane began to grasp how much Tellington was using him, and he suddenly felt Ashley's fear invade his insides like some kind of contagious virus.

Now he was glad he'd gone to the extra trouble of disposing every shred of evidence he could think of that might link him to Pearl or to where her body lay. After returning the tools to the garage he had taken off his clothes and torn out the labels, burned them, and flushed the ashes down the toilet. He would have done the same with the clothes themselves but didn't want to deal with all the soot and ash. Nobody burned things around here, not even in the fireplace this time of year, and he wasn't in the mood for going out and digging any more holes. So he turned out every pocket, rolled out the cuffs on his chinos and shook out the dirt, making sure nothing, not even the most insignificant scrap of paper, had somehow wedged itself into the creases. Then he laundered the clothes, folded them, and with his cowboy boots, put them in a plastic bag and drove them to the parking lot collection container of a popular thrift store in Tempe. It was after nine in the morning when he finally returned home, exhausted, and crashed in his room. It was the last thing he remembered.

He looked at Ashley. "How'd you get in here, anyway?"

"That was easy. The door was open."

"Which one?"

"The garage door. I came by earlier in the morning and it was closed. I went around pounding on doors for about ten minutes before I was convinced you weren't here. I still couldn't get you on the phone. I was getting frantic. I remembered saying something to Wentworth the other day about entering an open cutting competition out near Tonto Verde, so I stayed away from there in case he went out looking for me. I drove out to Cave Creek, lying low, until I finally tried here again a while ago. This time your Cherokee was in the garage. You'd left the door up. I parked next to you and walked in through the garage and I've been sitting here ever since."

A strained silence filled the room and felt almost like a physical presence. In a softer voice, Ashley said, "This is all my fault."

Kane remained quiet. A shorter span of silence this time.

"All I had to do was keep my mouth shut," Ashley said. "But the way Wentworth was needling you the other day I couldn't just sit there and do nothing. The vibes had gotten tense in the kitchen, and when you came back in from the bathroom and said you had to leave, I didn't want you to go. I was only trying to lighten things up by mentioning the lawyer. I couldn't believe the way Wentworth reacted once you started talking about him."

"Well, believe it." Kane got up and went to the closet for a fresh shirt.

"Is he still going through with it?" Ashley said, "That crazy plan of his for stealing the inheritance? I don't see how he could possibly pull it off."

Kane selected a golf shirt with a Blackhawk logo embroidered on the left breast. While tucking it in he looked down on Ashley. "It's a crazy plan, all right. About as crazy as he is. And dangerous—for us."

He helped Ashley to her feet. Her tears had dried, her face now relaxed in a resigned sort of acceptance of inevitable doom.

She put her arms around him. Kane responded and they held on to each other. Ashley said, "Maybe we *should* go to the police, before it's too late."

"It's already too late for that," Kane said. "We'll have to play this out." He grabbed Ashley by the shoulders and held her out at arms' length and made sure she was paying attention. "But you're right—we don't know for sure what Tellington has planned for us. It could be anything, from cutting us in to cutting our throats. Or maybe he wants to set us up as fall-guys. Whatever it is, we're okay for now. Tellington needs me in the loop until the estate is ready to pay. They'll probably have questions for me, and I'll need to be around to answer them. I'll do what I can to keep us covered; in the meantime, stay here. I don't think Tellington knows where I live, unless you've told him—"

Ashley quickly shook her head. "No. I've never told him anything about you."

"Okay, then. As long as you stay here, you've got nothing to worry about."

Kane picked up his cell phone from the nightstand and punched it on.

"Who are you calling?"

"I've had my phone off—just checking messages." Kane paused to read the screen. "Figures. I've got one from Tellington." He put the phone to his ear. After listening to the message, he punched off the phone and stuck it in his pocket. He told Ashley not to wait up for him. "Go to bed early and try to sleep. You look like you need it."

"Where are you going?"

"Tellington wants to see me."

EIGHTEEN

KANE SPOTTED Tellington's Escalade in a dirt parking space in front of the picnic tables. He pulled up several spaces away and got out of his Cherokee. He looked around until he saw Tellington's familiar silhouette off in the distance, perched atop a huge sandstone boulder. It took Kane several minutes to make his way to the boulder and climb up next to him.

"Nice view."

Tellington turned away from the sun setting behind the Phoenix skyline and regarded Kane for the first time since he'd arrived. Tellington stood up.

"Like I said the other day—I like being outside, in our natural environment." He rose to his full height, arms outstretched. "This is a beautiful place. You can see for miles in almost every direction. I've been meaning to come here and check it out ever since I drove by from the airport my first time to Phoenix." He made a show of admiring the scenery, then leveled his stare at Kane. "Now I need to check you out."

"What do you mean? What did I do?"

Before Kane could react, Tellington braced him, running thick hands across his body, untucking his shirt and pulling it up to his armpits. When he was through, Tellington snorted approval and sat back down.

"What? You thought I might be wearing a wire?"

"Can't be too careful," Tellington said.

Kane looked past Tellington's shoulder. Their boulder extended over the edge of a wide butte overlooking the third tee on the Papago Golf Course. It was a public course Kane had played many times, especially while growing up in the area. That's where he'd learned, the hard way, the finer points of hustling from the course's blue-collar golfers, guys who would lull him into a false sense of superiority with their awkward, self-taught swings and aw-shucks modesty—until he'd realize, too late, how thoroughly they were picking his pocket. And if Kane looked in the right direction, past Papago, he'd be able to see the Kane Trucking complex just a few blocks away on McDowell. He made a point of not looking, turning instead back toward his car and seeing that every inch of the path he'd taken to the boulder was clearly visible.

"I couldn't figure out why you wanted to meet at Papago Park," he said, "but I get it now. You don't trust me."

"Relax. You passed the test."

"Did I?"

"For now."

"Why don't you lighten up? I've already buried a body for you. What more do you want?"

Tellington's eyes went steely. "Guys have been known to get cold feet when it gets heavy. If they think it'll save them, they might even cop a plea and agree to set up their partners." But then Tellington's stare softened. He nodded his head slightly to his right, indicating where Kane should sit. "Let's talk."

Kane followed instructions, wary of the rounded edge of the boulder several feet away. There'd be no walking away from a fall from that height. The rock's surface was coarse enough to keep from sliding off as long as he stayed on the relatively level area next to Tellington. More cause for being wary.

The sun had now dropped out of sight, leaving behind thin layers of tangerine-colored clouds in its wake. Tellington resumed his contemplative stare, and without looking away, he said, "So how'd it go last night? Any problems?"

"No problems," Kane said. "How about your end? Please tell me this is all going to be worth it."

Tellington remained silent, staring into the distance, until the trace of a smile creased the skin around his mustache. "It'll be worth it, all right."

Kane waited for more. When none came, he said, "Are you going to tell me what's happening? I think I've earned the right to know."

Tellington looked at Kane, that inward, sly smile still in place. "All right, Kane. What do you want to know?"

"What happens next."

"I expect they'll get in touch with Mona."

"What about me? Do you think they'll want to see *me* again?

"I don't know. But you're going to want to see them, right?"

"Huh?"

"The finder's fee, Kane. You remembered to hit up Holt for the finder's fee, didn't you?"

"Yeah, I remembered."

"You might want to follow up on that. They'll be expecting it."

"When will the rest of it start happening?"

"Real soon. Holt works fast. He almost caught me at my friend's house."

"What friend?"

"It was actually my friend's ex-husband. I had to bring him in on this. We needed a logical way for Holt to think he's finding Pearl's daughter on his own. As long as he believes he's making all the discoveries through his own investigation, he's less likely to question the results. The thing with the delayed birth certificate worked out nicely. Holt had a copy, and I was able to prep the father with our version of how they applied for the original. And best of all, it's a solid story. Other than the little white lie about the adoption, the rest of it's close to the truth."

"But now there's another guy involved."

"Don't get your panties in a bunch, Kane; it couldn't be helped. And it's not a problem. I'll handle my end, my way"

"Let's talk more about the ends. How are we actually getting the money, and how are we splitting it?"

"How does fifty-fifty sound? Just between the two of us."

"What about all the people you're bringing in, your *friends*, their daughter."

"That's what I mean about taking care of my end. You don't have to worry about them. Just like I won't have to bother with Ashley. If you want to cut her in, it's from your end."

"But how do we actually get ahold of the money? If it's paid to Mona, how does it get to us?"

"Two words," Tellington said. "Offshore banking."

Again, Kane waited for more information. A more detailed explanation, something to bolster his confidence or to at least convince him that he wasn't being played for a chump. He looked down and watched a foursome gather on the third tee beneath them. Those hard lessons he'd learned down there suddenly seemed more recent. Maybe it was because of the casual way Tellington mentioned *offshore banking*. It produced a queasy feeling in Kane's gut, like the first time he found himself in a high-stakes match and the struggling old yokel he was playing said, in that same folksy drawl Tellington had just used, *"Well, I'm down two holes; I guess that's an automatic press."* Somehow Kane had known, right then, that the game was over, that he was not only going to lose much more money than he'd bargained for, but that his opponent had been in total control all along. Kane remembered how helpless he felt, watching the old guy step up to the tee and drive the ball like the ghost of Bobby Jones had suddenly taken over his body. The ball flew in a perfect, long arc to the middle of the fairway, sending Kane a crystal clear message. And now his gut was sending him the same goddamned message about Tellington.

Kane couldn't shake off the memories from that day. A paralysis reminiscent of the kitchen table incident at Ashley's began to creep in on him. He sat there on the rock, still looking down on the course, but only saw images of past disasters, culminating in the scene with his late father's lawyer. At the time, he thought his life would never be able to sink lower. Even worse was the self loathing that came later, when he realized, on the few occasions he was honest with himself, that the riches he thought he had coming would no longer keep him from seeing what a pathetic, shallow, self-serving creature he had become.

But of course, he *had* sunk lower. Just about to the depth of Pearl's grave.

He finally stood up, keeping his face away from Tellington. He shut his eyes and tried to clear his mind. Tellington's voice mercifully broke his train of thought.

"What's wrong, Kane?"

"Tell me more about the offshore banking."

"What do you want to know?"

"Are you talking about numbered accounts, that sort of thing?"

"That's right. I've moved money in the past and I'm already set up. You must know as well as I do that the only way we'll be able to take quick possession of a large sum of money is electronically. I can lose it in the system and turn it into cash before they know what hits them."

Kane turned and faced Tellington. He could feel his anger overpower his fear and helplessness. He words came out slow, calm, and deliberately, with an edge that surprised him.

"And what about me? Where will *I* be while you're out getting lost in the system?"

"I won't be going anywhere, Kane. We'll just be a couple of buddies joined at the hip until we make the split. I said the *money* will get lost, not me. I can orchestrate everything from here. Of course, you'll have to leave the country to pick up the cash. You gotta passport, don't you?"

Kane felt his newfound resolve already begin to waver. "Why didn't you say anything about this before? It's going to look pretty suspicious for me to be out applying for a passport all of a sudden, isn't it?"

"This happened fast. At first it was only a crazy idea I thought would be fun to check out. I really didn't take it seriously. But everything fell into place. Hell, I couldn't believe it. My friends were available, the dates checked out . . . one thing led to another. What's left is the tricky part—getting the money from Mona. Right now she doesn't know this is a scam. She'll think it's all real. It'll make her reaction all the more authentic."

"I can't believe this," Kane said. "Are you telling me she doesn't know, that you'll lie to her about her parents—"

Tellington was on his feet, both fists clutching wads of shirt below Kane's chin before he could say another word. Tellington spun him to the ground, Kane's backside and head simultaneously hitting the rough sandstone. Tellington held on, bending over him, bringing him up to a sitting position by pulling on his shirt.

"What does it take for you to get it, Kane? This is a lot of fucking money. This is more money than a million guys like you or I will ever see in a million lifetimes. I will do whatever it takes. If that means threatening Mona with her life or the life of her family, I'll do it."

Tellington let go of Kane with a shove, sending him back against the boulder's surface. He glared down on him and said, "I didn't have time to mess around with you, make sure you were up to speed or had any questions. Ever hear of *need to know* ? Well that's where you've been, Kane, on a need-to-know status. What you needed to know to get the job done was all I had time to give you. Do you have a numbered account squirreled away? Do you even know how to set one up? How about a passport?

You got one? There was no time to dick around with that. We had to move, make things happen before it was too late. As for the rest of it—you'll either sink or swim."

Tellington turned away. He brushed the dust off his trousers and headed for the parking lot. He was still on the boulder when his cell phone chirped. He answered it and listened quietly, not moving, then slowly worked his way back to Kane, the cell phone pressed against his ear. It was bad news. Kane had no trouble figuring that out as Tellington pocketed the phone. Kane scrambled to his feet, which only made it easier for the big man to grab him under the shirt collar again.

Tellington was at a complete loss for words, as if he were too angry to speak. He backed Kane toward the edge of the boulder— the edge that looked out over the course a good seventy-five feet below them. Then a man's shout from across the way pulled Tellington out of his trance.

"Hey! Are you guys all right? You need some help?"

Tellington relaxed his grip. Kane looked over at a young guy and his female companion on the trail from the parking lot. The color continued to rise in Tellington's face, his jaw clenched tight. The fuse was lit, but instead of exploding, Tellington gave Kane a half-assed shove closer to the edge, then turned around and walked briskly down the trail. The couple stepped wide to let him pass.

Kane gave Tellington plenty of lead time. It was getting dark, and he waited until Tellington's headlights lit up the landscape before he took to the path. As he reached his Cherokee, a park employee drove up and reminded him of the posted hours before running him off. Kane pulled onto the narrow, winding road, followed it past an open gate, and from his rearview mirror watched the employee pull over to close it. He caught the nearby 202 freeway, transitioned onto the 101, and headed for home.

The drive was long enough for this latest encounter with Tellington to start bothering Kane more with each passing mile.

Other than asking about any problems with the body, Tellington hadn't said anything about Pearl. No mention of her name and not a word about killing her. He was obviously over it and felt no need to bring it up. That made his comments about threatening the life of anyone standing in his way even more chilling—and believable.

And what about me? Kane thought *How much longer until I'm expendable? I'll bet I haven't spent more than a couple of hours with the man. Why would he care about me at all? He doesn't even know me. He probably spent more time with Pearl, doing whatever he did at her place, getting to know her, convincing her to drive down to Scottsdale with him . . .and look what he did to her.*

Kane didn't feel any better when he pulled into his driveway. He made sure to close the garage door this time. Ashley was waiting for him when he walked by the open den next to the kitchen.

"I thought you were going to get some sleep."

"Are you kidding?" Ashley's hands were crossed in front of her, clutching her upper arms below the shoulders. She was curled up on the couch, the TV providing the only light, the volume turned low.

Kane said, "Have you had anything to eat?"

"I had some toast. Could barely get it down. Then I found some tea, and that helped."

Kane opened the refrigerator. The cans of Budweiser were the first things he saw, and he couldn't remember the last time he'd had a drink. They looked more than just refreshing. He grabbed one and joined Ashley on the couch.

"So what happened?" she said.

"Nothing's changed. Tellington's got it all figured out."

"And you're still going along with him?"

"I don't have much choice."

A quiet moment passed. Then, in a low, tentative voice, Ashley said, "Did he say anything about me?"

"He told me if I wanted to cut you in, it would have to be from my end of the take."

"Cut me in?"

"Yeah. I guess he figures you're part of it since you were there when we started things rolling."

"And that's all he said?"

"That was it. Your name never came up again." Kane cracked open the beer and took a drink. He set the can on the coffee table and looked at Ashley. "I don't think he knows you were there last night. In any case, he didn't seem the least bit concerned."

Ashley clutched herself tighter. "Who was she, Alan? You never told me who she was."

"Her name was Pearl."

"The woman you told me about? From Sedona?"

Kane just nodded.

"And where is it now? Her body. He didn't leave it at the ranch, did he?"

"Don't worry, it's not at the ranch."

Ashley looked hard at Kane, fear straining her voice again, like before, when Kane had first found her in his bedroom.

"How can you be sure? Did you actually see where he took it? Or did he only tell you?"

"Don't ask me how I know; just take my word for it. The body is gone. It's nowhere near the ranch."

Ashley began to relax. She let go of her upper arms and sat back into the couch. But there were still questions.

"I don't get it," she said. "I thought Wentworth wanted you to take the lawyer up to Pearl's house to meet her."

"That's what *I* thought. Until we got there. But Tellington had a little surprise in store for me. A woman I'd never seen before answered the door and introduced herself as Pearl. It was the first part of Tellington's scheme to substitute a shill for Pearl's daughter."

Kane spent the next ten minutes telling Ashley everything he knew about Tellington's plan. He omitted his own role in covering up Pearl's murder, and didn't admit to being at the ranch after it happened. Ashley listened quietly, barely responding. She didn't object when he led her to the bedroom.

NINETEEN

KANE DIDN'T feel much like getting up. His inner clock was a mess from sleeping most of the day before and he'd been up all night, worrying until daybreak, wishing it were all a bad dream. That's what it felt like. One of those bad dreams where something horrible happens and you're so caught up in it that it feels absolutely real, where you're actually planning how to adjust your life accordingly or have given up hope for any life at all, until that merciful moment when you wake up. How he wished for that moment right now, to feel that wave of relief wash over him.

He forced himself out of bed, careful not to disturb Ashley, and quietly put on his clothes. He decided to make an appearance at work. He'd been a fairly reliable employee up to now and thought it important to reestablish a degree of normalcy.

Half an hour later he walked up to Margo's desk at the golf school.

"You look like shit, Alan."

"I told you I haven't been feeling well," he said. "Have you covered my—"

"Nice of you to stop by, Mr. Kane."

Blackhawk's head golf pro punctuated his greeting by slamming the door he'd just walked through. He tossed a folder onto Margo's desk, put his hands on his hips and looked Kane up and down.

"You look like shit."

Kane raised his eyebrows at Margo. Before he could say anything, she said, "We've been able to cover for him, Mr. Stewart. His regulars don't seem to mind rescheduling, what with the condition of the driving range—"

Stewart raised a hand to wave her off. "All right. It's been a slow week. But we'll be getting rid of the mats and start hitting off the grass on Monday. Not only that, we're reopening the north course. I know it's a week ahead of schedule, but the rye has taken root and they want to start overseeding the south course right away, while the weather's cooperating." He paused to take another long look at Kane. "That means business as usual. You going to be ready?"

"Yes sir," Kane said. "I'm good to go right now."

Stewart looked over at Margo. "How's today shaping up?"

"We've got everything covered for today. You know how it is— the guys are always scrambling to pick up anything they can get this time of year."

"Okay, then." Stewart returned his attention to Kane. "Go home and rest up. We don't need you around here today scaring off what few customers we have."

Kane watched his boss turn around and exit through the door he'd just entered, wondering if Stewart had been serious or trying to be funny. Sometimes it was hard to tell with him.

Out of the abrupt silence, Margo said, "Did that answer your question?"

"Yeah, it looks like you have everything handled. Thanks for sticking up for me."

Kane left the club and drove to a restaurant in one of the strip malls by Pinnacle Peak. He indulged in a long, drawn-out breakfast, staring all the while at the folded corner of a newspaper like he was reading it. He sat like that through the morning rush, finally getting up to leave about the same time his waitress gave up on turning his table. He threw down a few extra dollars when he noticed her staring at him, suddenly realizing how long he'd been there. Behind the wheel again, he headed north on Pima for a few miles to Cave Creek, a small outpost at the edge of the populated desert where an air of nouveau gentility competed with Southwestern kitsch. He turned west on Cave Creek Road, away from the exclusive fairways of Desert Mountain, toward the commercial side of town.

The business district stretched for about a mile along the main drag on both sides of where Scottsdale Road ended. No strip malls, just a few independent, service-minded businesses scattered among the town's primary draw of old west trading posts and funky restaurants. The emphasis was decidedly more cowboy than Indian.

A remarkably preserved gas station stood at the far west end of town. It was one of the old prefabs from the late 1930s, and its slick, white porcelain wall panels and steel framed windows gleamed as brightly as they had seventy-some years ago. The signature service canopy, held up by the building on one side and by two supporting columns on the outside edge, came out almost to the shoulder of Cave Creek Road. There was only a painted cement slab underneath the canopy where the pumps had once stood.

Kane pulled into the dirt lot between the station and one of the last trading posts along that stretch of road. He walked through the station's front door, past a sign posted in one of the window frames. It read, CAVE CREEK MOTORCYCLE DESIGNS, and underneath, in smaller script, GUNNAR WARBURTON—PROPRIETOR.

When he came up to a counter partially blocking the entrance to the rear of the shop, Kane could see Gunnar and a couple of guys standing over a new-looking Harley, pointing here and there, nodding and gesturing in the universal language that bonded man with machine. When Gunnar notice Kane, he gave a slight nod and returned to the conversation. Kane walked back outside, took a seat in one of the aluminum lawn chairs under the canopy, and studied the merchandise next door overflowing onto the dirt parking lot, a collection of rusting steel silhouettes depicting desert landscapes and coyotes and dancing Hopi flute players all leaning against a weather-beaten wall like discarded stage props from a long-forgotten play. He watched the cars pass by. Eventually, Gunnar and the two guys came out, Gunnar lingering near the doorway while the two guys climbed into a big Mercedes parked diagonally under a shaded portion of the canopy. When they had driven off, Gunnar took the chair next to Kane.

"What are you doing here, man? You know I don't hold any shit on the premises."

"I'm not here for that. The pot from the other night kicks ass. I'm sure it'll last me awhile."

Gunnar relaxed into his chair, nodding approval. Kane continued talking.

"I just needed to get away. They didn't need me at the course this morning so I went for a big breakfast. Got wired on coffee and started driving around. No particular destination. I happened by and saw your shop was open and turned in to see what you're up to."

"That's it, huh?"

Kane nodded. Gunnar looked at him closely, about to say something, when Kane changed the subject.

"Who're your friends?" he said, nodding down the road in the direction the Mercedes had taken.

Gunnar followed Kane's gaze and said, "The older dude? The big guy driving the Mercedes? He's some kind of corporate president. Their headquarters is in Phoenix. The guy with him is one of his lackeys, VP of sales, or something."

"Weekend warriors?"

"Yeah, I guess. They're pretty cool, though. The president's name is Charles Oaks. We call him Stumpy, but I doubt he answers to that around the boardroom. He's been riding for a few years now and recently got a crew together—mostly guys from work."

"I suppose there are worse ways to suck up to the boss."

"I'm sure there are. But most of them would be a lot less expensive. Did you see Stumpy's bike back there? He paid close to twenty-five grand for it, and I haven't even got started on it yet. He likes that badass fat-tire look—the fatter the better. Says he wants the rear end to match the one sitting on it."

"*He* said that?"

"I'm not making this up. That's the kind of guy he is. He says he wants the bike's rear end slung down low and wide, just like he's built, to make everything look nice and proportional when he's cruising down the road. Not only will he look good, he says he won't feel so top heavy when he's onboard. We were discussing it when you showed up. I told him there's a lot more to it than putting on a big tire. He'll need a customized fender, a new seat, and I'll have to tweak the frame and make some transmission adjustments. We didn't talk about paint and chrome—he said he wants to think it over first. But I'll tell you one thing, however he wants to finish it off will be first class. He'll have over forty grand in that bike before he rolls it out of here."

"If he's got all that money, why not just buy a custom bike to begin with?"

Gunnar shook his head. "You're missing the point. This guy wants the real deal, something all his, something he can identify with. Something that will take him back to those days when he wanted to be free but went to work instead. Now he can capture a piece of it, and with more style than he ever dreamed of. And you know what? More power to him. I'll treat that bike of his like it was my own."

"You really like him, don't you?"

"What's so strange about that, man? Stumpy's good people. So what if I like him? I like some of his friends, too. There might be a few brownnosers mixed into the bunch, but a few of them are all right. Just because you got money doesn't make you a bad person."

"Yeah, and it doesn't hurt business, either."

"You *still* don't get it. I don't feel the same way about my customers that you do about the . . . what do you call them? Oh, yeah, the *mooches*—the guys who come to you for lessons and the suckers you set up for a friendly round of golf. The thing is, I *like* my customers. Or let me put this way: If I don't like 'em, they're not my customers. That's the difference between you and me."

"It must be nice to be able to pick and choose," Kane said, "and not have to put up with the public in general. Someone you don't like comes in here, you just show them the door. If I did that, I'd be out of a job."

Gunnar sat back in his chair, either deep in thought or figuring out what to say and how to word it. Finally, in a low voice, he said, "Have you ever thought, *Maybe it's me, not them.*"

"What do you mean by that?"

"Just what I said. Maybe if you gave some of those guys a chance, if you were just a wee bit nice to them, you might not only begin to like them a little, you might also start to like yourself."

Kane didn't know what to say. He was having a hard time getting past the *Maybe it's me.* A vague feeling of having had this conversation before washed over him. He sat silent while Gunnar continued.

"Why don't you try it some time? After you've beat some guy and taken all his money, why not help him out? Give him a few tips. Show him where he went wrong and how he might be able to do better next time. It's called promoting good will. You'd be surprised how it can turn around and smile on you."

Kane couldn't believe what he was hearing, and from Gunnar, of all people. But Gunnar was through talking now, and under the falling silence the routine sounds along the roadside drifted in and took prominence—a man across the street hosing off his driveway and children laughing in the distance and tires crunching across the gravel spread over the dirt lot next door.

After a while, Kane said, "I didn't know you were a philosopher."

Gunnar let out a low snort, staring across the road at the man with the hose. "I'm no philosopher, just an observer." He turned to Kane. "Now why don't you tell me the real reason you came by?"

Kane met Gunnar's stare. Then, without warning, he felt his lips tremble. Tears welled in his eyes and he prayed he could hold them back and not embarrass himself, but they came anyway, rolling down his cheeks in huge drops, like those first fat raindrops that come down at the start of an Arizona thunderstorm, a few at a time, hitting here and there, as big as eggs spattering against the hood of your car and only lasting long enough to turn the dust to mud and then going away instead of washing everything clean. His tears felt just as conspicuous, but there was no use turning away; the damage was done. Gunnar was witnessing a breakdown, worse than any of the others, and there wasn't a thing Kane could do about it. He couldn't even say anything until he regained some kind of control over his mouth, but the harder he tried to stop all the quivering and trembling, the more intense it flared up, until he finally brought his hands up against his face and covered his eyes and shouted out, *Goddamnit,* in a voice he didn't recognize. After a prolonged silence, he wiped the tears into smeared streaks across his face and lowered his hands.

He opened his eyes and looked warily at Gunnar.

"That's better, man," Gunnar said. "Let it out."

Kane came close to laughing, and he felt the tension drain away. He *did* feel better. Gunnar wasn't mocking him or putting him down or making him feel ashamed or embarrassed. Kane suddenly trusted him enough to start talking. He told him almost everything.

TWENTY

IT HAD been almost two hours since they rolled Susan into the OR. Holt's anxiety was already ramped up, then he saw her surgeon walk into the waiting room. Dr. Troman was wearing that grim, unfocused expression that could mean only one thing. Holt stared at him in disbelief as he tried to rise from his chair, but by now Troman was next to him and Holt followed his lead and sat back down, the surgeon's hand resting on his shoulder for a moment before he took the seat next to him.

Not wasting words, Troman said, "Susan went into cardiac arrest on the operating table. We did everything we could, but we couldn't save her."

Holt stared into Troman's eyes, willing him to come to his senses, to recognize the mistake he was making. He couldn't be talking about his wife, not *his* Susan. It had to be somebody else. A mix-up. This was just a simple procedure. Routine. They do it all the time, no more complicated than a biopsy . . .

Troman returned Holt's stare, focused now with the frank detachment necessary for him to do his job. "It wasn't the surgery itself," he said, as if directly addressing Holt's thoughts. "She had a reaction to the anesthetic. It triggered a rare condition called malignant hyperthermia."

Holt finally found his voice. "I've never heard of it."

"It's a hereditary skeletal muscle defect. Unfortunately, there's no way to pre-identify patients who may develop it, no straightforward test to diagnose the condition. All we can go on are patient and family histories. That's why we ask all the questions before we schedule a surgery."

"You obviously didn't ask enough."

Troman didn't respond. They sat in silence for a few moments, and Holt began to worry that Troman would get up and leave. He wasn't ready to be left alone yet. Not without some answers.

"How does a person die from a muscle defect?"

"You can have MH your whole life and never know it. You may even have a few surgeries and never be affected. When it hits, it's chemically induced by inhalation anesthetics that set off a chain reaction leading to hypermetabolism. This alters calcium function at the cellular level, causing increased muscle contraction, hyperthermia, and subsequent damage to the central nervous system . . ."

"Okay, you're losing me with the doctor-speak. I don't need the overview. How did *Susan* die?"

"About twenty minutes into the surgery, we noticed the tachycardia—her heartbeat was speeding up—which quickly led to cardiac arrest. We had already halted the surgery and anesthesia and had started the MH protocol, but we were unable to revive her."

"If it happened so fast, how did you know for sure what was causing it?"

"I'd seen it before, just one time in fifteen years. But in any case, there was no way our anesthesiologist would have missed it once the symptoms appeared. With the abnormal transport of calcium, rigidity or tetanus-like movements occur, and we could see it affecting her jaw muscles."

Holt couldn't bring himself to ask if she'd suffered. What could Troman tell him, the truth? Lie? What he'd already described was obviously a horrible way to die, and the realization flooded Holt with an profound ache that reached into places inside he never knew existed.

The conversation over, Troman rose quietly and turned for the hallway outside the waiting room.

Holt stood up and followed him, grabbing an arm when he caught up. "I need to see her."

Troman paused, as if considering Holt's statement. It wasn't a request.

"Of course," Troman said. "Come with me."

* * *

Holt drove to Benny's school on autopilot, his mind still numbed by the lingering image of Susan's body lying beneath a white sheet on a gurney, about to be wheeled away. His first sight of it, after he'd turned a corner behind Dr. Troman, had hit him like a silent thunderclap, shaking the very structure of the building until he realized it was his knees that were buckling. Troman helped him to a chair, then left him alone.

Holt had called the school before he left the hospital and the principal was expecting him when he walked into her office. She sent an assistant to fetch Benny from his classroom. When he arrived at the office, Benny looked surprised to see his father there. Holt thanked the principal, took Benny's hand, and hurried out. Holt tried to hold himself together as they walked through the parking lot, fending off Benny's questions with, "I'll tell you when we get to the car."

Once they were seated inside, Holt said, "We're going home, Benny, but your mom's not going to be there."

Benny's expression turned from expectant to confused. Neither Holt nor Susan had told him about her surgery this morning. They'd put it off too long, and when the morning came they felt it was too late. No need to worry him, they'd rationalized, never considering that it might come to this. *He's worried now*, Holt thought, trying to find the right words. He slid as close to Benny as the console between them would allow and rested a hand on his shoulder.

"There's something I have to tell you that can't wait. You'll have to be brave . . ."

"Why won't Mom be home?" Benny said. Tears were already welling in his eyes.

"Mom had to go the hospital today. We didn't think it was serious. That's why we didn't tell you."

"When will she be back?"

"Mom's not coming back, Benny. She died at the hospital."

* * *

It was a long, tense drive home. Benny jumped out of the car before Holt had rolled to a full stop in the driveway. He ran to the front door and it was locked and he was about to run off, anywhere, Holt thought, just to run. Holt sprinted across the driveway just as Ruth Featherstone, Susan's mother, opened the door. She stood at the threshold, hugging Benny, as Holt came up. Benny buried his face in the folds of his grandmother's slacks and wouldn't look at him.

"Go away," Benny said. "I want my mom!"

"It's not your dad's fault," Ruth said, gently patting Benny's head and running her fingers through his hair. "He tried his very best to help her."

Benny kept his face hidden, choking back wet sobs. Ruth looked at Holt and he wondered how many times a heart can break in one day.

The three of them finally walked inside. Holt closed the front door behind them and Benny bolted up the stairs. The door to his room slammed shut. With Benny gone, Ruth seemed to deflate. She steadied herself with a hand on the staircase railing and sank onto one of the lower stairs. Holt sat next to her and she clutched his nearest arm and drew him close.

"Who can *I* blame?" she said. "The doctors? God? Is it my fault? I've never heard of this condition . . . what did you call it? Hyper-something?"

"Malignant hyperthermia."

Ruth repeated the two words, as if it would help her understand. Holt gave her an abbreviated version of the explanation he'd received from Dr. Troman. He had tried to be more specific earlier, when he first broke the news to Ruth over the phone, but at the time they were both too upset to make much sense of anything.

"I should have insisted on being there," she said, "instead of futzing with the house . . ."

"Like you told Benny—it's not anyone's fault. There wasn't anything you could have done."

"But I should have *been* there for her."

Maybe she should have, Holt thought, but Susan hadn't agreed. She didn't want her mother anywhere near the hospital, reliving her own ordeal of surviving a radical mastectomy and the ensuing treatments that almost killed her. Susan's situation wasn't anything like that, and she had downplayed this morning's surgery as a minor inconvenience, convincing Ruth to stay home and warm up the place for her quick return.

They talked awhile longer about the malignant hyperthermia. Ruth wasn't aware of it running in her family. To her knowledge, nothing like that had ever surfaced. Holt didn't want her to start feeling guilty about it and steered the conversation toward Benny. He looked up the staircase and said, "I think I should go check on him."

"Not yet, Ben." Ruth renewed her grip on Holt's arm. "Benny's stronger than you think. Nature will have to take its course, but he'll be okay."

* * *

Holt sat in the leather chair behind the desk in his study, thinking of Benny upstairs in his room. He'd peeked in on him a while ago and Benny was still mad at him, as if the boy needed a tangible target for his anger. He'd made it very clear once again that he wanted to be left alone.

There were framed photos of the family scattered throughout the study, wherever Holt looked. Not overdone, but tastefully positioned among the books and knickknacks on the shelves across from him and on his desk. On the wall was a family portrait taken only last summer. He looked at it and focused on his son. The picture was professionally done, and out of the half-dozen different proofs, this was the one Holt and Susan had loved the most. Benny was seated between them, the camera catching him just as he had glanced toward his mother, that pure quality of innocence and happiness written all over his face. How do you get it back, Holt wondered, once it's been taken away?

He forced himself out of the chair and into the kitchen, killed time making coffee, then brought a fresh cup with him back to the study. He found his briefcase and pulled the contents out and stacked them on the desktop. He'd let Maxine finish up the Logan Bigelow business. As far as he knew, she was still in San Francisco. As soon as he had the opportunity, he'd let her know what had happened and have her take over. He shuffled through the paperwork from his briefcase. It gave him something to do, a feeble attempt to distract himself.

He grabbed the clasped envelope Maxine had given him yesterday. Not much weight to it, he thought, and set it aside. The rest of the loose paperwork in front of him offered no new insights. Thinking of Maxine had him wondering why she hadn't called yet, and it brought to mind the birth certificate, the one Maxine had originally found for *Baby Girl Norwood*. He stared at the freshly organized notes and documents and couldn't recall seeing it. He rechecked the stack of papers a couple of times, then opened the clasped envelope, knowing it wouldn't be inside but dumping the contents onto the desktop nevertheless.

The last page to land on the stack was a photocopy of a current California driver's license. The copy had been enlarged, the details grainy, but the desk was well lit and Holt's initial vague recognition took root and twisted his sense of reality inside out as he stared at the picture.

It was Pearl Norwood.

Holt kept staring at the photocopy, his eyes darting back and forth between the picture of Pearl and the name Clarissa Morrison printed next to it. He tore into the rest of the papers from the envelope and found the marriage and divorce records for Saunders. Thirty-five years ago he had married a woman named Clarissa Jackson. In the divorce papers her name was Clarissa Saunders. Holt figured Morrison was either her latest husband's name or anybody's guess.

He picked up the photocopy, holding it close, his mind turning as he tried to manufacture a sensible explanation more bearable than the truth—he'd been played.

He tried to fully grasp what had happened, only to be overwhelmed by more questions: How did Kane find a stand-in for Pearl? Where was the real Pearl Norwood? Did she even exist? And most of all, how did Kane find out about Bigelow?

The answer to that last question crept up on Holt as he thought it through. It had to be the birth certificate. It would have told Kane everything he needed to know, and Holt had conveniently left it within Kane's reach when he took Susan's call during that first meeting at Blackhawk.

Holt needed Dr. Janus now more than ever. The doctor's cryptic message held the only hope Holt had left. He picked up the phone and punched in Maxine's cell phone number. The call went straight to voice mail. Holt got up and paced the floor for a few minutes, then collapsed onto the leather sofa under the window.

* * *

He'd lost track of time and where he was when Maxine finally called, his head spinning after jumping up from the sofa too fast.

"What have you got?" he said. "Have you talked to Janus?"

"Not exactly." The line went quiet, and Holt waited it out, sensing that Maxine needed a moment to collect her thoughts before she continued. "I'm sorry, Mr. Holt, but I don't know if Dr. Janus is going to be of much help. I got in to see him last night but he was pretty much out of it. This morning was even worse."

"What do you mean, *Out of it*? Was he unconscious?"

"No, he's been awake, but not lucid. He was hallucinating again this morning. He thought I was one of the attendants from the morgue he'd been watching all night at the foot of his bed, whispering amongst themselves while waiting to take him down to the basement."

"He's imagining it—people in white coats waiting to take him away?"

"Yes. He's *seeing* and *hearing* this stuff. This morning, I followed Annie as far as the foot of his bed. He created quite a scene when he saw me standing there. He looked as old as Father Time and was clearly agitated, like he was trying to get out of the bed. Then he raised his arm and shook his finger right at me, saying that I was one of them, one of his tormentors from last night. Needless to say, I had to leave before they could calm him down."

"Shit," Holt said, reclaiming his chair behind the desk. "So is this a permanent condition? Was he like this before the surgery? Is it Alzheimer's?"

"His daughter assures me he doesn't have Alzheimer's. She thinks it's a reaction to the drugs they're giving him. They had applied a transdermal patch to his back to control the post-operative pain, and apparently it didn't stay attached and he'd been in a lot of pain for who knows how long. When they figured it out, the doctors administered painkillers into his IV drip. Annie found out one of the drugs was Ativan, an antianxiety agent. It's also a hypnotic. It's what makes you feel so good when they're wheeling you into surgery. But Janus can't handle it, especially when they combine it with a painkiller like Darvon. Annie says it'll have him behaving like a raging schizophrenic as soon as it hits his bloodstream. They were both aware of this beforehand and supposedly it's on his chart, but the doctors here don't seem to care. She says they're treating him like any other old man, doctor or not, suffering from the effects of dementia or Alzheimer's. They see it every day. They tell her Ativan is what they *give* schizophrenics and that it shouldn't affect him like that. One of the doctors wrote it off as *ICU psychosis,* and said to give it a while and he should come out of it."

Doctors, Holt thought, his earlier scene with Troman still crowding his mind. "So what do *you* think?"

"I think I should go back this afternoon," Maxine said. "I'm here at my hotel room and have extended it for another day. I just got off the phone with Annie. They seem to have his pain under control, and she assured me he won't be getting any more Ativan. I'll see how it goes."

"Stay as long as it takes," Holt said. "We need Janus, and you'll have to handle it. I'm done."

"You're done? What do you mean by . . ."

"Susan's dead. She died this morning . . . on the operating table."

The line went quiet for a long while. Holt couldn't speak. Saying the words brought back the pain, made it real all over again, and they packed a punch almost as devastating as when he'd heard them from Troman.

"My God, Ben, I'm so sorry. I had no idea it was this serious."

"It wasn't supposed to be," Holt said, surprised that he could continue talking. "Just a routine procedure. Don't you love that word, *procedure*? It makes knocking you out and cutting you up sound so harmless."

"How's Benny taking it?"

"Not well. If his grandmother weren't here, I don't know what I'd do. Right now she seems to be the only one he trusts."

"This is such a shock . . . I can't imagine what he must be going through." A brief pause, then Maxine's voice was back, gathering resolve. "Don't worry, I'll do my best. If Janus comes around, maybe we can resolve this quickly."

"I don't think it's going to be that easy," Holt said. "I just opened the envelope you gave me yesterday, the stuff you found on Saunders and his wife."

"Is there a problem?"

"Yeah, only I don't know how big yet. Turns out we were almost the victims of a hoax. If you hadn't found the driver's license for Saunders's wife, it could have been a disaster. They're using her as a stand-in for Pearl Norwood. If it weren't for you, I would have bought it."

"What are you talking about? How could—"

Holt told her. He covered everything he knew and everything he thought he knew. And even as he spoke, he realized he'd have to stay involved and see it through to the end. The authorities had to be notified. There would be questions only he could answer, and more questions he couldn't, such as, where was Pearl Norwood? The *real* Pearl Norwood.

Maxine had follow-up questions, and Holt answered the best he could. Then another silence settled in over the line, longer than before. Finally, she said, "Mr. Holt, I like you. I like working for you. I hope you know that."

Back to *Mr. Holt*. Not *Ben*, like before, when she'd heard the news about Susan.

"I like working with you, too, Max." Holt didn't know what else to say, and he had to listen closer when Maxine continued, her voice lowering.

"Despite my feelings about you and our work, I'm afraid my loyalty has always been with the firm. That's where my paycheck comes from."

"Where are you going with this?"

"Please, don't talk. Just hear me out." Maxine paused for a long breath, then continued. "When they made you partner? That's when it started. Stratton told me to keep an eye on you and file reports on everything you did. He wasn't happy about elevating you to a full partner, the way Mr. Bigelow forced it through. He resented it, even though you were doing a good job. I think he'd rather see you fail."

"I guess that explains how Logan's insurance document found its way to Stratton's desk before I could tell him about it."

"I'd put it off as long as I could."

"Why are you telling me this now?"

"Never mind that," she said. "There's more. The other day, while I was attending to something in the executive suite, I overheard the tail end of a phone conversation out of Stratton's office. He was on the line with a member of the board of trustees that now runs Mr. Bigelow's foundation. They were talking about the ten-million-dollar payout. I didn't hear the specifics, but they were working *something* out." Susan brought her voice up a notch, as if she wanted to be sure Holt heard her. "Those board members? They're highly educated accountants—glorified bean counters. If anyone can get creative with all that cash, they can."

"What are you implying? You think Stratton was working out some kind of kickback—"

"I'm just telling you to watch out for yourself. As far as Stratton is concerned, you won't be employed here much longer, no matter *who* gets the settlement. You can use this information for leverage, make a deal with him."

"You mean sell my conscience to keep my job?"

"What else can you do? You're on your own, with a son to raise. That's going to be hard to do from the unemployment line. A middle-aged, overpaid lawyer out of work—what are your chances of landing on your feet in *this* economy?"

"So am I supposed to thank you for turning the tables on Stratton?"

"I'm sorry, Mr. Holt. This has been eating at me all week. And now, with what's happened . . ."

"We'll talk about it later, when I'm up for it. For now, stay with Janus. Contact me when you have something."

Holt broke the connection and tossed his phone onto the desktop. He looked up at Benny's image in the family portrait and followed the boy's gaze toward Susan. Her expression seemed to have changed, forever frozen now with the haunted eyes Holt sometimes saw in old photographs of family ancestors.

He looked away, not liking where his thoughts were leading. He couldn't allow them to paralyze him any longer. He found the contact number for Pearl Norwood and made the call, not sure how he would handle it. It went directly to voicemail. He called Alan Kane, whose phone rang several times, then went to voicemail as well. Holt gathered the paperwork on his desk and stuffed it into his briefcase. He walked out of the study to find Ruth.

She was sitting in the living room. The family members rarely used it themselves, reserving it for entertaining guests and acquaintances outside the inner circle. The atmosphere in the room always felt sterile and unlived-in, which now seemed appropriate. Holt sat next to her on the sofa.

"I need your help, Ruth. If there was any way around it, I wouldn't ask, but I don't know what else to do."

Ruth took his hand but otherwise didn't acknowledge hearing him, her eyes blank beneath red, swollen lids.

"It's about my job," Holt said. "I'm about to lose it."

She turned to him, her eyes searching his, looking for something to focus on. "What can I do?"

"I need to be gone for the rest of the day. Something's come up. It's a problem that I created, and if I don't fix it, I'm through."

"And you're worried about Benny," Ruth said.

"I'm worried about all of us. Life is going to be hard enough for Benny as it is, but if I couldn't take care of him . . ."

"I'll be here for him, Ben. We'll be okay for now."

"Thank you for this," Holt said, squeezing her hand. "I'll be back tonight."

TWENTY-ONE

THE DRIVE from Sky Harbor to Sedona was still fresh in Holt's mind from his previous trip. He had the interstate displayed on the nav system and found his way to I-17 without a hitch. The desert stretched out before him and he felt better now that he was on the move, away from the press of indifferent strangers crowding him on the plane and rushing around him in the terminal. He tried to suppress his dark thoughts by concentrating on Clarissa Morrison and Alan Kane and how to avoid any collateral damage when the shit hit the fan. Hopefully, there would be enough time to settle the inheritance issues before the news got out.

Holt figured Clarissa would be at the cabin or close by. She had to be available for corroborating the identity of Bigelow's heir. She'd want it done quietly, without raising suspicion from the Red Rock Lodge's staff and neighbors, and Holt squirmed in his seat as he remembered how he'd agreed to do just that—to keep it quiet and confidential. He was lucky to have stumbled onto what was happening, yet at the same time Holt felt a grudging admiration for their plan—it was audacious enough to have actually worked. All they had to do was convince him that he'd found Pearl, then everything else would have fallen into place—proof positive, from collateral evidence to DNA testing, that Mona McBride, an unsuspecting housewife in Ojai, was the legal heir named in Logan Bigelow's trust.

* * *

The signpost came up quickly from around a bend in the road, surprising Holt even though he was on the lookout. He braked hard and managed to pull into the lodge's parking area, at first ignoring the emergency vehicles. He climbed out of the rental car and walked past an ambulance and a red pickup truck with an unlit light bar mounted on top of the cab. A couple of paramedics were talking to a man in navy blue trousers and a white shirt with military style epaulets on the shoulders. Holt couldn't read the lettering on the side of the pickup truck from his angle, but he assumed it belonged to the local fire chief. Holt walked by without saying anything.

He came up to the footbridge and slowed down. He hadn't really noticed the smell until that moment. He realized it had been there all along, that he must have unconsciously assumed, despite the emergency vehicles, that it was just the normal smell you get out in the woods, from a campfire or from the wood smoke out of a cabin chimney. He hurried on to the bridge. When he was halfway across he saw the fire engine and the men rolling up hoses, unhurried, adrenaline spent, the crisis over. Some of the firefighters had soot on their faces and fresh, black streaks across their yellow turnout coats. The engine was parked along the narrow unpaved driveway that served the cabins across the creek. It must have pulled up from somewhere on the far side of the cabins, out of Holt's view. The smell of wet, smoldering wood grew more noticeable and was getting stronger as Holt reached the far side of the bridge. He hesitated again before stepping off, looking for a clear path between pools of dark water collected in the low spots of the muddy path in front of him. Ash was everywhere, some of it drifting in the air, most of it clinging to the nearby shrubs and trees or coating the surface of the path, and Holt trudged through the gray muck knowing what he was going to find, shocked nevertheless when he turned a corner and saw the empty, black ground where Pearl's cabin had once stood.

Holt looked closer and saw there was a layer of charred rubble covering the high ground in front of him, crowned by portions of the stone fireplace and chimney that remained standing. Some of the nearby trees were scorched, and the studio out back had a partially burned roof, but otherwise the surrounding structures and foliage remained unharmed. A low haze of smoke and ash still hovered over the scene, and a couple of firefighters sifted through the smoldering debris with pikes and hooks, looking for hot spots, or perhaps human remains. Another firefighter stood alone where the front porch had been. He had his helmet off and was watching his two partners. Holt approached him and asked, "Did they make it out?"

The firefighter turned toward him, surprised, as if he hadn't heard Holt come up, or perhaps his mind was somewhere else and he'd just been distracted from his thoughts. Before he could speak, Holt repeated, "The people who live here—did they make it out okay?"

"Who are *you*?" The firefighter put on his helmet and started walking back to the staging area. "Are you related to them?"

"No relation," Holt said, hurrying along to keep up. "I'm a friend, here to see Pearl Norwood. Around here they know her as Peal Diamond. It's her cabin. Do you know if she's all right?"

The firefighter stopped walking. He looked at Holt and shook his head. "I'm sorry. Two bodies were just found, side by side, in what was left of the bed. They were burned beyond recognition. A fire that burns that hot . . . well, there were also the remains of several oxygen tanks in the bedroom. That pretty much tells the story." The firefighter started to move on, then paused for a closer look at Holt. "I can tell you this," he said, turning his chin toward the rubble. "There's no sign of Pearl Diamond in there."

"How can you be sure? You just said the bodies were burned beyond recognition."

"The fire didn't destroy their teeth. Both bodies had a full set, badly charred but still intact. With the surrounding flesh burned away, it was hard to miss. The thing is, I know for a fact that Pearl wore dentures. I was on the call, assisting the paramedics, when her husband had a stroke a while back. It was late at night, and Pearl was too upset and preoccupied to think about her dentures and I wound up retrieving them from the bathroom counter and delivering them to her at the hospital."

"So you know her."

"Yeah, I know Pearl. And I don't have a clue what the hell is going on around here."

With nothing more to say, the firefighter walked away, leaving Holt standing in his wake. Holt turned back toward the charred ground and it looked different to him now that he knew about the bodies.

He was the only onlooker. The fire had been out for a while and there was nothing left to see. He walked back to the footbridge and watched the fire engine back away down the narrow access lane. He heard men climbing into other vehicles, slamming doors, starting engines. In the parking lot, a county medical examiner's van idled next to the ambulance he'd seen on his way in, waiting, Holt assumed, for the departing fire engine and support rigs to make room along the access road. The chief's pickup was gone and the attendants were all inside their vehicles. Holt stood by his rental for a last look around. The sound of laboring diesels echoed through the trees, followed by quick glimpses of the fire engine and a hook-and-ladder truck making their way along the road north of the parking lot. The ambulance and medical examiner's van slowly moved out.

* * *

His cell phone was useless. Holt glanced up at the towering red rock visible here and there through gaps in the trees and remembered he was traveling along the bottom of a deep canyon. He tossed the phone onto the passenger seat. He'd check for text messages and voicemails later, when he could pick up a signal in Sedona.

The old part of town sat on a ridge high enough for cell phone reception, where Holt's phone received a clear signal but showed no messages. He parked in front of one of the restaurants crowded among the tourist attractions lining the main drag. He was hungry, and a Mexican restaurant across the way looked inviting. Somewhere between the tortilla soup and the enchiladas, he decided to call Bryce Saunders.

He finished his meal, then walked across the street and down half a block from the Mexican restaurant, looking for a quiet spot to make the call. He found a lone park bench that faced away from the sidewalk at the edge of a scenic drop-off that took in an almost surreal view of the surrounding red rock buttes. He opened his briefcase and pulled out his notes for the phone numbers Saunders had given him. Holt was getting used to the tension by now, the way it would ebb and flow throughout the day. Once again it began to tighten, one notch at a time, a little tighter with every ring that went unanswered. Bryce Saunders finally answered just as Holt was about to give up.

Holt identified himself. Saunders said, "I thought I might be hearing from you."

"Why's that?"

"Didn't Clarissa tell you—?"

"Clarissa? What would she want to tell me?"

"I told her I couldn't go through with it," Saunders said. "I had the business card you gave me and I told her who you were. I gave her your number—"

"Slow down, Saunders. I haven't heard from anybody. Why don't you take it from the top. First of all, what do you mean, *You can't go through with it*?"

"Just what I said. I can't do it. I'm not going to let my daughter get involved with any of this."

The line went quiet. Holt concentrated on what Saunders had just said. "So your daughter really doesn't know what's going on?"

"Fuck no. And I'm pissed at Clarissa for even thinking of doing something so stupid—and dangerous. That guy she sent over here scared me."

"What guy?"

"The guy who came barging into my house the other night, threatening me to play along, or else."

"I'm still lost. What night?"

"Wednesday night. The night before you came around. He was still here the next morning when you knocked on my door. He'd kept me up all night, telling me how to act and what to say and that you, or somebody like you, would be coming around with a shitload of questions and that I'd better be ready with the right answers."

"Is that why you sent me away? To meet me at the restaurant?"

"Yeah, and he didn't leave until after I told him what we talked about."

Another pause on the line. Holt quickly rethought his snap assumption that Saunders was talking about Alan Kane. Holt had been with Kane on into Wednesday evening, and while it would have been possible for Kane to make it out to LA later that night, it didn't seem likely. He'd appeared lethargic and ready for bed rather than in a hurry to leave town. Besides, Holt couldn't see Kane scaring anyone. Not like this. Saunders sounded truly afraid. Holt asked, "Who is this guy?"

Saunders didn't reply right away, and Holt wondered if he was still there. After another drawn-out moment, Saunders said, "I don't know."

"C'mon, Saunders. Who was he? I don't have time to—"

"I really don't know. He just came up here and started in on me. He never told me his name."

"Just like that—you let in this stranger and he forces you to commit a major felony?"

"It wasn't like that. He knew all about me. He said he'd known Clarissa for years, and that she'd told him everything he needed to know, including stuff about our daughter. He said if I knew what was good for me, and if I didn't want anything bad to happen to her, I'd do what he asked."

"Then why are you backing out now?"

"I've had time to come to my senses. While he was here, I thought it best to go along with him. I didn't want a big confrontation. Not here. Not until I had time to figure out what to do. But everything happened so fast. First he's here, then you come by. There was too much shit raining down on me to let me think straight. So I play along and do what he tells me. But after everybody goes away, after you're gone and he's gone and it's quiet enough for me to calm down, I start to get mad. I call up Mona and I can see right away she doesn't know what's going on, so I don't say anything about it. I tell her I'm trying to get in touch with her mother, which by now is true—I want to see Clarissa in the worst way. Mona knows I haven't seen her in years. I don't have a number for her or have any idea where she lives, but Mona's kept in touch and gives me a couple of numbers. I try Clarissa's cell and home phone numbers and get an out-of-service message on one and an answering machine on the other. I leave a message on the machine and get a callback an hour or so later."

"Where'd she call from?"

"I don't know. It didn't come up. We just got to talking about what the hell was happening. What bothered me most was her willingness to lie to our own daughter. I mean, how could she put Mona through it, to let her believe she was adopted?"

"Hold on. Let me get this for the record; you're telling me that Mona is your real daughter—you're the father, Clarissa is the mother?"

"That's right. The bullshit I fed you the other day? It was close to the truth. The only thing I lied about was the adoption."

"Then why did I find a delayed birth certificate?"

"Clarissa was always into holistic cures and medicine, way before it was popular. She wanted to have a natural childbirth, at home. She knew about a midwife who came highly recommended and the woman agreed to assist us. The only problem was that she was from Guatemala and in the country illegally. But Clarissa liked her, and we went ahead and Mona was born at home. Clarissa was never too worried about how it would turn out. She believed that everything happens for a good reason and that things would work out. Sure enough, a few years later the midwife finally got a green card and agreed to sign the paperwork they needed for the birth certificate."

"And Mona still doesn't know about the inheritance scheme?"

"The guy insisted that I not tell her. He wanted her reaction to be genuine when she was told officially. He said you can't fake something like that, and that everybody would be watching her closely."

Holt imagined the emotional response evoked by finding out after thirty years that you'd been adopted. He could picture a variety of reactions—shock, anger, confusion. And then you throw in the inheritance. What a bombshell. Whoever was running the show had it right. Better to exploit real emotions rather than fake them. And on top of it all, Holt knew he would have believed it.

"And Clarissa," he said, "was okay with all this?"

"That's what really pissed me off, even more than the guy coming over with his threats and hard-ass attitude. I told Clarissa flat out it wasn't going to happen. I told her to get ahold of whoever the fuck her friend was and tell him to back off or I would go to the cops."

"Have you?"

"Not yet. Thought I'd give it a while and see what happens. I'm getting nervous, though. I almost didn't answer the phone just now, thinking maybe I ought to lay low until this blows over. I'm thinking of heading over to Mona's to make sure she's all right, then maybe take a little vacation."

"That might not be a bad idea."

The line went silent again. Then Saunders asked, "Why do you say that?" Before Holt could answer, he said, "Why are you calling, anyway? If Clarissa hasn't talked to you—"

"Let's just say Clarissa has delivered the message."

"What do you mean by that?"

It had to have been Clarissa in Pearl's burned-out cabin. If it wasn't Pearl herself, who else could it be? Did that mean Pearl was dead? Now that he'd talked to the firefighter, Holt knew Pearl Norwood had been alive and well right up until he started looking for her. That meant the Social Security Card he'd looked at was the real thing, that they didn't fabricate an identity out of thin air. The odds she was still around couldn't be good, not with her invalid husband burned to a crisp beside her imposter. He needed to warn Saunders, but Holt also needed to be sure of the facts. And facts were hard to come by when you were drowning in lies and clutching at false leads.

"I don't know what's going on," Holt said, "but I'm starting to believe you. You need to look after yourself, and your family."

"What about the cops? Should I call them?"

"I think some police involvement would be a good thing, but they're going to want more information. You can tell them you've been threatened, but by whom? They'll need a name, or at the very least a good description. Now that his plans are washed up, the only question is whether or not he'll be mad enough to come after you. If he's a pro, he'll walk away."

"But if he's a psycho . . ."

"Let's hope for the former. You can't cause him any more trouble. Without knowing his name—"

"That's not entirely true," Saunders said.

"What? C'mon, Saunders, don't do this to me. Who is he?"

"I didn't lie to you. He never told me his name. But when I talked to Clarissa, *she* told me. Only it's not his real name."

"Anything would be helpful," Holt said, thinking, Great, more lies. "So who is he?"

"He's using the name Wentworth Tellington."

"She say anything else about him?"

"Not really. She didn't want to talk about him at all. I'm sure she wasn't looking forward to talking *to* him, either. I guess I put her on the spot, but that's the way it goes. She got us into this mess; she can get us out."

"So what does he look like?"

"Big and mean."

"Can you be a little more specific?"

"He's a white guy. Well over six foot, weighs maybe two-fifty. He's an older dude, a lot of gray . . . no, it's more like silver. Silver hair and mustache."

"What do you mean by older? Forty-five, sixty-five . . .what?"

"Probably not as old as me. If I had to guess, I'd say late fifties."

"Anything else?"

"Like I said, he's a scary guy. Gotta a hell of a mean streak."

Holt jotted down Tellington's name and description on the notepad beneath Saunders's phone numbers. He underlined *scary*, as that seemed to be Tellington's most noteworthy feature.

"Go see your daughter," he said. "That little vacation is looking better and better."

* * *

Back on the road, Holt was thirty-some miles north of Phoenix when the call came. The caller ID number was unfamiliar, but he recognized Maxine's voice.

"It's me," she said. "I'm on a landline in the intensive care unit. They plugged in a phone next to Dr. Janus's bed. He wants to talk to you."

"Put him on."

Holt listened to the sounds of the phone changing hands. Then a hoarse, scratchy voice came on the line.

"Hello . . . can you hear me all right?"

"I hear you fine, Dr. Janus. How are you feeling?"

"Aw, my voice is shot. It's from the trachea tube they use when you're under general anesthesia. Annie tells me I scared off your girl when she came by earlier. Sorry about that."

"No problem. Sounds like you're doing better."

"I'd like to say I can't remember acting like such a mental case, but what I was experiencing seemed all too real at the time. I hope it won't prejudice you against taking me seriously now."

"Your daughter told us about your problem with the medication. Add on the post-operative pain and stress, and I can understand how things went sideways."

"Thank you for not mentioning my age—too many birthdays is the biggest stress maker of all." Janus wheezed a few weak coughs into the phone for emphasis. "I just want to assure you that all this hasn't affected my long-term memory, at least not yet."

"That's good to hear," Holt said, "because we need to go back thirty years to find what I'm looking for."

Holt waited for a response but heard only the old man's breathing. It didn't sound labored as much as it seemed just plain tired. Muffled sounds came over the line while Janus moved the phone or readjusted himself, then he was back.

"Thirty years doesn't seem that far away," Janus said. "and I clearly remember Logan Bigelow. Scottsdale was a smaller town back then, and I generally didn't have famous patients. I guess that's why I remember Logan and his girlfriend so well. Don't get me wrong; it's not as if I've been thinking about them all these years. But when Annie mentioned his name before my surgery, and when she asked about Pearl's daughter, it all came back to me."

"Why the message?" Holt said. "What's the *terrible mistake* you had referred to, and how can you set things straight?"

"As I understood it, you were trying to find Pearl's daughter through the girl's adoptive parents. That was your mistake—there are, and never were, any adoptive parents."

"So what happened? Did Pearl raise the girl herself?"

"No one raised the baby. It never left the hospital." Janus paused. A few more ragged breaths. "It died within days after it was born."

It took a second for the last few words to sink in. Holt stared at the highway in front on him, an asphalt ribbon stretched out on a blank, dirt-colored expanse of nothingness.

"Didn't you tell Logan?"

"No. He was gone by then. He had arranged everything earlier and wasn't there for the birth."

"What about Pearl? How did she take it?"

"There was no reason for her to know. She had planned to give up the baby, so I didn't tell her."

"But she had a right to know. If there was some kind of congenital defect she needed to be aware of it. So did Logan Bigelow . . ."

Holt backed off. Janus's breathing was getting noticeably worse. What had been a faint rasp was fast becoming an alarming rattle as his evident discomfort came through over the phone line. This was no time to start preaching to an old man trying to recover from major surgery. What was done, was done, Holt told himself. Just stay focused on the task at hand. With a conscious effort to keep his voice calm, he said, "I don't see how we missed it. I'm sure we searched for a death certificate."

Holt heard the phone change hands again. In the background he heard Janus's voice say, "Here . . . tell him what I told you."

"This is Ann Warren, Dr. Janus's daughter. I don't know what you said, but it's got Dad stressed out . . . just a minute." More muffled background conversation, then Ann was back. "He says you missed the death certificate because you didn't know what to look for. He doesn't know the exact date, but it was issued as a Jane Doe about a week after her birth. It's got Dad's signature. I hope that helps; now I have to go."

And she hung up.

* * *

Holt watched the miles tick by on the odometer. He'd give Maxine five more miles before he tried her cell phone. She beat him to it, calling him halfway past the three mile mark.

"I assume you heard Dr. Janus's side of the conversation," Holt said. "Can you talk?"

"I'm outside the hospital, heading for my rental. I heard the whole thing, including the bit about the death certificate. I'll get on it as soon as possible. I've made some friends over at the Arizona Office of Vital Records, and I'll call them right away. I also have my laptop with me. I'll email you whatever I get, when I get it."

"Any idea why he issued the death certificate under a Jane Doe?"

"Not a clue. But something was bothering him, something that seemed more than physical pain or discomfort. He was clearly upset."

"How about his daughter, Ann? She didn't seem too happy with me, either, before she hung up on me."

"She wasn't. But I'm sure most of it was out of concern for her father and the way he was behaving."

"I guess it's out of our hands now. I'll stop by the office as soon as I get back in town. Forward anything you get to my office email address."

"Where are you?"

"On the road, somewhere between Sedona and Phoenix. The situation is now completely out of control and has escalated way beyond looking for Logan's daughter. Innocent people are dead, and I have an obligation to tell the authorities what I know. I can't just let it go."

"What happened?"

"I was unable to contact Kane or his accomplice. I decided to fly out and resolve this, one way or the other. When I got to Pearl's cabin, it was burned to the ground with two bodies inside—Pearl's common-law husband, and someone I have to believe is Clarissa Morrison."

"Why do you think it's Clarissa?"

"Trust me. I have it on good authority. Whoever set the fire thought Clarissa would be mistaken for Pearl, at least for a while. Pearl is still missing. She hasn't surfaced since this all began."

"You don't think Kane is behind it?"

"Maybe I'm being naive, but I can't see Kane as a cold-blooded killer. I don't think he's the guy. Not since I learned about Wentworth Tellington."

"Who is Wentworth Tellington?"

"I have no idea. That's why I have *you*, if you're really working for me."

TWENTY-TWO

S O THIS Wentworth Tellington is a killer, huh?"

Gunnar's question startled Kane out of his daydream. He'd been watching Gunnar all morning, waiting for a response to his confession, but up until now Gunnar had kept focused on his work, concentrating on Stumpy's bike and taking quick trips every fifteen minutes or so out to the paint booth behind the shop to spray another coat of acrylic lacquer onto a customized frame. He went about his work with a determined yet somehow detached proficiency, speaking to Kane only when he needed a hand with some heavy lifting or wanted a wrench or some other specific tool out of his reach.

Of course, Kane hadn't *really* confessed. Not about Pearl. That was something he was going to have to keep locked inside, a dark secret with a life of its own, digging in deep, establishing permanent residence. And he thought, Maybe it shows. Maybe that's why Gunnar hadn't said anything. Maybe he suspects me of holding back and is waiting for me to come clean with the whole story.

He was relieved now that Gunnar was talking, and he answered with an affirmative nod. Gunnar didn't see it, having already headed for a workbench on the far side of the garage.

"You've really gone and done it this time, man," he said over his shoulder. "Looking for that free ride. It ain't ever going to happen. You know that, don't you?"

Kane sat still and remained silent. He was perched on another workbench, his feet dangling over the edge, the hard surface numbing his butt.

"I still don't get how you hooked up with the guy," Gunnar continued. "I mean, What were you thinking?"

"I don't know," Kane said. "It just happened. Like I said, we were over at Ashley's place, having lunch. We started talking about this inheritance . . . all of a sudden Tellington's talking about claiming it. He sounded like he knew what he was talking about. He sucked me in. In any case, Ashley seemed to know him pretty well."

"Yeah, right," Gunnar said. "And where is she now? Still over at your place?"

"I think so. She's afraid to go back to the ranch."

"I don't blame her." Gunnar wiped his hands with a shop rag as he looked over at the dismantled parts of Stumpy's bike, then finally turned toward Kane. "I think we should go see how she's doing . . . take her out for a late lunch. I'm at a good place to stop. The frame out back needs at least twenty-four hours to cure and I can get back to this anytime."

There was something about Gunnar that Kane had failed to notice during the years he had known him. But on this long, quiet morning, when he had taken the time to really look at him, at first frustrated by Gunnar's apparent indifference and then seeing past it, Kane recognized a noble spirit hiding behind all the rough edges and the fuck-you attitude. That's when he knew Gunnar was going to help him. Gunnar was going to take charge of the situation the same way he had torn into Stumpy's bike, and with the same sure-handed finesse he had used to lay on those coats of lacquer out back. Kane's hopes were realized when Gunnar jerked his head toward the door. Without a word they walked out of the shop. Gunnar locked up, then climbed onto the passenger seat of the Cherokee as Kane keyed the motor.

They traveled in silence. Gunnar seemed content to sit and watch the scenery drift by and Kane didn't want to say anything, afraid that he might put the kibosh on the welcome turn of events. On the way up Kane's driveway they saw Ashley waiting by the front door. She ran around to the garage at the back of the house and met them as they stepped out.

She grabbed Kane around the waist. "I'm glad you're back. I've been going crazy, listening to cars going by on the road, waiting for them to turn in, hoping they didn't, not knowing—"

"Hey, don't worry. Everything's going to be all right." Kane gave her a squeeze, then held her out at arm's length. "Everything's cool. Nobody's been here, have they?"

"No . . ." Ashley looked over at Gunnar, as if she had just noticed him standing there. She wiped away a stray tear and tried to smile. "Hi, Gunnar."

"How ya doin', Ashley?"

She hesitated a moment, glanced at Kane, then back to Gunnar. "Did Alan tell you . . . about what I saw at the ranch?"

"Yeah."

"What are we going to do? What's going to happen to us?"

"I don't know. All you can do now is take it as it comes."

Gunnar's answer didn't seem to pick up her spirits. She pushed away from Kane. Gunnar came over and offered a comforting arm around her shoulders. She leaned into him. He asked her if she'd eaten today.

"I've been too worried to eat," she said.

Gunnar led Ashley toward the house. "You'll feel better with some food in you." He looked back over his shoulder. "C'mon, Kane, get in here and make your guests some lunch."

The back door was still locked and Kane passed in front of them to unlock it and ushered them inside. Gunnar and Ashley sat at the kitchen table while Kane went to work. Beers all around. Chips and salsa to hold them off until Kane served up platefuls of *huevos rancheros*.

A little color had returned to Ashley's cheeks when she said, "I'd feel better if I had some of my stuff. I can't go on wearing these clothes, and my horse needs looking after."

"Okay," Kane said. "We'll go over and take care of it."

"I said I needed some things; I didn't say I'd go back to the ranch. I went out this morning, but I couldn't do it, despite needing a change of underwear and some fresh makeup."

"What do you need makeup for?" Gunnar said. "You look as sweet as a just-washed peach, fresh off the tree."

"Thanks Gunnar, but this ol' peach needs some help. When I was out I bought a toothbrush and a few things to get by. I'll be all right for a few days. I just need some of my clothes—a pair of shorts and tennis shoes or sandals, and maybe a couple of tee shirts. It's too hot for ranch-wear if I'm just going to be hanging around here."

She was dressed in her Levis and boots and had on one of Kane's dress shirts, tails out, sleeves rolled up past her elbows. Kane looked her over and said, "I guess I could go by and pick them up. I don't know much about horses, though."

"We'll both go," Gunnar said. "Better let *me* handle the horse."

"Thanks, Gunnar. Alan can show you where his stall is. You just have to make sure he's got fresh hay in the feeder. If it's empty, tear a couple of flakes off one of the bales stacked in the vacant stall next to his. You'll find some oats in a stainless steel container in the feedroom next door. Take a scoopful and spread 'em on the bottom tray of the feeder. His water should be okay; the trough's got a water leveler to keep it full, but you might check on it to make sure. Don't worry about mucking out the stall, it's cleaned every morning—"

"Don't they feed him when they clean up?"

"I can't count on it. The owner took a lot of the stock and his best hands to a horse show in Nevada. While everyone's gone there's only a couple of Mexicans left to maintain the place, and I haven't seen them around all week. They're used to seeing me take care of my horse, and if they show up and clean out his stall and notice an empty feeder, they might toss in some hay, but that's it. With so many horses temporarily gone from that end of the stable, who knows if they'll even check on him?"

Ashley got up and grabbed her purse. She handed Kane a ring full of keys. "Everything should be locked up. You know the pegboard by the door? Where I keep the key to the tack room? It should also open any padlocks on the stable doors."

"When's the owner coming back?" Kane asked.

"Not until Monday night, at the earliest. Probably more like Tuesday. If you run into the Mexicans, tell them you're there to feed my horse. They'll recognize my SUV if you take it instead of your Cherokee." She pointed out the key to her Explorer, and the one to her bungalow.

"They understand English?"

"They get by. Don't let them fool you."

Gunnar stood up. "Okay, then. Let's go."

* * *

Kane didn't need the key to Ashley's bungalow. The doorknob turned in his hand and the unlatched deadbolt allowed the door to swing open. He walked inside and noticed the tack room key was missing from its peg. Gunnar moved past him to check all the rooms.

"Grab some clothes for Ashley and whatever else you think she might need," Kane said. "I'm heading over to the stables."

He passed by the tack room adjacent to the stables and on to a Dutch door large enough to handle horse traffic. The bottom half was locked, but the top section hung open, secured to the wall with a king-sized doornail. Kane peered inside down a dim corridor that separated rows of stalls facing each other. At the far end of the corridor stood a similar door, both sections wide open in a wash of white light from outside. He climbed over the bottom half of the door on his end and walked down the corridor.

The bridge-plank flooring was littered with loose straw and hay that muffled his footsteps. As he passed a stall, he was almost run over by Tellington's horse. Tellington had him on a lead, and they were all startled, especially the horse. He reared up and let out a loud whinny, front hoofs kicking out, steel shoes flashing in shafts of errant light streaming in through the open eves overhead, then coming down hard on the wood floor. Tellington regained control of the leader whipping about from the horse's halter and winced in pain when the frightened animal gave it a sharp tug. Tellington switched it to his left hand and glanced at the burnt, open flesh of his right palm where the leather strap had been torn from his grip. He glared at Kane.

"Goddamnit, Kane. You scared the shit out of us. You shouldn't be sneaking up like that, on man *or* beast."

Kane looked past Tellington and the horse. Through the open doors in back, he could make out a horse trailer hitched to Tellington's Escalade. A quick moment passed, then he refocused on Tellington. "Going somewhere?"

"That's right. And it's fucking up my other plans. I only needed a few more days to finish my business here. Now everything's shot to hell." Tellington came closer to the horse and stroked his flank, keeping his voice calm. The horse began to settle down but seemed reluctant to unwind, as if he'd be happier kicking a few planks from his stall before bolting into the sunshine outside.

Kane said, "What happened? You get the money already?"

"You *are* an idiot, Kane. Of course I haven't got the money. That was going to take some time. Not that it matters. There's not going to be any money. Not for any of us."

"What happened?"

"Didn't you hear? Pearl died."

"What . . . what are you talking about? What does that have to do with anything?"

"I guess you *didn't* hear," Tellington said. "Pearl's body turned up. At least that's what the cops will think. For a while, maybe, if we're lucky. It appears she died in the cabin with her old man. It burned to the ground. I guess keeping those oxygen tanks in the bedroom can be hazardous to your health."

The news took Kane by surprise, but he shook off the swarm of questions begging to be asked, refusing to let Tellington sidetrack him. He gathered his thoughts, then said, "How does that change things? Can't your friend's daughter still make the claim? I'm assuming it was her mother in the fire; why wouldn't their ID match still work?"

Tellington shook his head. He laughed, but he didn't smile. "You're pretty goddamned cold, Kane, I'll give you that." He turned his attention to his horse, ignoring Kane. "Okay, boy," he said, "let's get you back in the stall. I'll give you a few minutes to yourself . . . let you settle down . . . we'll get into that trailer a little later."

The horse stood half in, half out of the stall. Tellington tried to back him all the way in, but still the horse resisted, tossing his head to test the grip on the halter. His nostrils flared with every breath, as if he could smell the tension behind Tellington's calm voice. The large muscles running from his chest down to his forelegs quivered and his hooves fidgeted and stomped. Tellington finally managed to wheel him around and lead him inside the stall, murmuring soothing words all the while, especially while he worked himself back toward the stall's shoulder-high door so he could pull it shut.

Kane stood in his way.

"I don't have time for this, Kane."

"Make time."

"For what?"

"For telling me everything. Why can't we get the money?"

"What difference does it make? It's over."

Tellington shoved Kane aside.

Kane lunged back and hit Tellington squarely on the jaw.

Both of them stood there a moment, neither one saying anything or even believing what had just happened. Kane felt an angry flush warm his cheeks. He'd been angry at so many things and at so many people for so long and now it was finally coming out. It felt good. But as he looked at Tellington, he realized he had only lit that fuse again. He had lashed out with everything he had, or so it felt, yet Tellington just stood there, glaring at Kane like a batter ignoring the pain from where he'd been hit, getting ready to charge the pitcher. Kane glanced back over his shoulder, looking for Gunnar. He thought he saw a silhouette out by the half-closed door, but he couldn't be sure.

"What are you looking for, Kane? A way out?"

Kane turned back toward Tellington and a fist exploded in the middle of his face. A flurry of punches hit him. Hard knuckles pounded his body when he raised his arms to protect his face. Headshots slipped past his fingers and more punches tore into his arms, beating them down. Kane was learning firsthand and too late what a real fight was all about—no rules, no time-outs, and the possibility he might not live through it. By now all he wanted to do was get away from Tellington's wrath, but when he doubled over on the floor, Tellington went to work with his boots. Brutal kicks guided Kane farther into the stall as he tried to crawl away, sliding across hay and horseshit, the stomping hooves and the panicked bellows from Tellington's horse echoing off the walls.

Then something rang out, a loud, metallic clang. The blows to his body ended abruptly. Kane opened his eyes, and through a veil of blood and muck he watched the blurred image of Tellington's body topple over, slowly at first, then gathering speed on its descent. No hands came up to break the fall, and Tellington landed face down next to him.

It was all too much for the horse. He let out an unholy scream and bucked and kicked and reared up inside the close confines of the stall. Kane felt a pair of hands grab him by the ankles and drag him across the floor. He heard hooves splinter the side of the stall and drum on the floor and then change resonance when they trampled on what could have only been flesh and bone. Then the horse flew out of the stall, skittering on the straw-littered bridge planks in a wild fight for traction down the dark corridor, heading for daylight.

Gunnar bent over Kane and used both hands to gently prop up his face. "Hang tight, man. You're gonna be okay. I have to go catch that horse."

TWENTY-THREE

A COMFORTING silence lulled Kane into a half-conscious stupor. He hurt everywhere, but nowhere in particular. He'd found a soft place to lie down on the hay bales stored in a vacant stall. He was unsure of how long he'd been there when Gunnar returned.

"Lucked out with the horse," Gunnar said. "All the gates were closed and I just let him run himself out. Cornered him against the fence and he was too tired to fight when I led him to that horse trailer outside the stable. I assume it belongs to your friend . . . or what's left of him."

"What do you mean?" Kane said. He lifted his head off a partially broken down hay bale and tired to focus. "Is he—"

"He's dead." Gunnar looked at Kane, shook his head, and slid down against the side of the stall until he was sitting on the floor. "Didn't you see him?"

"I didn't look. It was all I could do to just make it over here to lie down."

"Well, it's not a pretty sight. That fuckin' horse ran right over him on the way out the stall."

"Shit." Kane groaned and pulled himself to a sitting position. "Now what?"

Gunnar stared at him. Said nothing.

"Should we call the police?"

"Call the cops and I'm outta here. I'm not getting mixed up with a dead body and the law."

"It was an accident," Kane said. "You said so yourself, that his horse ran over him."

"The horse trampled him only after I'd knocked the shit out of him with a shovel."

"Is *that* what I heard before he fell?"

"Yeah. I really rang his bell, didn't I? The shovel was the only thing handy when I came up behind him. You looked like you'd had enough, and I didn't think I should waste any more time."

Kane nodded. "I guess I owe you."

"I guess you do."

They sat in silence for a few minutes. Gunnar finally got up, took off the tee shirt he was wearing beneath his Levi vest, went to a spigot at the nearest water trough and wetted the shirt down. He came over to Kane and said, "Let's see how bad the damage is."

The dried blood covering Kane's face had come from that first punch on the nose. When Gunnar had wiped it clean, he stood back for an overall impression.

"How's your nose? Can you breathe through it?"

"I think so," Kane said, touching it gingerly.

"It doesn't look broken . . . hard to tell, though, what with all the swelling. Main thing is if you can breathe okay. Same goes for your ribs. You took some pretty good kicks."

Kane got to his feet. He couldn't stand very straight and his first steps were wobbly. He hugged his ribs as he walked to the neighboring stall to look at Tellington.

Gunnar stood beside him and said, "We've been lucky, so far. I didn't see the Mexicans around when I was chasing down the horse. It must be siesta time."

"How much more time do you think we've got?"

"Good question. It's best to assume they could show up any minute."

"So what should we do?"

"The way I see it, we have one of two choices: leave the body here, or get rid of it."

"Maybe we should just leave him here," Kane said. "It's obvious what happened to him. We'll let the horse out of the trailer, leave everything the way it is, and let someone else find him."

"Just an accident, huh?"

"Yeah. Accidents happen. Tellington's horse got spooked. Tellington fell down and got run over. I'll bet this shit happens all the time."

Gunnar came around and squatted down on his haunches for a closer look at the body. "Maybe. But you see this?" He pointed in the general direction of Tellington's head. "The horse didn't kick him in the head at all. The torso and lower body are a mess, but I'm not sure those injuries would have been fatal right away. On the other hand, *I* was the one who caused the damage to his head. Probably cracked his skull, and that could very well be what killed him. The rest is just window dressing."

"So what? Couldn't he have been kicked in the head first, before going down and getting run over?

"I'm not arguing with you, man. There's a good chance they'll see this as an accident. But if they get suspicious and take a close look, there could be trouble. What if they're able to tell it wasn't a hoof that nailed him in the head? If they're scientific about it, how hard can it be to figure out? When they know it wasn't the horse, you'll have a full-blown investigation. They'll start looking real close for clues, questioning everyone out here." Gunnar stood up, dusted off his hands, and looked at Kane. "Your nose is leaking again."

Kane wiped his upper lip and studied the red smear across his fingers.

"I wonder how much of your blood is splattered around here," Gunnar said.

Kane didn't bother to look.

"See how it gets?" Gunnar spread his arms in a mock imitation of an innocent man with nothing to hide. "No matter how well you've got it figured, ya never know what's gonna happen when there's a body lying around. And once they get a whiff of something fishy, it's too late."

"What's the downside of getting rid of the body?"

"Other than getting caught?"

"You know what I mean."

"If we get rid of the body, and if no one finds it, there's no murder. Not for sure. And best of all, there's no crime scene."

Kane and Gunnar stood silent for a while, looking down at Tellington's remains. Kane finally said, "You willing to risk it?"

Gunnar looked around, as if buying time. "If we're going to do this, we better move fast."

Kane nodded toward Tellington's rig outside the stable. "I don't know about the trailer—I wouldn't want that horse to freak out again. Maybe we should stuff the body in the back of the Escalade. I think I know where to take it."

"Where would *that* be?"

"There's miles of empty desert around my place, and we could get him there without too much exposure."

"And do what? Dump him out there?"

"I've got something else in mind."

Gunnar flashed a quick, hard stare at Kane. "Okay, man. If you say so."

Kane emptied Tellington's pockets, transferring their contents, including the tack room key, into his own. They found an old saddle blanket to wrap around Tellington's body and carried it out to the Escalade. Once the body was taken care of, they went to work on the stall. Gunnar took on the heavy lifting. He used a pitchfork to toss fresh straw over the bloodstained muck covering the floor where Tellington had fallen, then scooped it all into a wheelbarrow and wheeled it outside to the top of a ramp and dropped the load into a Dumpster. He returned to the stall and scattered the remaining uncontaminated muck and straw across the damp bald spot on the floor.

Kane found Ashley's horse. The feeder had hay in it and the water looked good. When they were ready to leave, he locked the bottom half of the Dutch door Tellington had unlocked earlier. He was on his way back to Ashley's bungalow to replace the key on the pegboard when he remembered the tack room. He hadn't checked to see if it was locked. He thought about Pearl as he walked over, then pushed aside the memory of seeing her body lying on the floor. He was thinking about what else was in the tack room—Tellington's stuff. It had to be where he'd kept his saddles and bridles and who-knew-what-else. Kane almost panicked when he stepped into the room and saw all the saddles lined up on their stands.

Funny how he hadn't noticed them before. He couldn't remember what Tellington's saddle looked like, couldn't see much difference between the individual saddles in the lineup, anyway. He looked for places where there might be a name or number and came across an owner's name branded on the underside of a leather stirrup strap. Some of the others were branded underneath the seat. On the third saddle he knocked over, he found Tellington's name. Then he looked around at all the saddle blankets and bridles and halters and he knew there was nothing he could do about finding the right ones. He'd have to be satisfied with the saddle. He fetched Gunnar to carry it out and throw it on top of Tellington's body in the back of the Escalade.

Kane stayed back to replace the tack room key on its peg and to lock Ashley's bungalow. He took a last look around and met Gunnar who was now sitting behind the wheel of Tellington's rig.

"Gimme the keys," Gunnar said.

After starting the Escalade, he waited for Kane to open the gate, drove through, and stopped on the other side while Kane went back for Ashley's Explorer. Gunnar was still sitting there when Kane pulled up next to him and got out to shut the gate.

Kane climbed into the Explorer and opened the passenger window to talk to Gunnar on the other side.

"So far, so good."

"Let's not go admiring ourselves just yet," Gunnar said. "I'm not comfortable driving a dead man's car, especially with him in it." He gave Kane another hard stare. "You sure about taking this to your place?"

Kane returned the stare and said, "Trust me."

* * *

Ashley let out a gasp when she saw Kane's face. "Holy shit, Alan, what happened?"

"What . . . oh, this? Kane brought up a hand to his face, then shrugged. "You should see the other guy."

Ashley slid off her stool to come up for a closer look. When Kane walked in, she'd been sitting at the wet bar in the den, nursing a beer.

"Did Wentworth do this to you?"

Kane ignored the question. He gave her another dismissive shrug and said, "It's safe for you to go home now."

"You mean right now?" She went back to the bar and grabbed her beer. "I don't know if I'm ready to do that yet."

"It would be best if you did. It's important for everything to appear normal out at the ranch."

"Appear normal?"

"Bad choice of words. Everything *is* back to normal."

"But what about Wentworth Tellington?" The exasperation in Ashley's voice rose. "Are you going to tell me what's going on?"

"You don't want to know."

Just then Gunnar walked in. He noticed the beer in Ashley's hand and asked Kane to get him one and took the stool next to Ashley. Kane grabbed two bottles, keeping one for himself. He remained standing behind the bar. Gunnar took a long pull from his bottle. No one said a word until he'd drained it empty and placed it on the bar top. He looked at Kane and broke the silence.

"You better find a place to sit before you fall down."

Kane had moved in against the bar and was leaning on his elbows. "You're probably right. This beer went straight to my head."

Ashley said, "Shouldn't you see a doctor?"

"She's got a point," Gunnar said. "At least get a tetanus shot. No telling what you've picked up in that barnyard. You ever hear of lockjaw? It's a nasty way to go."

"First things first," Kane said. "Right now we need to get Ashley back to the ranch—" Ashley started to protest, but Kane waved her off and turned back to Gunnar. "Why don't you follow her out there? You know, show her everything's okay. You can use my car."

"This is bullshit," Ashley said. "What am I, a piece of furniture? You could at least have the decency to talk to me directly."

Kane and Gunnar ignored her. They looked across the bar top at each other. No words were spoken. Ashley kicked back her stool and stormed out of the room.

"She's not very happy," Gunnar said. "What did you tell her?"

"As little as possible. No reason for her to get any more involved than she already is."

"She doesn't know about Tellington?"

"Not unless she's figured it out on her own."

"You're probably right. If she doesn't know anything, she doesn't have anything to hide."

"Yeah, a little tip I picked up from Tellington. Keep everyone in the dark." Kane paused for a tentative sip of beer. "Sooner or later they'll come looking for him, asking questions out at the ranch. One little innocent stare from Ashley will be worth a thousand explanations."

Kane pulled the keys to his Cherokee out of his pocket and dropped them next to his beer bottle on the bar. He brought his voice down.

"Where'd you park Tellington's rig?"

"Out back. Behind the garage."

"That's no good. We need to move it farther out, where Ashley won't see it when she goes to her car."

"I see your point. Give me a few minutes, and make sure she doesn't go rushing out of here in a huff until I've moved it." Gunnar picked up the keys to the Cherokee. "Once I've got her squared away at her place, I need to make some discreet inquiries. It may take a while, so don't get excited if I'm not back right away."

"*Inquiries*? About what?"

"We'll talk about it when I get back."

TWENTY FOUR

HOLT WAS halfway to the elevator when the man approached him. He was big, middle-aged, wearing a dark suit, no tie.

"Mr. Holt?"

Holt slowed, but didn't quite stop walking. Until now he hadn't noticed how dim the lighting was in the parking structure, and the man was too far away to clearly see his features. In any case, Holt didn't recognize the voice.

"Do I know you?"

The man was walking briskly, trying to close the gap from about twenty feet away. "We haven't met. My name is Leonard Greenstreet. I'm a federal marshal."

Holt waited for the man to catch up. "What's this about?"

"I'm looking for Wentworth Tellington."

Holt looked around. Just the two of them. He flashed on Bryce Saunders's description of Tellington—*big and scary*, and the man now standing next to him could easily fill the bill.

"Do you have some credentials, a badge—"

Greenstreet produced his credentials with a practiced ease before Holt could finish his sentence. Holt looked at the picture ID next to the badge but didn't bother studying them closer. He wouldn't know whether they were fakes or not.

"We need to talk," Greenstreet said. "Privately."

"All right. I was just on my way to my office."

"I'd prefer we do it here. My car's around the corner, a few spaces down."

A tinge of fear flared in Holt's gut. "I'm not going *anywhere* with you. If this is official business, we can take it upstairs. If not—" Holt shrugged and resumed his way to the elevator.

"That's the thing," Greenstreet called after him. "This *isn't* official."

Holt stopped again, his curiosity getting the better of him. Greenstreet said, "*Your* car, then. Just let me get a folder out of mine and meet you there."

Holt waited while Greenstreet grabbed a briefcase out of a black sedan parked two rows over. Holt recalled Bryce's description again, this time remembering the silver hair and mustache as he looked at Greenstreet's clean shaven face and dishwater blond hair. Holt attributed his apprehension to an overactive imagination once they were inside his Mercedes. Greenstreet settled in and handed him a thick manila file folder.

Holt placed the folder on his lap. "How did you connect me with Tellington?"

"An online inquiry from your office found its way to our database. I located the source without too much trouble, did some more digging, and learned it was your assistant, Ms. Brennan, who set off the bells and whistles. Then I flew out here, *post-haste*."

"That's fast work," Holt said. "You must really want him. I didn't know he existed until a few hours ago."

"Do you know where I can find him?"

"I'm still trying to figure out how you found *me*. I just now got into town. How did you know—"

"A man's car is a dead giveaway when you have access to DMV records. I'd already called your office, found out Maxine Brennan worked directly for you. The rest was easy."

"So why are you looking for Tellington?"

"You're good," Greenstreet said. "I start out asking the questions, yet here I am on the wrong end, trying to explain myself." He eased back in his seat. "How about we put what we've got on the table? We're both looking for Tellington; maybe we can help each other out."

By now Holt was thumbing through the folder. He came across mug shots and printed documents and handwritten notes. Too much to digest all at once.

"What did this guy do, anyway?"

"Okay. Stop with the questions." Greenstreet shifted in his seat to better face Holt. He took back the folder, looked for something specific, and handed over a photograph. "Tellington's an alias. We know him as Thomas Dryden." Greenstreet paused, pointed at the mug shot now in Holt's hands. "Until a while ago, he was in the Witness Protection Program."

"This is Tellington?" The silver hair from Bryce's description was still fresh in Holt's mind. The man in the eight-by-ten photo had salt-and-pepper hair, no mustache.

"So . . ." Greenstreet said, "you haven't actually seen him."

"No. But I thought I had a reliable description. The man who gave it to me was very clear about Tellington's silver hair and matching mustache."

"Maybe I'm talking to the wrong guy. Who gave you this information?"

"Look," Holt said. "There are other people involved. Two of them are now dead, maybe a third, all of them alive and well until I came around and literally ruined their lives. I'm not going to involve anyone else until I know what's going on."

Greenstreet sighed. "All right, Mr. Holt. I'll play ball." He pulled another photo out of the file. "*This* is Wentworth Tellington."

Holt studied a photo of an older gentleman in a western suit, a bolo tie, and a Stetson in his hand. There was no mistaking the color of his hair, even though the photograph was taken from a distance and was in black and white, like a copy from a newspaper article.

"Wouldn't be too hard to impersonate an old guy like that," Greenstreet said, "if you had the girth. Kind of like playing Mark Twain or Colonel Sanders—you get the hair and clothes right, who's gonna tell the difference. Anyway, Mr. Tellington had a ranch in Montana. He wasn't really a horse breeder, more like a collector. The way rich guys collect cars. He disappeared around the same time Thomas Dryden dropped off our radar."

"While you had him in Witness Protection?"

"Yeah. Dryden had made a deal with the FBI to turn on his boss, a major crime figure in Philadelphia. Dryden cooked the books for him, knew all the dirty little secrets. They convicted the boss, then gave us Dryden. Guess where we relocated him?"

"Montana?"

"You catch on fast. I wish I could say the same thing for myself. Dryden had us going from the beginning. In fact, I don't think *Dryden* is his real name, either, but that's the only identity that matches our fingerprint and DNA records. In any case, he used us to get away clean after stealing from his boss. Turns out he cooked more than one set of books."

"And you think Dryden is responsible for Tellington's disappearance?"

"Disappearance? Let's stop being polite. Tellington's most likely dead. Dryden steals your identity the old fashioned way— he kills you for it. We figure he took on the persona of Wentworth Tellington, moved all that blue ribbon livestock out of state, and sold the cream of the crop at a big auction they hold every year in Oklahoma."

"But where's your proof?" Holt said. "Two men are missing. Is that all you've got?"

"Dryden worked for Tellington. I helped him get the job. Then Dryden goes missing, and lo and behold, Tellington's nowhere to be found. We sent out BOLOs and set up database alerts and got a hit from the sale in Oklahoma. By the time we got there, a silver-haired gent had made off with over three million for the sale of half a dozen prize thoroughbreds. Paid by wire transfer, and now lost on the other side of the digital banking system. What's worse, Tellington hasn't been reported missing, and to this day no one is looking for him. It's not a crime to abandon a ranch and sell off your assets. In this economy, people are walking away from all kinds of situations."

"What about the buyers? Do they get to keep the horses?"

"If the horses turn out to be stolen, they'll be confiscated."

"And they're out the three million?"

"Only if we find Dryden. The paperwork was in order and everyone believed they were dealing with Tellington. Without Dryden to prove otherwise, there's no crime. Those ol' boys in Oklahoma wouldn't lose any sleep if Dryden, a.k.a. Wentworth Tellington, stayed gone forever."

"Does anyone else believe your theory?"

Greenstreet almost laughed. "Spoken like a true lawyer, and a lot like my boss. What did he tell me? Oh yeah—theories are hard to prove." He gazed out the windshield, away from Holt. "My superiors think I'm either incompetent or crazy, depending on which ones you talk to. After the fiasco in Oklahoma, they *suggested* I take some time off. Probably to give them a chance to decide what to do with me. And not only am *I* toxic, can you imagine the shitstorm that will come down on the whole program if the media ever gets ahold of this?" Greenstreet rearranged himself again on the car seat. "Getting back to my theory—I do have a few facts. All the horses were sold, except one, an appaloosa stallion. It's worth a lot of money, especially to a breeder, and I figure that's the only reason Dryden has surfaced again under Tellington's name. He's looking for that special buyer who's willing to keep the sale low-key."

"Theory or not," Holt said, "it fits with what's happened here. I came close myself to buying what Dryden was selling. Now, like

I said, people are dead. I've got no choice but to inform the local authorities in Sedona."

"You've always had a choice," Greenstreet said. "Why haven't you made it yet?"

Now Holt was on the wrong end of the questions. "Let's say I've had confidentiality issues, along with my own media worries."

"Now we're getting somewhere." Greenstreet smiled agreeably and gestured for Holt to continue. "I've spilled *my* guts; let's hear *your* story."

Holt mulled it over for a while, then thought, What the hell. He told Greenstreet about the inheritance scam, leaving out Bigelow's name and a text message he'd received from Maxine less than an hour ago about the death certificate. He kept the focus on Alan Kane, the obvious link to Dryden, and the man he held as responsible as anyone for Pearl's likely murder and for the two dead bodies in her cabin.

When he had finished, Greenstreet said, "If we're going to find Dryden, it'll be through Kane. If he's still alive, I need to get to him before that sonofabitch ends their relationship."

"That's a lot of ifs," Holt said.

"Where can I find him?"

"You can try Blackhawk Golf Club in North Scottsdale. That's where he works."

"A home address would be better."

"All I've got is a cell phone number and a PO box."

"Okay, give me the numbers."

As he jotted them down, Greenstreet asked, "What about a car? What does he drive?"

"A late model Cherokee. Red. Don't ask me the license number."

"Anything else?"

Holt was about to shake his head when he remembered his conversation with Kane's brother.

"Dynamite Boulevard," he said. "Kane's brother told me he was taking care of a house in North Scottsdale, near Dynamite Boulevard. He said it's a big place, off by itself."

"That's good," Greenstreet said. "Maybe something obvious will turn up on archived satellite images. How long do you think it will take me to drive out there?"

"To Scottsdale? I'm not sure; I've always flown. Probably around six hours, closer to five if you're in a hurry and the highway patrol cooperates."

"Like I said, this is unofficial. Those superiors I was telling you about? It's best they don't know about this. Ditto for anyone else. I hope you can keep this conversation quiet, just between the two of us."

"What happens if I don't?"

"Nothing good."

Greenstreet's smile had disappeared, and Holt's earlier apprehension crept in on him again, only this time it came at him from a different angle. He sat in his car for a few minutes after Greenstreet had gone, not sure if he'd been threatened or given a little friendly advice. Holt wanted to think Greenstreet was trying to save his job and spare his agency any undue heartburn, but if that were the case, why act alone and unofficially? There was also something unsettling about the familiar way Greenstreet had mentioned the *ol' boys in Oklahoma*. As Greenstreet had hinted, they had plenty to gain if Dryden permanently disappeared. So did the Feds. Earning the gratitude of all parties involved, and perhaps a lucrative bonus from the former, would settle a score for the marshal. In that light, the one-man crusade made sense, now prompting Holt to regard Greenstreet's parting comment as a threat.

He left his car and rode the elevator to the penthouse suites and had to unlock the main entrance. It was quiet inside, not even the cleaning crew around as he made his way to his office. He fired up his laptop docking station and opened his email account. He found the email attachment Maxine had mentioned in her text message—a scanned copy of Jane Doe's death certificate. Maxine had managed to expedite the paperwork, but it would still take a few days to receive the certified copy in the mail. In the meantime, Holt could appease Stratton with a forwarded copy of the attachment.

Before he shut down his laptop, a thought occurred to him and he Googled the name Pearl Diamond. There were over a million search results—jewelry sites hawking pearl necklaces and diamond rings and every other combination you could think of. Over half of the first page was filled with *Pokémon Diamond and Pearl* sites, whatever the hell they were. Holt scrolled through a few additional pages, then tried more specific search requests.

He was about to give up, then thought of trying *stained glass lamps + Pearl Diamond*. He scrolled through a dozen pages of more garbage, and on page thirteen finally came across a blog out of Sedona dated seven years ago. There was a thumbnail photo, and Holt got his first look at the Pearl he'd been looking for.

He clicked on the image and studied the enlarged photo. Holt recognized the studio in the background. The expression on Pearl's face reminded him of Susan's in the family portrait, as if it were some kind of proof that Pearl was really dead. He knew it was only his imagination, but it was working overtime. He thought about Logan Bigelow and all the what ifs. Wouldn't Pearl now be alive if Holt had been on the Gulfstream the other night? What if the plane hadn't crashed? Would he have found Pearl under completely different circumstances? Would Logan have met her again? Holt's earlier assessment of himself, that this wasn't about him and that he was only a bystander, was dead wrong. He'd been in the middle of it all along, a pivotal cog in the machinery, free to tip off Kane with a careless remark that would change everything, whether initiated by fate or by a series of random coincidences that began with a routine mammogram.

Holt printed a copy of Pearl's photograph. It was a footprint in the sand, physical proof of Pearl's existence, and he wasn't going to allow the incoming tide to wash it away.

TWENTY-FIVE

Gunnar pulled out a tin of Altoids. He snapped open the lid and offered Kane a mint. Kane waved him off without a glance.

"Suit yourself, man," Gunnar said, pushing aside the mints and plucking a fat, pre-rolled joint out of the tin box. "I like to keep something on hand for emergencies, and if this don't qualify, what does?" He struck a match to light the joint, drew in a long hit, then held it out to Kane.

Kane stared at him "Didn't you recently give me a lecture about smoking it too much?"

"It's true." Gunnar's voice was tight, trying to hold in the smoke as he talked. He finally blew it out and said, "And it's obviously fucked up your judgment. But at this point, what the hell's the difference? How much more fucked up can you get?"

"Yeah," Kane said. "Fuck it."

He reached for the joint. He hadn't been high since that day at the ranch, when he'd first met Tellington. He wondered about it now as he sucked in a lungful of smoke. Wondered about how things might have turned out if he'd been straight.

He passed back the joint, and Gunnar said, "Think of it as medicinal usage. You look like you need it."

"I look that bad?"

"Maybe it's just the moonlight, but you look kinda pale. You must be getting pretty stiff by now."

"I ache everywhere. I hope this will take the edge off."

He was sitting on the ground, his back against a smooth boulder large enough to share with Gunnar. He leaned his head back until it rested against the granite as well. He said, "I guess I'm not much of a fighter. To tell you the truth, that was the first fight I've been in since the fifth grade."

"I could tell," Gunnar said. He took another hit and seemed content to just sit there.

"I got beat up that time, too." Kane said. "He was little guy. I still remember his name—Frankie Lucero—and man, he came on like gangbusters. First, he waited for a bunch of kids to gather round, you know, the usual crowd you get with the advertised after-school fight, and then he was all over me. No style at all; that's what I remember most. He just windmilled his fists out in front as fast as he could, not taking aim, or anything. Just throwing enough shit against the wall until something stuck, my face being the wall, most of the shit sticking. Got a bloody nose and my jaw ached for the rest of the week." Kane instinctively reached up to check his nose. "It didn't feel anything like this. I don't remember if he knocked me down; he might have, but I sure remember those flying fists. I didn't even get in a punch."

Gunnar handed him the joint. "Yeah, those little guys can be hell on wheels."

"So can the big ones."

"At least you got in a punch this time."

"Maybe so, but I obviously wasn't ready for what happened next. That school-yard lesson wasn't much preparation. Like comparing Little League with the Majors."

They sat and smoked quietly for a few passes. Then Kane said, "I used to beat up my brother, but that doesn't count. It's not really a fight if the other guy's so much younger and smaller that he can't defend himself. Of course, my old man could defend him. Jeffrey was my parents *miracle baby*, and he could do no wrong. If I ever fucked around with him, look out, there'd be hell to pay. Man, would I cringe whenever Mom said, *Wait until your father gets home.*"

"So the old man used to smack you around?"

"Not like that. It was all very formal. First, I'd have to think about it all day, dreading the moment he'd walk through the door and hear the bad news. Then I'd have to go wait some more, up in his bathroom. He liked to take his time, make me sweat it out a little longer, then come up and grab his tortoise-shell hairbrush and whack me half a dozen times with the flat end. There'd be a few tears, but I don't know why. It never really hurt. I know it sounds weird, but I was always disappointed about that."

"About it not hurting?"

"Yeah. After the big buildup it was kind of a letdown."

"Don't ever let anybody hear you complain about *that*. Those punches you took today? How would they have felt to a ten-year-old kid?"

Kane didn't answer. Gunnar said, "I know you've had your run-ins with your old man and all, but you didn't have it so bad."

"There are more ways to hurt someone than with your fists."

"Yeah. You got your boots; you got your pool cues . . . you ever been hit with the skinny end of a fungo bat? My old man used to take my—"

"Come on, Gunnar. You know what I mean."

"No, man. I don't. I would have gladly traded you just one good smack in the chops for a year's worth of your mental anguish."

"Okay. You've made your point." Kane stared at the joint in his hand. He couldn't remember if it was his turn to take a hit or to hand it back to Gunnar.

Then the horse made some noise behind the palo verde tree where he was tied up. Kane looked around at the moonlit landscape and felt the now-familiar paranoia of the other night begin to work on him. He handed Gunnar the joint and said, "I think it's time to get out of here."

Kane used one of the shovels to lean on and to help himself up. The pot had dulled some of the pain, but he was still stiff and sore. He looked down at the freshly filled grave.

"Gotta hand it to you, man," Gunnar said. He had untied the horse and was bringing him around. "Using Tellington's horse to pack him in was a stroke of genius. Think we can find our way back to your place?"

Kane surveyed their surroundings. The moon was getting low, but the sky was clear and the long shadows cast from a thin stand of saguaros nearby reached out to him like skeletal fingers. Despite the therapeutic effects the pot had on his pain, Kane wished he wasn't stoned. They had dug the grave on the same slope as Pearl's, only farther down south by a good half mile. It had been a long trek, but there was plenty of natural cover and they were able to pick a site far too rugged for motorized vehicles. As best he could tell, they were out of sight of the paved roads in the area and he saw no other signs of civilization from where they stood. But you never know—strange things can happen in the desert. Kane tried to tell himself it was only the pot, but he felt as though he'd just awakened in a new and dangerous environment that had gone unnoticed until now.

He realized Gunnar was staring at him and said, "All we have to do is follow the fall-line until it levels out, then head northwest. There'll be enough moonlight to see our way back."

Kane shouldered most of the digging tools. Gunnar took charge of the horse, as he had on the way out. He carried the digging bar over his left shoulder. They walked side by side wherever the terrain allowed, the horse following behind on a leader. They kept their voices low.

"You doing okay?" Gunnar said. "Maybe we should strap *you* on the horse."

"Yeah, that'd be great. Falling off a horse would make my day complete."

"He looks pretty docile to me."

Kane stared at the horse for a few paces. He turned back to look straight ahead and said, "I'll make it. We'll be there soon."

"Then all we gotta do is get rid of an SUV, a horse trailer, and this goddamned horse." Gunnar tugged on the leader to keep the horse on track. "By the way, they still hang horse thieves?"

"Well, we live in Arizona. With our luck, they probably do."

"You mean *your* luck. I've already made some plans. After I got Ashley settled, I looked up some guys I know. They can handle Tellington's ride, no problem. Escalades are a hot item and it'll be gone forever, probably to Mexico by lunchtime. As a favor, they'll also take care of the trailer for me. I don't know about the horse."

Kane looked at the horse again. He *did* look docile, for the moment. "It would take a helluva a hole to bury him."

"No shit. It would take a backhoe to bury that fucker."

"So what should we do?"

"I don't know. I have no idea where we could take him. As it stands now, it looks like Tellington took his horse and split. It'd be nice to keep it that way. We did a good job of cleaning the stall, and I don't think anyone's gonna go poking around in all that horseshit in the Dumpster out back looking for clues. Not with both him and his horse gone. We've gotta find a way to get rid of it ourselves."

"It's probably worth a lot of money," Kane said. "I don't know much about horses, but I know quality when I see it."

Gunnar paused to appraise the horse. "Yeah, he's a fine animal. I wonder what something like that goes for."

"Kind of makes me wonder how Tellington got ahold of him in the first place."

"What? . . . You think he stole him?"

"Take a look at this," Kane said. He handed Gunnar the wallet he'd taken earlier from Tellington's pocket.

Gunnar grabbed it from Kane's outstretched hand. "Good thinking. I'm glad we didn't bury him with his ID on him."

"Take a look inside. He's got three different sets of IDs. Back at the house, while I was waiting for you, I looked them over. There's different names in there on three different driver's licenses with the same picture."

Gunnar slowed down to study them closer. The light wasn't good enough to read them clearly, but he acknowledged that the names were different. He folded the wallet and handed it back.

"We'll check 'em over when we get to your place, also the glove box in the Escalade, in case we missed anything. Maybe we can find out where he lived. It would be nice to find papers on the horse."

"Good point. No telling how much he's worth without the paperwork. But maybe for the right price we could unload him, no questions asked."

Gunnar was shaking his head. "No, we can't be stupid. What if he's a famous show horse, or maybe not famous, but well-known enough to be recognized by the locals? We can't be connected to him through a sale, questions or not."

They walked awhile in silence. Then Gunnar said, "You find anything else on the body?"

"Not much. No more paperwork. I found this, though." Kane handed over a small leather case.

Gunnar opened it up. "Lock picks."

"Ashley had mentioned he was pretty handy at opening her door," Kane said, "without a key."

"I see what you mean about this guy," Gunnar said, handing back the picks. "By the look of those IDs, makes you wonder if Tellington was his real name."

"Nothing wrong with that. Maybe nobody will be looking for him, and if they are, they might figure he doesn't want to be found."

They walked on, thoughts to themselves, until they saw the familiar silhouette of Kane's house visible beneath the white glow of the moon in front of them. They came up to the garage, their footsteps crunching through the gravel driveway—

CLICK-CLACK.

"Don't you just love that sound?" A man stepped out from shadows, next to the garage wall. "Always an attention getter," he said, leveling a pump shotgun directly at Kane's chest. "Now you boys got about two seconds to drop to the ground, face down. Hands out in front."

Kane and Gunnar did as they were told. Their digging tools clattered to the gravel and Kane heard the horse run off, hoofbeats fading in the distance. The man stepped up closer and dropped a nylon strap next to Kane's head. It had one end already looped into the slip-lock fastener.

The man stepped back a few feet and said, "Slip that tie over your friend's wrists, behind his back, and cinch it tight. Do it now."

Kane picked up the nylon tie. Gunnar cooperated by positioning his hands behind his back. Neither one of them spoke. When Kane was finished, the man ordered him back on the ground.

"This is kind of awkward, trying to do this with my finger on the trigger. I suggest you two don't make any sudden movements."

Kane watched the man's shoes move behind him until they were out of sight. The man ordered him to place his hands behind his back and Kane felt another stiff nylon tie being slipped over his wrists. The man tugged at it awkwardly with one hand, then Kane heard him set down the shotgun for a quick moment so he could use both hands to cinch it home. It was tight, cutting into Kane's flesh. His arms already ached.

The man went through their pockets, pulling out wallets, cell phones, and keys. He stepped back a few paces.

"Let's see what we've got here," he said, squatting down on his haunches, almost low enough for Kane to see his face, but not quite. Kane quit straining and turned his head to rest it on the ground as the man flicked on a flashlight and took a few moments to go through the wallets. When he was through, he said, "Okay, you two can roll over, just keep your butts on the ground."

Kane and Gunnar managed themselves into sitting positions, hands behind their backs.

"That's it," the man said, encouraging them with a casual wave of the shotgun. "Slide in close, side by side, just one easy target."

"Who the fuck *are* you?" Gunnar said.

"Where I come from, the man with the shotgun gets to ask the questions." He held the gun with his right hand, brandished Tellington's wallet with the other. "How deep did you bury him?"

No answer. The man said, "I don't have all night." He glanced up. The night was about over, the sky showing a hint of gray light. "If you'd rather I call this in, just sit tight and we'll wait for the cavalry. I doubt they'll need a Navajo tracker to follow your trail back to the grave."

"We buried him deep," Gunnar said. "He won't be turning up any time soon."

"Good to know . . . Mr. Warburton, is it?" The man had shuffled through the driver's licenses and was looking at Gunnar's. "How do *you* figure into all this?"

"It's a long story."

"I'll bet it is. How about you, Mr. Kane? Got anything to say?"

Kane looked down at the ground and kept his mouth shut. Why the conversation, anyway? What was there to talk about?

"Okay," the man said, stepping in close to Kane. "Play it that way. But you know what? I don't give a shit about you, or your friend. You can either go down for this, or you boys can run a little errand for me and walk away when you're done. The choice is yours."

"Talk to him," Gunnar said, shoving his shoulder against Kane's "It's not like we've got a lot to lose."

Kane acquiesced with a shrug.

The man seemed to relax. He stood up straight and finally pointed the shotgun away from them. "I need to make a few calls, then we'll talk." He stared at them an extra beat before moving away "Just stay put. Don't do anything stupid."

He walked over to a dark sedan parked in the shadows alongside the garage door. He had a clear view of them through the windshield as he busied himself inside.

"The guy's a fed," Gunnar said, his voice low and urgent. "You see the plates? The fucking riot gun? Looks like government issue to me."

Kane kept his eyes on the man and his voice just as low. "Where the hell did he come from? How did he find out about us?"

"This isn't *about* us," Gunnar said. "He already made that pretty clear."

"Who, then? Tellington?"

"Who else? He didn't seem too broken up about the desert funeral."

"It still doesn't make sense, him being here by himself. No backup, not even a partner."

"Yeah," Gunnar said. "We should be in the back of a squad car by now."

"And what's the *little errand* he wants us to run?"

"You can bet it's not cool. Looks to me like he's gone rogue. He's either some kind of vigilante nut, or in business for himself."

"That's just great," Kane said. "It could be as bad for us, either way."

"I don't like it any more than you do, but there's not a whole lot we can do about it. For the time being, try not to piss him off."

They sat there for a while, shoulder to shoulder, watching the moon turn pale over the horizon. The man stepped out of the sedan, walked toward them, and hunkered down to talk to them at eye level.

"Here's how I see it," he said, shaking his head. "I've got you boys dead to rights, with a dead man's horse, his vehicle and trailer, and the tools you used to bury him. All we've got to do is follow the horse's trail back to the body. I mean, talk about evidence—you boys handed it to me on a platter. What I want to know now is, how were you planning on getting away with it?"

Kane started to speak. The man shut him up with a hard stare. "It's a rhetorical question, son, you don't have to answer. But I *would* like to know if you'll play ball. You could use my help, and your cooperation will go a long way toward seeing you get it."

"What's the catch?" Gunnar said.

The man considered him for a moment, then stood up and looked toward Tellington's Escalade, the roof and part of the trailer visible out in the stunted mesquite.

"There's no catch. I'm just offering you a way to get rid of all the evidence, including the horse."

"Is *that* what this is about?" Kane said. "The horse?"

"The horse is part of it," the man said. "No question about it. But there's a bigger picture that I'll need to keep to myself. If you want to stick your nose into that, then I guess we'll have to head back into the desert and dig a couple of more graves."

"Fuck that," Gunnar said. "Let's talk about getting rid of the evidence."

"Let's do that," the man said, holding his stare toward Kane. "All you need to do is round up the horse, load him into Tellington's trailer, and head out I-40 toward Oklahoma City." The man paused, letting the two of them get a handle on what he'd said, then looked at Gunnar. "Warburton, you drive the Escalade. Kane will follow you in his Cherokee. I'll be bringing up the rear, with the contents of your wallets and your cell phones in my possession. You can keep your driver's licenses, but I strongly recommend that you don't get pulled over. If you do, you're on your own. Try to run, and I'll have an APB out on your vehicles before you can say, *death by lethal injection*."

"What do we do," Gunnar said, "when we get to Oklahoma City?"

"We're not going all the way to Oklahoma City. There's a truck stop where you'll drop off Tellington's rig. You'll just leave the keys in the ignition, and walk away. Kane will be there in his Cherokee to pick you up."

"And then we're free to go?"

"That'll be it. You can drive off into the sunset."

"So we get our lives back," Gunnar said. "I appreciate that. But I'd like to know why. What's in it for you?"

The man shook his head again, a crooked, wry smile on his face as he lazily swung the shotgun toward Gunnar.

"That's *my* business." the man said. "I thought I'd made that clear to you."

"Fair enough." Gunnar glanced over at Kane, then returned the man's smile. "You've got yourself a deal."

TWENTY-SIX

STRATTON DIDN'T set a meeting with Holt until Wednesday morning, the day after Susan's funeral. The only communication Holt received until then was a reply to the email he'd sent Stratton informing him of the Jane Doe death certificate. The reply offered a lukewarm congratulation on a job well done—so far.

Other than that, Holt had stayed away from the office and didn't try to reach Maxine. He felt bad about missing the memorial service for Logan Bigelow on Saturday, but he wasn't willing to leave Benny again while he attended. There were other services as well, funerals for the other Gulfstream passengers— Mel Kingston, Bigelow's top accountant, and his admin, Marsha Fuller; the real estate guy, Jeff McElroy; Debra Hurley, the facilities and logistics VP; and, of course, the co-pilot, Danny Swansborough. Holt knew them all, considered them friends, and he hoped their families would understand his absence from their services.

He never heard from Greenstreet again. A couple of days after their only meeting, Holt had found a blog, the *Red Rock News*, and used it to keep tabs on the investigation into the fire at Pearl's cabin. At first the coverage centered on the fire itself. Oak Creek Canyon was a tinderbox, and it was a minor miracle that the fire had been contained. Then the focus turned to the mystery woman who died in the cabin. Pearl Diamond was officially ruled out as a victim of the fire, but her whereabouts were unknown. The body next to Cornel Diamond had yet to be identified. Holt wasn't ready to get involved. He'd think about it later, after he buried his wife.

Benny had surprised him the morning of the funeral. The boy dressed himself just like his mother would have, and he came downstairs ready to go. He held it together all through the service, never wavering. Holt knew how Benny really felt and how hard it must have been for his boy to suck it up, especially when he took his father's hand at the gravesite. Holt was about to lose it, right there in front of God and the pastor and a hundred mourners, when Benny looked up at him and said, "Don't cry, Dad. We have to make Mom proud of us." When Holt heard that, he felt his life change. His six-year-old son was showing more guts than Holt ever had or could ever hope to have—until that moment. Holt vowed, over his wife's grave, to always be there for their son, to make sure Benny had the opportunity for a good life, whatever it took. If that meant Holt had to find a way to keep his goddamned job, so be it.

* * *

It was early, even for Holt, when he entered Stratton's office. The senior partner was sitting in one of the chairs angled in front of his desk. He stood when Holt came in and offered his condolences. Holt thanked him for the flowers. Stratton plucked a document from his desk and handed it to Holt.

"This came in yesterday via an express courier from the Arizona Department of Health Services," Stratton said.

The men sat down. Holt politely studied the stamped certification on the death certificate, then handed it back. "Looks like it's in order."

"We're all very pleased to see this sorted out," Stratton said. He glanced again at the certificate, a slight frown on his face. He leaned back in his chair. "There are still a few things, however, that need clarification. For instance, I don't see a parental name on the death certificate. What do we have by way of proof that Logan Bigelow fathered this child?"

"We have the doctor who filled out the certificate. He'll be sending us a signed statement confirming that the Jane Doe on the certificate was Logan and Pearl's baby. I haven't heard the details yet, but I'm confident he has a reasonable explanation."

"Not good enough, Ben. We're *lawyers*. Our clients pay us to be anal, and I've assured the foundation's board of trustees that we've gone beyond normal due diligence."

Due diligence. There's a lesson to be learned here, Holt thought. A little more due diligence on his part earlier on might have made a difference. Like researching Pearl *Diamond* and finding that photo as soon as he'd learned about her using Cornel's name, instead of later, when he was feeling guilty.

"So you'll want something that's legally binding."

"That's right," Stratton said. "I want Dr. Janus to sign an affidavit and I want you to have it properly witnessed, notarized, and filed with the rest of our paperwork. That way we're covered."

"You mean that way we still have a client, the board of trustees."

Stratton's jaw dropped. "What are you insinuating, Ben?"

"I'm not insinuating anything. I just want in on the global view. I want to know if I'll still be employed tomorrow."

Silence filled the room. The certificate rested on Stratton's lap, his hands folded together, arms on the armrests. He sat that way, stone still, for at least a full minute.

"All right," he said. "Here's the global view. If the foundation receives Logan's life insurance payment, promptly, quietly, and without controversy, your future here remains intact. If not, you're through."

At least he's being honest, Holt thought, not worried in the least that Stratton would renege if he delivered the goods.

Stratton might keep things from him or lie by omission, but he'd never break his word. He was too vain to stoop that low.

"In that case, I better work out the details," Holt said. "I'd like to fly up to San Francisco after Janus is released from the hospital. He was having a rough time of it in the ICU—our phone conversation ended badly, and it upset him. I want to make this as easy on him as possible."

"Sounds reasonable." Stratton rose from his chair. "As long as it doesn't take too long. You were lucky to find him after all these years. Lucky he survived the surgery. It would be a shame if he had a relapse—"

"Don't worry. I'm on this."

They walked to the door, Stratton's hand on Holt's shoulder. An avuncular gesture that took Holt completely by surprise.

Once out of Stratton's clutches, he ran into Maxine in the hallway and had her follow him to his office.

"How'd it go with Stratton?" she said, closing the door behind her.

"It ended strangely. He almost acted as if he likes me."

"Sounds like the worm has turned."

"It's not that. More like I'm finally a big enough asshole to join the club and he wanted to welcome me aboard, one asshole to another."

"I guess that's a *good* thing," Maxine said, "as long as you know where you stand and don't lose sight of who you really are."

"That's the thing. I really am an asshole."

"You'll never convince me of that."

"We'll see. But thanks for the kind words. And thanks for helping me through this."

Maxine acknowledged the thank-you with a smile, then pulled a document out of a folder she was carrying. "This is the affidavit Stratton wants you to have signed."

Holt shot her a knowing look. "Any word when Janus will be released from the hospital?"

"He's already home. I've been talking with Annie, and she tells me he's relatively comfortable." Maxine went back to the folder for an envelope. "If you don't dawdle, you can make the early flight to San Francisco. Here's your boarding pass."

"Looks like you thought of everything."

"Oh, that reminds me," Maxine said, pointing at the envelope "There's a phone number in there for a licensed notary. Stratton arranged for him to meet you. You might want to give him a call when you land, firm up the time."

* * *

Holt headed out to Presidio Heights from the airport, preferring to drive a rental rather than endure a lengthy cab ride. He knew the way, having played golf at the Presidio recently. Dr. Janus's house was only a few blocks away from the golf course, and Holt caught glimpses of the bay soon after turning down his street. The house sat on a corner lot at the bottom of a hill, close to a greenbelt.

A vintage, red brick retaining wall held up one end of the house and compensated for the slope of the hill, allowing the house to sit level. A two-car garage served the same purpose around the corner, and it was hard to tell at first sight exactly how many stories were stacked above it. Holt found a place to park across the street.

On his way to the front door, Holt remembered the notary public. Preoccupied with the usual airport issues, he'd forgotten to phone him. Once across the street, Holt called the number Maxine had provided and was forwarded to a man named Barton Jayne who answered in a stiff accent that wasn't quite British. He told Holt he could be there at the house within thirty minutes—closer to fifteen, if the traffic cooperated.

Sounds like someone Stratton would know, Holt thought, slipping his cell phone into his pocket and continuing on to Janus's front door.

He was greeted by Ann Warren. She looked tired, but not down. Right away she put Holt at ease, apologizing for her abrupt manner over the phone from the intensive care unit the previous week.

"I was the one who was out of line," Holt said. "And I'm sorry if I upset your father."

"I don't think it was what you said, Mr. Holt. More like the circumstances. The surgery was tough on him, but he's already come a long way. He'll be glad you're here. He's been anxious about seeing you all day."

Holt followed Ann upstairs to a spacious study. Holt soon realized the vertical windows really opened up the room. It was like being inside a huge bay window with views of blue sky and green treetops and a street below that exuded Old San Francisco charm. The vaulted ceiling and the narrow jambs between the windows were painted white. Polished hardwood flooring shined along the edges of a tan rug that ran the length of the room, at the far end of which Dr. Janus sat in a leather easy chair. He appeared to be asleep.

"Dad?" Ann walked up softly and placed a hand on his shoulder. "Mr. Holt's here to see you."

Holt approached tentatively. Janus opened his eyes and turned toward him. "Is it still morning, or afternoon?"

"It's still morning," Holt said.

"Well then, good morning, Mr. Holt. We meet at last."

Ann stayed close, smiled at her father, and said, "Can I get you anything?"

Janus patted her hand on his shoulder and said he was fine. She turned to Holt.

"How about you, Mr. Holt? Coffee? We'll be having lunch soon, would you like to join us?"

"Please, call me Ben. I'm not sure about lunch just yet, but a cup of black coffee sounds great."

Ann went away, and Holt set his briefcase on a desk close to Janus. Holt pulled out the desk's chair and sat facing him.

"Thank you for agreeing to see me. I'm truly sorry for the intrusion at a time—"

Janus waved him off with a surprisingly spry gesture. "Not to worry. I'm glad to have the company." He set his hand back on the armrest and briefly lowered his head for a self-deprecating glance at himself. "Don't let appearances fool you. I'm sure I look worse than I feel. They had me standing up hours after the surgery, walking the next day. The medical profession doesn't believe in coddling these days."

"How's the pain?"

"It's retreated into an overall soreness. Nothing I can't handle. As long as I'm not moving, I feel pretty good."

Holt was relieved. Janus didn't look bad, considering. He reached back for his briefcase and pulled out the affidavit Maxine had prepared.

"This won't take long. To save time, we've prepared your statement. It's basically what you told me over the phone about the birth and death certificates for Pearl Norwood's baby girl. I have a notary public on the way over to witness your signature. In the meantime you can look it over, see if we got it right."

Janus took the document and gave it a cursory glance. "I'll need my glasses to actually read this."

"Do you have them handy? I'll get them for you."

Janus pointed to the desk. "Try the top drawer, on the right."

Holt found the glasses and handed them over. Janus didn't put them on right away. He seemed to have other things on his mind.

"I don't remember much about our phone conversation," Janus said. "I had some trouble with the medication, and my stint in the ICU is pretty much a blur."

He rambled on for a while, and Holt let him talk, killing time while they waited for the notary. The old man finally put on the glasses and read the affidavit. A few short paragraphs. When he was through, he handed it back to Holt.

"Not much to it, is there?"

"Nope," Holt said. "Just your verification, for the record."

"Was it really that important for you to fly up here? All this fussing about, waiting for a notary . . ."

"With an estate the size of Logan Bigelow's, you can't be too careful. There was a provision in one of the trusts that needed to be finalized, and you've just wrapped it up for us."

"So it's true. I wasn't hearing things when Ann told me Mr. Bigelow wanted to bequeath something to his child—Pearl's baby."

"That's right. He'd only started looking for her a few weeks before he died."

Janus sank back in his chair. "Well, that *is* disturbing. I didn't want to say anything more to Ann until I heard it from you myself."

Ann came in with the coffee. Holt looked over at Janus while she set the cup on the desk next to Holt. She followed Holt's gaze and said, "Are you okay, Dad? You look kind of pale."

The doorbell chimed. Ann looked quickly at Holt again before turning for the stairs. Holt listened to a muffled exchange from the foyer, followed by footsteps rising toward the landing outside the study. Ann ushered in Barton Jayne, and after another quick glance at her father, shut the door behind her on her way out.

Introductions were made, the document signed, witnessed, and stamped. Jayne packed his tools of the trade and offered a curt nod to Dr. Janus that appeared to end the proceedings. Holt picked up his briefcase and shouldered the strap. He walked over to shake Janus's hand.

"Thanks again for your help."

There was still some steel in Janus's grip. He held on tight and pulled Holt down closer. "We need to talk."

No harm in humoring the old guy, Holt thought. "Sure, just let me walk Mr. Jayne out."

When he returned, Dr. Janus was still in his chair. Holt took his seat again and waited for the old man to speak.

"I need some legal advice."

"In regards to . . .?"

"Is there a statute of limitations for kidnapping?"

Where did *this* come from? It was the last question Holt could have imagined Janus asking. He thought for a moment before answering.

"I'm not a criminal lawyer, and I'm not sure about Arizona, but I believe kidnapping is a class two felony. The statute of limitations runs out in seven years." Now his mental wheels were turning, and Holt thought of something else. "But falsifying public records? That's another story. It's as serious as murder— no time limit."

"I hope the penalty is a little less severe," Janus said. He slowly massaged his right temple. "Did you happen to keep the affidavit with you?"

"I've got it right here," Holt said, patting the briefcase on his lap.

Janus straightened in his chair the best he could. He pointed at the briefcase.

"Then you might want to tear it up," he said, the color returning to his face. He looked at Holt with a clear and steady gaze. "I'm afraid I have a confession to make."

TWENTY-SEVEN

HOLT WAITED out on the patio this time. The heat wasn't as intense as it had been before. The dry desert air, not really cool yet, blew gently off the golf course and swirled about in random eddies that caressed the hairs on his exposed arms and charged them with some kind of current that stood them on end. It was a pleasant distraction, reminding Holt of the Santa Ana winds that sometimes blew into Newport Beach this time of year.

When he saw Alan Kane through the glass wall separating the patio from the rest of the dining area, he rubbed his arms and broke the spell. Kane spotted him at just about the same time and made his way out to the table.

"I don't like you hanging around here," Kane said. "I'm trying to hold on to my job, and you're not helping."

"If you'd answered my calls, I wouldn't have had to track you down."

Holt watched Kane stand there and look around. Other than his table, the patio was empty, the lunch hour long past. Through the windows Holt saw a group of golfers at the bar, scorecards out, discussing their round over beers. A couple of tables inside were occupied with stragglers left over from lunch, and just on the other side of the glass sat another foursome getting ready to leave. Kane finally sat down.

"You don't look so hot," Holt said.

"I'm getting tired of hearing that."

"Who beat you up? You piss off somebody with a golf club in his hand?"

"Look, I'm barely hanging on here. It wasn't easy begging my boss to keep me on the schedule. I'm not in the mood to do any more explaining."

"You tell him the truth?"

"What do you mean by that?"

"I'm just wondering what kind of story you came up with. What was it, a car accident? You got mugged out on the back nine—"

"What do you want from me?"

"I'm not really interested in what happened to you. I want to know what happened to Pearl."

Kane slumped back in his chair. "She's dead. Her cabin burned down with her in it, along with the other guy."

"You can do better than that," Holt said. He slid closer to the table and moved the bread plate and silverware out of the way. He rested his arms in their place, looked directly at Kane. "First, let's get this out of the way: we found the death certificate for Logan Bigelow's kid. I had a meeting recently with the doctor who issued the certificate, and I have his sworn conformation to verify its accuracy. Ten million dollars in life insurance proceeds will now be paid to Bigelow's charitable foundation, the contingent beneficiary named in the policy."

Holt paused, just to make sure Kane got the message, then said, "I know about Clarissa. I know she died in the fire instead of Pearl. I know about Tellington . . ."

The unbruised portions of Kane's face turned a whiter shade of pale at the mention of Tellington's name. "I don't know what you're talking about."

"That's okay. I wasn't expecting anything from you, least of all the truth. You've had me going from the beginning, why change now?"

Kane didn't answer.

"When I saw the light, when I found out about Clarissa and then Tellington, I knew it was my fault. I fucked up, and you took advantage of it." Holt looked through the glass at the empty table where they'd had their first meeting. "Being here, in this place again, brings it all back. Like watching reruns of a movie, the scene where I get a phone call and hurry out to the lobby for some privacy. Me leaving my briefcase behind. You taking a look inside and finding the birth certificate. That's all you needed, wasn't it? Then you worked out a plan. You used me, and it cost innocent lives."

Kane still didn't say anything. He sat there with that vacant stare, reminding Holt of his first impression of him.

"And you know what?" Holt said. "It didn't have to be like this. If you'd only played it straight with me, it would have turned out so different."

Kane's eyes finally focused on him. "What are you talking about?"

"You first. Tell me what really happened."

Kane shrugged. "That day we talked? After you took off I went out looking for Pearl, on my own, just like I told you when we drove up to Sedona."

"But when we got to the cabin, that wasn't Pearl."

Kane had nothing more to say.

"We're just talking here, Alan. You and me. I don't even have my briefcase with me. Want to search me for a wire or a tape recorder? Wouldn't do me any good, anyway. I have a feeling that the powers that be just want this to go away."

"Then what do you want?"

"I want some kind of closure, as corny as that sounds, and you're the only one who can help me. Nothing's going to happen to you."

Kane sat there some more, then said, "All right. I'll tell you this much, Pearl didn't die in the fire, but she died."

"Who killed her? Was it you, or Tellington?"

"You figure it out. By the time you and I drove to Sedona, things had gotten out of hand. I'd already talked to Pearl the day before, asked her about Bigelow and her daughter. She told me they had planned on putting the baby up for adoption from the beginning. She couldn't remember any of the details. I don't think she wanted to. She put it all behind her after Bigelow left, and she was happy to keep it that way."

"So you bring in someone to take Pearl's place," Holt said. "Someone with a daughter about the same age as Pearl's and with a sketchy enough background to mold her into the girl we're looking for. That's a pretty tall order. How'd you find her? Is this where Tellington came in?"

"Pretty much. You know the rest."

"Not really. I don't know how you can sleep at night. I know I can't."

"Well, that's too fucking bad about your beauty sleep. We've all got our problems."

"You're right. Losing sleep over a stranger's death can't compare with losing out on ten million dollars. You must be devastated."

"Is that why you're here, to gloat?"

"Not really. It's more like I'm here to share my pain. You deserve a little payback for what you've dished out."

"You're nuts," Kane said, pushing back his chair.

"Before you leave, can I ask you a personal question?"

"That depends. Will you leave me alone then?"

"Yeah, I promise."

"What the hell," Kane said, relaxing again for the moment. "Make it quick."

Holt eased back from the table, found a comfortable position in his chair. "When you talked to Pearl that first time—the real Pearl—did she say anything about her pregnancy? Did she mention anything about her room at the hospital? Did she have to share it?"

"What difference does any of that make?"

"Humor me for a few more minutes. Then I'm out of your hair."

Kane shrugged, sat up a little straighter. "I guess Pearl shared a room with my mom."

"Just a guess?"

"That's what Pearl told me. I think she brought it up because that's when I was born. That's how Pearl met my mom and later became my babysitter."

"Cute story," Holt said. "But you don't have the details quite right. Pearl didn't share a room with your mom. Your *mom* shared a room with Roberta Kane."

Kane looked at Holt as if he were out of his mind. "What are you talking about? Roberta Kane *is* my mother."

"Is she?"

"She was. She's been dead for years."

"And I understand your father passed away recently."

"Yeah, a couple of months ago."

"Your brother's alive, though. You might find it interesting to compare blood types. See if your DNA matches up." Holt leaned in close again, brought his voice down to a conspiratorial whisper. "It might be even more interesting to check your DNA against Pearl's, if they ever find her."

Kane was on his feet. He tried to laugh. "Oh, I get it. Maybe I can even claim the inheritance; is that it? How stupid do you think I am? You think I'm going to lead you to Pearl's body and claim my fortune? You think I'd actually fall for such a crock of shit?"

"It's no crock. It's just our little secret. Between you, me, and the doctor who delivered a couple of babies thirty years ago."

Kane started pacing. At first Holt thought he was heading for the door, but he changed direction and shuffled aimlessly around the patio, the yellowish, crescent-shaped bruises under his eyes looking angrier, the scabbed-over scrapes on his face more swollen.

Holt brought his voice back up to a normal conversational tone. "Babies switched at birth—it's not really so hard to believe, is it? An unwanted healthy boy for an unfortunate but very-much-wanted baby girl, barely alive, and without a chance for survival. Then you throw in a rich and powerful father. The doctors tell him it was their only chance, that his wife wouldn't be able to have another child. Then providence intervenes. All of a sudden the father can provide his wife with the joy of a healthy son instead of the devastation and life-long heartbreak of a dead daughter. It's a fleeting opportunity requiring a quick decision, and with the help of the doctor who delivered both babies, the switch is made."

Kane came back to his chair, stood behind it, and grabbed the top of the backrest with both hands. "I don't even know why I'm listening to you." He stood there, looking around as if he had somewhere to go. After a long moment, he said, "Okay, for the sake of argument, how the fuck do you know all this?"

"I already told you," Holt said. "I had a meeting with your doctor. Before our conversation, when he had found out about Bigelow's last wishes, can you believe that he felt sorry for you? He wanted to confess to the switch so you could collect."

"So why didn't he?"

"I told him the real story, that you were involved somehow with Pearl's murder. How it was all about the money, to hell with anyone who got in the way. It didn't take much persuasion on my part to change his mind, especially when I passed along a federal marshal's advice to keep my mouth shut. The good doctor realized he'd only succeed in stirring up trouble for himself. He also knew there was no one left to corroborate his narrative and no trace of Pearl to prove your identity."

"Who else was involved? How'd they rig the birth certificates?"

"That was the easy part. The doctor was the one who filled them out. All he had to do was assign you to the Kanes and an unnamed baby girl to Pearl and Bigelow. But when the baby died, he had a problem. He didn't want to connect the wrong parents with the genetic abnormality that killed her, so he tried to hide it with a the death certificate issued to a Jane Doe. That's why we had such a hard time finding it."

"Thanks for *sharing*. But all this sounds like a conspiracy to me. You're breaking the law. Let's see what happens when I file a suit."

Holt stood up and faced Kane. "You're damn right I'm breaking the law, and you're going to have a hard time proving it. Without my confession, you think they'll believe you? That doesn't mean I won't talk. In fact, I'd actually feel better getting this off my chest and out in the open—your fraudulent scheme, the kidnapping and murder and the cover ups. Talk about conspiracies. I might even be able to help solve the mystery in Sedona. In any case, you'll never survive. The only way you can prove who you are and claim the insurance money is to produce your mother's body. Good luck with explaining how you know where it is."

Holt stared for a while longer at Kane, saw the rapid beat of his pulse pounding in his neck. *The Tell Tale Heart*. Holt could finally see the truth staring back at him.

A soft, rustling gust swept in and charged the air again, and when it died away Holt heard only the sound of his own footsteps. He felt Kane's eyes on him as he pulled open the glass door to exit the patio and just then Kane's voice rose above a crescendo of clattering table settings and breaking glass. Holt paused with the door half-opened, thought better of looking back, then pulled it wide and walked away.